The Dark Menace

by

I0653860

William Blackwell

The Dark Menace

Published by WILLIAM BLACKWELL PUBLISHING
Paperback ISBN: 978-1-7389714-5-9
Version: 2023.04.12

Do not go gentle into that good night,
Old age should burn and rave at close of day;
Rage, rage against the dying of the light.
—Dylan Thomas

Of such great powers or beings there may be conceivably a survival... a survival of a hugely remote period when... consciousness was manifested perhaps, in shapes and forms long since withdrawn before the tide of advancing humanity... forms of which poetry and legend alone have caught a flying memory and called them gods, monsters, mythical beings of all sorts and kinds...

—Algernon Blackwood

Victims worldwide have reported seeing this man peering into their homes, their bedrooms, their baby cribs, their cars and even—into their souls.
—Heidi Hollis, author of *The Hat Man: The True Story of Evil Encounters*

PROLOGUE

The muffled scream echoing eerily from the hallway leading to Noah's bedroom didn't alarm Barbara Janzen enough to stir her from her couch-potato, channel-surfing position. She reached into the glass bowl cradled on her lap and shoveled a mouthful of potato chips into her mouth, unaware of a few chips that slid down her gray sweatshirt, one lodging in the crotch of her sweatpants, a few others spilling onto the sofa. She grabbed the remote, adjusted her bulk, and cranked up the volume. The crotch-pinned chip crunched into powder. Oblivious, she flicked the channel quickly six times and finally stopped at *Bride of the Monster*, a 1955 B-grade cult horror film. She leaned back and grinned, exposing crooked, decaying and nicotine-stained teeth.

"Mooommmmy... heeeeeelp me!"

She craned her neck, scanning the dimly lit hallway. The shrieking cry for help echoed off the walls and then the house grew quiet and still. She frowned slightly. *Damn kid,* she thought. *Always having nightmares about monsters. There are no monsters. Only on TV.* Raising the volume a second time, she refocused on Bela Lugosi's cult classic, a movie she thought would take her away from the bleakness and despair of her own existence.

Five minutes later, she was lost in the movie.

The front door swung open so violently it crashed into the wall, rattling a window and knocking a cactus plant onto the floor, shattering the clay pot and spilling dirt on the beaten carpet. The cactus miraculously stood upright, a prickly phallus

3

defying all odds. A long-haired motley-looking man dressed in torn denim stepped inside and grinned.

"You drunken idiot," Barbara said, her eyes narrowing. "You scared the shit out of me. Look what you've done. What the hell's wrong with you?"

Through glazed eyes, the man gazed at the TV, then at Barbara. He took a long swill from his Molson Canadian beer can, chucked the empty outside, and slammed the door. "Honey, I'm home."

Barbara paused her movie and put the glass bowl on the coffee table, along with the remote. She gritted her teeth and clenched her fists. Her first instinct was to erupt like a volcano and she struggled to control the rising flow of lava. It wouldn't do any good to argue with Garrett now. Not in his current condition. He could be extremely confrontational when he was drunk. And not just verbal abuse; a few times he'd come close to striking her. Besides, he'd just called her 'honey,' a word he rarely used when speaking to her, even though the term of endearment was alcohol-induced.

She rose and approached him quickly, helping him off with his jean jacket and leading him over to a tattered La-Z-Boy chair. She plopped him into it.

He melted into the chair, slouched his head to one side, and focused on the screen vacantly. "You watching that crap again?"

Not wanting to rouse his ire, she ignored the comment, grabbed a dustpan and broom from a nearby closet and kneeled down to the mess he'd made. She swept up shattered remains of the clay pot, deposited them into a kitchen garbage can, and returned with an empty glass and a dish cloth. She swept some soil into the glass and, using the dish cloth as an improvised glove, carefully picked up the cactus plant and inserted it into the dirt inside. In the kitchen, she added a little water to it and placed it on a kitchen window sill, out of the way of future intoxicated paths of destruction, she hoped.

She cleaned the carpet as best she could and evaluated her effort. It would need a vacuum to get everything, she knew. But the vacuum was broken, and had been for more than a week. She sighed heavily, returned to the couch and plunked herself down.

She studied Garrett. His head lolled slowly to and fro, eyes opening and closing.

"I should get you to bed," she said. "You're wasted."

His eyes opened. "Barney's got a new hottie. Sweet little thing she is..."

"Barney's always getting new girlfriends. He wears them out faster than you do a pair of socks."

She searched his bloodshot eyes for a response, but they were closed now. She watched Garrett for a minute or two as spittle began dribbling from his open mouth. He emitted a loud nasally snore, the first of many to come. She debated trying to help him to bed, but quickly changed her mind. No sense waking the fool now. Let him sleep it off in his favorite chair.

She resumed watching *Bride of the Monster* with a sigh, thankful that she hadn't married this loser. He couldn't hold down a steady job, drank like a fish, and relied on government hand-outs to survive. And his demeanor and disposition were far from that of a model citizen. But, just like all the others, he'd probably be gone in a month or two.

Five minutes or so into the movie, even over Garrett's snoring and the blaring TV, Barbara heard a loud crash, followed by another ear-piercing scream. This time she did react, standing up so fast, she tilted her chip bowl, spilling its crunchy contents all over the sofa and carpet.

Garrett stirred, inhaled a nasally snore, and muttered something incomprehensible—the beginning of his night-time symphonic somniloquy.

At the far end of the hall, the bedroom door burst open and Noah sprang out, crashing head-first into the wall and falling on the floor. Although she didn't rush, Barbara walked purposefully down the hall, stopped in front of her son, and knelt down. His long brown hair was sweat-matted to his head. A small cut above his left eye leaked blood down his face. His mouth was open in a large O of shock and his green eyes were wide open, fixated and frozen on the ceiling. Holding his arms stiffly at his sides, he appeared to be in a state of catatonia. She grabbed his shoulders and shook him.

He blinked, opened his eyes, and looked at his mother. "The Hat Man," Noah said, the color draining from his face. "Help me, Mommy, help me... he tried to kill me."

CHAPTER ONE

A kaleidoscope of brilliant colors flashed before his eyes. Deep greens, dark purples, vibrant pinks, reds and blues. Inside the colors, images appeared—faceless apparitions with indistinct and undulating shapes. Some of the ghost-like images were black, some white. They twirled in the rainbow of colors, shrinking and growing, shrinking and growing. Then the black images began attacking the white images, slicing them with machetes, stabbing them with knives, biting into their heads and bodies with menacing fangs. Horrifying screams punctuated the eerie silence and Noah, his eyes opening in shock and terror, bolted upright.

Where am I? He surveyed the darkness and saw large trees looming in the distance, illuminated faintly by the white glow of a full moon. The ghostly combatants had disappeared. *A forest. But where?* Brushing off dirt and leaves from his clothes, he stood up, trying to make sense of his surroundings. But try as he might, he couldn't figure out how he'd gotten here. Worse, he couldn't remember events of the last week. He tried to take a step, but felt a numbness and an electric tingling sensation in his body that strained his efforts. He managed one step and stopped, frozen to the spot. A terrible feeling of cold dread surged through his veins. He felt his heart begin to pound in his chest furiously; struggling to escape its rib cage prison cell and leave him to fend for himself. After three or four panicked gasps, he managed to restrain his cardiovascular prisoner.

"What's going on?" Noah asked. "Where am I?"

In Noah's panic-tinged tone, the forest echoed back a response: "What's going on? Where am I?"

Fighting paralyzing protestations, he took a step, crunching into the forest carpet. It brought him renewed confidence, helping to diminish the fear demons. *That's it. You can do it.* Noah needed to leave the forest and search out some city lights. That way, he could find his apartment in downtown Charlottetown, Prince Edward Island, get to his bedroom, resume his sleep and wipe this nightmare off the map; if indeed that's what it was.

Locating a path in the forest, he crunched his way along, rubbing his shoulders and arms in an effort to eliminate the tingling numbness and the bone-chilling cold that was slowly enveloping him. He was still looking down at the path when he felt its evil presence. He looked up instantly, knowing, but not wanting to know what he was about to see.

But it was different this time. He was different. Noah stopped dead in his tracks.

Illuminated by the ominously glowing moon and the black looming trees, the old man grinned. He produced a machete and held it high in the air, adjusting his tattered straw hat and scratching his stubble with his free hand.

"You've finally come to meet your maker," he said. Then he cackled in an incongruously high-pitched voice.

The cold chill coursing through Noah's veins turned to ice. *Oh my God, no.* He had seen the man in many forms in his childhood years, and wasn't wasting any time on small talk now. He turned around and ran, taking some measure of satisfaction in the realization that the ice in his body had miraculously thawed and his legs willingly complied.

Noah turned a corner on the path and glanced back. The man was coming for him. He knew that if he caught him, there would be no mercy. As in his childhood nightmares, he would be sliced and diced to smithereens.

You're dreaming, you're dreaming, you're dreaming, Noah thought as he ran. *Hide.*

As if he'd been reading Noah's thoughts, the man replied, "You can run, but you can't hide."

Panting and puffing, Noah rounded another bend and came into a clearing in the forest. In a corner, just inside the tree-line, was a large hollowed-out log. Quickly he bent down and crawled inside, curling up in a fetal position as soon as he was out of sight, hoping against all hope that the menacing man was wrong. He could hide. He would hide. He would wake up and return to the comfort of his bed.

He struggled to control his breathing as the twig-snapping footfalls grew nearer. Then it became quiet. Unnervingly quiet. But in the silence, Noah heard the sound of breathing, not his own—a raspy, nasally inhaling and exhaling that grew louder. In a terrified instant, he knew it was too late. He was caught. Time to die.

"I got you now," the man said, the sound of his footfalls nearing. "You can run but you can't hide."

Before he could move, Noah heard a splitting sound and he knew right away what it was. Metal on wood. The man was chopping at the rotten tree trunk with his machete. Chopping through to him. But a split-second later, instead of the sharp metal of the blade, Noah felt the stomping of a boot heel on the small of his back and a bolt of red hot pain shot up his spine.

He tried to scream. Nothing. He tried to move. Nothing. He was frozen, once again.

The man cackled. "I bet that hurts. What I'm gonna do next will really mess you up."

Noah tried to crawl out of the log but he was paralyzed. He pressed his eyes shut tightly, gritted his teeth, and tried with all his strength to break free.

The sound of a distant wailing siren suddenly snapped him back into reality.

When he opened his eyes, he was sitting bolt upright, staring at the small green nightlight that instantly told him he was back in his house, back in his bedroom. With a loud sigh, he curled up in bed. His heart stilled, and the fear slowly melted away. *A terrible nightmare. Nothing more.*

But it wasn't long before a dark presence invaded the room—thick and palpable. His heartbeat once again thumped louder, faster. Beads of perspiration sprouted on his forehead. His throat became dry and the numbing, tingling sensation returned. Green dots danced in front of him and he tried to reassure himself. *It's from the nightlight. Don't worry.*

But he was too afraid to open his eyes, in case the inbred-looking hillbilly had returned. Finally, it became too much. He felt like he was being completely engulfed by this dark and evil presence, as if it was swallowing him whole and turning him into some kind of a monster. Emotions swept through him—anger, rage, anxiety and finally a powerful sadness that slowly gave rise to fear.

He opened his eyes. *Oh God, please. All this time. Why now?*

The darkly cloaked man stood at the foot of his bed, staring at him. Looking at him as if he was trying to reach into Noah's soul and snatch it away. The man raised a hand and touched his wide-brimmed black hat. Noah tried to shout, scream, move, but it was no use at all. He was frozen like a chunk of ice. The Hat Man walked around to the side of the bed and leaned down, his black face, a dark mask with no discernible features whatsoever, moved in closer.

Like an incubated alien fetus, Noah was sure his pounding heart would snap his ribcage, tear his muscles and flesh, leap right out of his chest, and escape its humanoid incarceration once and for all. His mind filled with the sudden image of a slimy extraterrestrial creature exploding onto the Hat Man and wrapping its deadly tentacles around his throat and face, constricting and suffocating the life out of the monster. If he wasn't paralyzed with fear, he might have grinned.

The black face moved closer and stopped six inches or so from Noah's face. Noah's breathing became labored and he felt a painful tightening in his chest. The small of his back still stung from the hillbilly's heel. *Time to die. This is what it feels like to die. Not now, oh please God, not now.* With raw panic rising up his throat like a sick green bile, he mustered all his strength and jerked. His body twitched and convulsed and he instantly sat upright, gasping for breath as sweat streamed down his face. Eyes wide with terror, he watched the Hat Man shrink, retreat and disappear out of sight, trailed by a green dragon tail emanating from the glowing green nightlight.

It took a few minutes for Noah to calm himself down. When his breathing finally returned to something approximating normal, he glanced at his digital alarm clock:

3:33 am. He climbed out of bed, wincing as the small of his back ignited with fiery pain. He was still trembling by the time he reached the bathroom. Still too terrified to look in the mirror, he wiped his face with a towel, relieved himself, sat down gingerly on his living room couch and flicked on a table lamp. He needed some incandescent comfort right now to try and make sense of the nightmare that had seemed so much more than a nightmare.

The Hat Man had returned. With a vengeance. He had been only six the last time he'd seen the Hat Man, thirty-four years ago. But he remembered the haunting experience as if it had happened yesterday. As a child, he'd suffered from frequent nightmares, many of them paralyzing. There were variations of many themes, but most involved some kind of a monster chasing him with murderous intentions. And while they'd terrified him, none of the monster sightings had resulted in physical injury. Except for the Hat Man. As a child, the darkly cloaked intruder had bent down to his bed, wrapped cold fingers around his throat, and began choking the life out of him. He remembered gasping for breath. He remembered the constricting pain he'd felt as he leaped out of bed, rushed from his bedroom in terror, and face-planted into the hallway wall. He'd suffered a concussion that dislodged much of his cognitive functions for two weeks and kept him out of school for three weeks. He absently rubbed the scar above his left eye, the result of the concussive cut that had required six stitches to repair.

But, after that ill-fated evening, the nightmares had stopped. All the monsters and the Hat Man had vanished. Maybe the concussion—which doctors had described as moderate to severe—had helped. Whatever the reason, Noah had managed to banish the Hat Man, along with all the other shadowy creatures, from his waking and sleeping world. Blocked them out and successfully expelled them from his existence.

Growing up in Calgary, Alberta, had been tough too, but he'd also managed to block that out. He'd been eighteen when his stepfather, Garrett, and his mother Barbara combined lethal doses of opioids and alcohol one night during a horror-movie binge-watching session. The irony at the time hadn't been missed by Noah. They'd been watching a remake of a Jack the Ripper slasher movie when the grim reaper, with his death-dealing scythe, had decided to pay them a life-ending visit.

But, like the Hat Man, Noah had put it behind him like a fading shadow, and had focused full-tilt on work, not willing to admit to himself, on any level, that at best the workaholic cure would only serve as a Band-Aid solution to a gaping traumatic wound. In spite of himself, images began to float into his head, images of Barbara slumped over on the couch, her glass of vodka and orange juice, her signature poison, still held tightly in her hand. Garrett, the loser that he was, nestled in beside her, his head slumped on her shoulder, his mouth open wide, his venom of choice, a Molson Canadian beer, spilled onto his lap.

But, as he'd done successfully throughout his life, Noah, in spite of a knot of sadness and grief tightening in his stomach, pushed the dark shadows into the dark recesses of his mind. In his mind's eye, he grabbed the Hat Man forcefully and tossed him into the cavernous hole along with the others, locked the closet door, and threw away the key.

He smiled. He was starting to feel better already. "Mind over matter," he said, trying to boost his confidence. "That's all it is. Mind over matter."

A few minutes later, as he drifted off into what would be a dreamless and peaceful sleep, the only thought that crossed his mind was one that brought anticipatory chills of excitement. Last week, he'd asked Angela Rosewood, a cashier at a nearby Wendy's fast-food restaurant, out on a date. And, finally, after the fourth entreaty, she'd accepted. Tomorrow was the big day.

As he drifted off, her acceptance speech echoed in his head: *"I used to think you were weird. And I probably still do. But you're weird in a positive sort of way. You're five times lucky. I guess I'll go."*

CHAPTER TWO

Angela hurried through her chores that Saturday afternoon, wanting to keep her mind busy so she wouldn't think about *him*. She finished vacuuming the small galley-style kitchen, pulled the cord out, and wheeled the upright machine into the single small bedroom of her modest main-floor apartment a few blocks from the downtown core. The cord got stuck underneath the partially open door and momentarily impeded her forward momentum. She tripped over the vacuum and fell on her bed, which was littered with dirty laundry and cosmetic items. She landed on an open tube of ruby red lipstick, smearing a slithering serpent on her sweatshirt as she struggled to get up.

"Shit," she said, rolling over on her back. She placed the cap on the lipstick tube, thought of wiping the serpent with a hand, and then quickly changed her mind. She grabbed a few tissues from a nightstand and wiped the white cotton fabric of her sweatshirt. All it did was elongate and fatten the snake but it would have to do. She got the cord unstuck from the door, plugged it in, and resumed vacuuming.

A few minutes later, satisfied with her work, she carefully rolled up the cord, not wanting another lipstick-tainted fall. She was a little clumsy, a little unorganized, but she tried hard to counterbalance her genetic predisposition with determination, hard work, and thoughtful planning. After putting the vacuum cleaner away in a hall closet, she returned to the bedroom and began picking away at the items on the bed, trying to organize clothing, jewelry, cosmetic items, scraps of paper containing TO DO lists, and her collection of Prince Edward Island beach pebbles. She started with the clothing, throwing it all into a nearby dirty laundry hamper, realizing, but not caring, that some of the items were actually clean. Once she finished with the clothing, she started into the pebbles, fingering them and placing them into a black ornate jewelry box she'd purchased expressly for that purpose.

She picked up a heart-shaped pebble, shuffled toward the nightstand, and looked out the window. A lone maple tree stood in the middle of the backyard, its leafless branches coated with a layer of freshly fallen snow. The sun was beginning to set behind the peaked roof of a neighborhood house, a shiny orange background to a brilliant blue sky. But she knew it was cold, a little below -15 degrees Celsius according to the Weather Network, which she had religiously watched this morning, as she did every morning. A blue jay fluttered in and landed on a branch of the tree. It looked at her for a moment, chirped, and disappeared, a plume of white dust trailing its hasty exit.

Maybe he knows there's a storm coming, she thought. *Doesn't wildlife operate on a different frequency of awareness than us humans?* She thought so, but she wasn't sure. She rubbed the heart-shaped pebble, admiring Mother Nature's perfect creation, and thought about returning it to the jewelry box but changed her mind. She set it on the nightstand, but slid it a little too far and tipped over the framed-glass photo of *him*. Along with the heart pebble, the image fell off the table, landing with a muffled crash on the carpet.

"Oh shit," she said, her plump cheeks flushing. "Can't you do anything right?" She picked up the picture, leaving the heart under a mound of broken glass, a shard of which pricked her index finger, triggering a small bubble of blood to trickle to the surface.

"Oww," she said, wiping her finger on her already stained sweatshirt.

Her eyes moistening, she studied the image of Case Blackthorn; short-cropped black hair, thick pointy mustache, broad inviting smile, and dark brown eyes. His mammoth arms were crossed over his muscled chest and his bulky frame was back-dropped by the signature red sand of PEI, deep blue ocean water, and a bright blue sky dotted with white puffy clouds.

It had been seven months since Angela and Case had parted company, but the heartbreak was still as fresh and raw as the wound on her finger. Clutching the broken frame in both hands, she reclined on her bed amidst her toiletry and cosmetic items, barely feeling them pressing into her back, but not caring. Involuntarily, her mind reeled back to that heart-wrenching moment when it all had ended.

She closed her eyes, watching the drama unfold in her mind, as if she was watching a romantic movie. But unlike a movie, she was deeply attached to the scene in a painful, unprocessed sort of way. She and Case sat on a colorful beach blanket on a bright sunny summer day, drinking white wine and eating brie cheese and crackers, after a refreshing dip in Cavendish beach's wave-washed waters. It was their three-year anniversary and Case had hinted in the months leading up to this moment that there would be a big announcement coming. Angela had mistakenly believed it would be a marriage proposal. Remembering that day as the tears flowed freely down her cheeks, she realized now that she should've known better. He'd been cold and distant in the past four or five months and she'd ignored the signs, foolishly believing it was just a "guy thing" and he would come around.

"I wanna spend more time with the guys." *Guy thing.*

"I don't know how long I'm gonna be gone. My boss might want me to work late." *Man stuff.*

"I think it's healthy for our relationship if we spend time apart; I mean more time apart." *Male malevolence. Normal.*

She snapped back into *Broken Dreams*, the title she'd given to the tear-jerker soap opera of her shattered hopes. After some mundane observations about the scenery, Case had grabbed his khaki cargo shorts and reached into the back pocket.

Angela's heart skipped a beat. *The ring. He has the ring.*

But instead, he removed a crumpled greeting card and handed it to her. But Angela wasn't dismayed. First, he'd give her a card for their anniversary, and then a ring. Afterward, she could surprise him with his anniversary gift—a Rolex watch she'd purchased by maxing out the single credit card she owned.

Beaming with delight, Angela opened the card. There was an animated image of a monkey resembling Curious George on the front. The monkey, grinning broadly, leaped into the air while holding a wine glass, its contents managing to stay put in spite of his excitement. The caption on the top of the card said *YOU'RE GREAT!* She opened it up with a big sigh, sure that the mushy romantic stuff would be contained inside. But all she saw was an image of the monkey, face-first on the green jungle carpet. Evidently he'd taken a spill but managed to preserve his wine. Below the sprawled monkey, the card said, *EVEN WHEN YOU FALL DOWN!*

Underneath the caption, Case had written, *I love you, Angela. I'm sorry it's not in the way that you want. I hope we can still be friends.*

And as the tears streamed down her face, he'd tried to console her. "I know you want more, but I'm just not able to give it. I want to be friends with you, honey. I really do."

What? Nothing about the anniversary? Breaking up with me on our anniversary. Nothing about the marriage proposal. Insensitive bastard.

But she didn't say any of those things. She hastily grabbed her belongings, including the Rolex watch, and stormed off. Twenty minutes later, while she stood on the highway trying to hitchhike a ride home, he pulled up beside her in his silver Toyota Camry.

By that time, the full weight of his rejection had hit her like a lead balloon. And she was finally able to say something. She remembered it as clearly as she recalled the painful break-up.

"Why don't you go and fuck yourself!" Then she watched as his Camry drove off and slowly disappeared.

She shook her head, bringing her back to the present, and wiped her tears away, smearing blood on her face from the injured index finger. She grabbed a tissue, blew her nose, wiped away more tears, crumpled the tissue into a ball, and tossed it on the nightstand.

She let her mind slip back to *Broken Dreams*, trying to rewind the movie to the good times. But they were harder to find. And then, she remembered something else about

Case—he had a vindictive streak that she'd managed to block out for many years. She tried to give it shape.

Bing-bong. The doorbell rang.

The sound shattered her grief-stricken reverie. "Oh my God." She looked at the clock. Six-thirty, exactly the time Noah had agreed to pick her up. *What happened to the time? Why did I even say yes?* She wasn't emotionally prepared for a date. She hadn't yet moved on from Case. She wasn't ready to meet someone else.

Bing-bong.

She hurriedly went to the door, wondering if she should just tell him she was sick or something and apologize.

From behind the protection of the door, she asked, "Is that you, Noah?"

"Yes, it's me."

"I'm sorry. I don't know if I can do this."

"Are you okay?"

Her mind raced. *What to say? What to say?* She certainly couldn't let him see her in this condition—blood and tear-soaked face; blood and lipstick-smeared sweatshirt; frumpy gray sweatpants; her long hair matted to her face. "I fell while I was cleaning, and I... I lost track of time."

"Are you hurt?"

Yes, she was deeply hurt, but probably not in the way that he meant. "No. But I'm not ready."

"I can come back if you want, in an hour or so."

She knew there was a storm coming. She couldn't leave him hanging out there for too long in the cold. He was probably already freezing. "Where were you planning on taking me?"

"The Pilot House. You know it?"

"Yeah. Nice ambiance."

"If you're not feeling well, we can do this another time."

He was giving her an out and she wanted to take it. But some self-preservationist need to save herself from the dark and poisonous tentacles of heartbreak, misery and despair, prompted a change of heart. "I know where it is. Give me an hour to clean up and I'll meet you there. Is that okay?"

"Are you sure you're up for this?"

She realized with a pang of sadness that Noah had showed her more consideration in the last five minutes than Case had in the first month of their relationship. "I'll be fine. I'll meet you there. Okay?"

"I can pick you up, if you'd like. There's a storm coming, you know."

"It's only a few blocks. Thanks, but I'll meet you there."

"Okay."

She heard the crunching of snow growing fainter as his footfalls retreated down the walkway of the main-floor suite she rented in an old two-story home.

CHAPTER THREE

"Excuse me, sir, do you have the time?" Noah asked.

The man removed his glasses, wiped the foggy lenses with his sleeve, replaced them and looked at his watch. "It's 8:33."

"Thanks."

Noah nursed a beer in a booth in the cozily lit and crowded Pilot House pub. Angela had said an hour. She was already about an hour late. As he'd left her apartment, the storm had begun asserting its fury full-force—pounding winds, driving snow, and temperatures expected to drop to a frigid -22 degrees Celsius overnight. He'd parked his pickup in the rear stall of his apartment, and walked the few short blocks to the pub.

When he'd arrived, he'd tried to enter from the front door, and then realized it had been closed to the public for some time. He saw arrows pointing to a side door. The Pilot House had a separate dining room, pub and bistro. He'd mistakenly entered the bistro door and a friendly staffer had asked him if he was an early guest, since the venue had been booked for a private party that night. Apologizing, he turned to leave, and then it caught his eye. Directly in front of him in the hallway entrance, there was a colorful abstract painting showing people drinking amicably at a table, vibrantly colored cocktails in their hands. One man, an almost three-dimensional image of the Hat Man, struck him. But, far from menacing, the Hat Man was smiling at him, eyeballing him with an oversized black and white eye and oddly angled full brown lips. However, the black gaucho-style hat was unmistakable.

He thought about it now. What did it mean? Was the Hat Man actually a benevolent presence as opposed to a powerful evil force? Noah had no idea. Since the Hat Man had disappeared from his life so many years ago, he had no reason to do any research on the subject. But things were different now. *Note to self. Check this guy out.*

His recent nightmare and its associated feelings of terror and dread overshadowed any sense of positivity the Hat Man might exude, and the hastily assembled theory of the monster being good melted like the snowflakes on his winter jacket. That terrifying experience had opened an emotional can of worms that he would just as soon see resealed and frozen in time. He'd managed for so many years to successfully forget the Hat Man. He wanted to keep him buried, keep the Dark Menace in a cryonic state indefinitely.

He took a sip of his Budweiser beer and looked beyond the exposed brick walls and wood beams of the pub to the window. A dark shadow caught his eye. It stopped and peered through the window of the closed-to-patrons front door. *Was that a hat?* It was too dark to tell.

He shuddered, feeling a coldness on the nape of his neck as prickly hairs strained against layers of cotton fabric. Squinting to get a better look, he realized it was a shadow, the shadow of a man fighting blinding snow and reduced visibility to reach his parked car. And now that he thought about it, Noah wasn't even sure if he'd stopped and peered through the window or not. He reached for his phone, about to call Angela.

He felt a cold hand touch his shoulder. He started and swung around quickly.

Angela looked down at him with an embarrassed grin. "Sorry. Didn't mean to scare you."

"It's... it's okay."

She removed her purple toque and sat down in the booth facing him. "I'm sorry I'm late."

Noah hoped his expression didn't show how irritated he was at her tardiness. "It's okay. At least you made it."

The waitress came. Noah ordered another beer, Angela, a glass of house white wine. They talked about the weather until their drinks arrived. It was a favorite conversation for Canadians anyway, and it helped lessen the initial tension a little. Even though Noah had started to get a little upset, even slightly angry at Angela's lateness, seeing her bright fresh face buried the negative emotions in the drop of a hat.

She had a mischievous smile, sandy-blond hair, and deep blue soul-searching eyes. He also noticed a kindness and gentleness to her demeanor that he'd immediately found attractive when he first met her four months ago. Of course, her large pendulous breasts added more of the right ingredients to the recipe of attraction.

"Did you say you fell in your apartment?" Noah asked, beginning to peel the label off his beer bottle.

Her eyes met his. "I'm a little clumsy sometimes." She held up the index finger of her right hand, exposing a Band-Aid-wrapped fingertip. "It's nothing, really."

"I'm glad you're okay. With this weather and all, we're lucky we live close."

"You have a place around here?" Her eyes moved to his label-peeling hand.

He stopped tearing at it and took a sip. "Just a few blocks away. Third floor apartment on Kent Street. I'm just down the street from Rochford Square."

"I know it," she said. "It's not far at all. Where do you work?"

To Noah, the conversation seemed a little wooden and forced. He hoped it would flow naturally soon, once the boring stuff was dispensed with. "I'm a grants officer for PEI Arts Council. Along with a committee, I decide who gets government grants and who doesn't."

"Is that provincial or federal?"

"It's a branch of the provincial government, but we get money from the feds."

"It sounds interesting."

"It's not, really."

"How long have you been doing that?"

"Six years."

"And before that?"

"I graduated from UPEI with a bachelor of Fine Arts. Photography emphasis."

"You like taking pictures?"

"I love taking pictures. Some of them have even ended up in the Arts Council's promotional stuff." An introvert by nature, Noah didn't feel at ease talking about himself, although he did love talking about and taking photographs. His mind was very visually oriented. Still, he would rather be the interviewer than the interviewee.

"I'd love to see some of them one day," Angela said as she wiped a wet strand of hair away from the frame of her glasses.

"I'll show you. Many are pretty abstract stuff, though. I'm not sure you're into that."

"I'm sure I'd love them." She smiled and a little dimple formed on the right side of her pleasingly pudgy cheek. Then she frowned a little and the dimple exited, stage right.

Noah seized his opening. "Do you have any aspirations beyond working at Wendy's?" He realized with a slight grimace he'd just jammed the toe of his boot into his mouth.

Over the din of loud and jovial conversation, she looked down at her wine glass.

"Sorry... I didn't mean it that way," Noah said. *What other way could I have meant it?*

"It's okay," she said. "I ask myself the same thing sometimes. If I could only get my shit together."

Now here was a can of worms, if he wanted to open it. He did. "What happened? I mean, you don't have to talk about it if you don't want to. Maybe it's the wrong question for a first date. Jesus, I'm not very good at this."

"It's okay," she said, some of the color draining from her rosy cheeks. "It's part of the process, right? Getting to know each other."

Noah nodded.

She continued. "Five years ago, I lived in Toronto. I was born there. Anyway, I was engaged to be married. I was in a relationship for twelve years with Seth, my high school sweetheart. He was a successful accountant who had his own big firm and all that. He never wanted me to work, never wanted me to go to school. He said he'd provide for me... do you really wanna hear this?"

"Sometimes it's therapeutic to vent," Noah said, as if he actually knew anything about that. "Carry on."

"Well, to make a long story short, Seth dumped me. I guess he likes eighteen-year-olds because that's what he married. What a cliché—being left for a younger woman. Do I look old? I mean, I'm only 35."

"You look great," Noah said. And he meant it. "You're beautiful."

"People have called me cute, but not beautiful. But thanks, anyway."

"I mean it."

She smiled. The dimple returned. She finished her glass of wine and waved over the waitress for another. Just to be hospitable, Noah ordered another beer, even though he wasn't close to finishing his second one yet.

An uncomfortable silence gathered while they waited for the drinks.

Noah didn't want to change the subject with small talk. He sensed the floodgates were opening.

Once the waitress brought their drinks, Angela took a small sip of wine and continued. "Anyway, as I said, Seth didn't want me to have a career, or even get any post-secondary education. He wanted me to be a stay-at-home housewife and raise the three kids we'd planned on having. And, like the bimbo I am, I willingly complied. Now look at me. I have no skills whatsoever."

"He sounds like an asshole, frankly. And, I'm sure you've got talent. You're not too old to discover and develop it."

"With what?" Angela said glumly. "I'm flat broke."

"Maybe you've got an undiscovered artistic bent," Noah said. "If you did, I could help you. There's a little-known division of the Arts Council that also offers small business loans and grants. We just need to figure out what you're good at."

Her eyes glazing over, Angela took another sip of wine. She looked unconvinced. "We'll see what happens. But before I go ahead and screw up this entire date, why don't you tell me a little about yourself?"

"You're not screwing anything up. What do you wanna know?"

"I'm getting tired of talking about past relationships, I mean old boy-fiends."

Noah burst out laughing.

So did Angela.

"You just said 'boy-fiends,'" Noah said, grinning.

"I know," she said with a chuckle. "Must have been a Freudian slip. You don't have to tell me about your ex-girl-fiends though. I'll let you off the hook for now. What about your family? Any brothers or sisters?"

She'd hit on the one topic that Noah was most uncomfortable talking about. He hadn't had a real relationship in sixteen years. And with Natasha, there had been no drama. They'd just grown apart and after five years of relative stability it had ended amicably. He'd just simply lost interest in relationships after it had ended. Or that's what he'd told himself, anyway. Until he had met Angela. She'd rekindled that long-dead flame. Even now, he found her vulnerability and candor refreshing. Angela was fanning the flames of a long dormant desire. And she'd been brutally honest. He should do the same. Or, as Emily Dickinson once said: "Tell all the truth but tell it slant."

He took a sip of liquid courage. "I'm an only child. My mother died of a drug overdose. I don't know who my real father is. My mom was, well let's just say a little promiscuous." *Not very slant, buddy. Not very slant at all.*

"I'm sorry," she said.

"Don't be. I'm not." *That sounds rather smug. Don't fuck this up.* "I mean, it was a long time ago. I'm over it," he lied. "And it's been a long time since I've been in a relationship."

"So you're all by your lonesome," she said. "Like me."

Noah nodded. "Any brothers or sisters? What about your parents?"

The frown returned. Another sip of wine followed. "I have an older brother and an older sister—Jerry and Selena. Jerry's a lawyer. Selena's a corporate executive for a big oil company based in Calgary. We don't talk much. They say I'm trapped in the past. Maybe they're right."

"You're here now in the present." He offered her a small smile. "What about your parents?"

"They're retired now. My father Jonah used to be a lawyer. Jerry runs the firm now. My mother Linda was a housewife, but you know that's a lot of work too when you have kids."

"I imagine," Noah said. "You get along with your mother and father?"

"I know what you're doing," Angela said, that mischievous grin that had so attracted him initially returning with a vengeance.

Noah smiled. "Really? What am I doing?"

"You're getting all this backstory out of the way so we can have some fun."

Noah didn't know if he'd consciously planned such a strategy, but it didn't matter. He liked where it was going. He grinned. "You got me. That's exactly what I'm doing. Now that you've figured me out, just go ahead and say you get along with your parents and all that, so we can move on to the really good stuff."

She smiled broadly, exposing straight white teeth. "Actually I *do* get along with my parents. I love them. They live in Toronto. I talk to my mom and dad at least once a week. There... over and done with." She had a twinkle in her eye. "Now, tell me, what's the good stuff?"

Noah was glad the conversation had steered away from relationships and the death of his mother and possible questions about the identity of a biological father he never knew. Unresolved issues with his mother still bothered him on many levels, but he didn't give a rat's ass if he ever found out who his biological father was.

For the time being, he was just glad he didn't have to go into any details about how neglected he'd been as a child, exposed to a hundred different father figures, and how the resulting lack of love and attention had for many years insulated him in a cocoon of self-reliance.

He wanted this conversation to be one of possibilities and positivity. "If you could have one wish granted, what would it be?" he asked.

Angela tucked an errant strand of hair behind her ear. "That's a tough one." After a few seconds of pensive silence, she said, "My first thought was to say I wanted to be the rich.

Then I thought immortality. But, you know, with the world the way is, who knows where we'll be in fifty years? We might've destroyed the planet by then and wiped out the entire human race. Then, of course, I thought of a soulmate, you know, everlasting love and happiness and all that. But in the big picture, that's still a little selfish. So I guess I'm gonna go with world peace."

"That's a selfless and noble wish."

"Yeah, but maybe I'd change my mind if it became a reality. What would you wish for?"

I'd make the Hat Man go away, was the first thought that crossed Noah's mind, but he quickly pushed it away. "Well, I was thinking world peace, end world hunger, end poverty, end the destruction of our planet, all that. Or I could just be selfish and wish for tons of money or a soulmate. Then, as you were talking, it came to me—I'd wish for God-like powers. If I had divine powers, I'd be able to do all those things and more. After all, it's only one wish."

"You're smart. I wish I would've thought of that."

"Given more time, you probably would've."

Time flew by for the next two hours and Noah learned a lot. They were both bibliophiles, logophiles and voracious readers, Angela preferring suspense, romance, thriller and paranormal while Noah's tastes leaned more toward non-fiction crime drama, horror, and post-apocalyptic fiction.

Like himself, Angela was somewhat of a recluse, often preferring the company of a good book over a real person.

During their often playful conversation, Angela would occasionally brush Noah's hand lightly with her own. Her touch sent warm and sensuous tingles through his body. She was really starting to grow on him.

Her face became serious. "Hey, since you mentioned God-like powers earlier, do you believe in God?"

Religion, politics and sex. The three things you should never talk about. Maybe it was all bullshit. "I used to think I was an agnostic. But then I realized I had the definition wrong. An agnostic believes that nothing is known or can be known about the existence of God, or of anything beyond material things. I'm actually spiritual, but don't attach that spirituality to any religious denomination. How about you?"

"I'd say the same, I think. I was raised a Catholic. I've often been told to pray to canonized saints, only they've never answered my prayers. And besides, the church has all those rules and regulations. Some of it seems a bit hypocritical to me."

"Well, if you believe in God in a Christian sense, then it stands to reason that you believe in the Devil, too."

"Well, I believe in evil forces."

Noah saw a dark shadow pass the large window fronting Grafton Street. And he was sure that this time, the shadow man was wearing a wide-brimmed hat. He shuddered as ice-cold fingers gripped his throat. The image of the Hat Man from his nightmares flashed before him, choking the life out of him. He started to panic. *Don't screw this date up.*

Angela saw his hand trembling and she touched it. "Are you okay? You just turned white as a ghost." Wincing, she suddenly removed her hand from his, as if she'd also felt the powerful evil presence.

He precipitously felt cold. His hand still trembling, he rose. "Sorry, be right back. Gotta go to the bathroom."

Enclosed in a stall sitting on the toilet, Noah studied his trembling right hand. He gripped it with his left, trying to stop it. At the mention of the Devil, a dark and sinister presence had washed over him. And he vividly remembered the Hat Man trying to strangle him. Was the Hat Man the Devil? *After he's done with me, will he go after Angela?* The thought made him feel sick to his stomach. No. He couldn't let that happen. *I need to see a doctor. Something's wrong with me.* Taking deep breaths, he waited in the cubicle until the trembling slowed. Not stopped. Just slowed.

About five minutes later, he felt calm enough to exit the stall. He ran the hot and cold water taps, splashed water on his face, dried it with a paper towel and stared at his reflection in the mirror. His dark green eyes were a little bloodshot and something new; his left lower eyelid quivered slightly—a nervous tic. *Yikes.* He ran a hand through his brown hair, noticing three pronounced worry lines in his brow. He tried to iron them out with the palm of his hand. It didn't entirely work, but it would have to do. He didn't want to leave Angela waiting. He hated doing that to people as much as he hated having it done to him.

Approaching her, he realized some of the color had also drained from her face. It bothered him. Things had been going so well until the Hat Man had come along and fucked it up. Until the Devil had come along and fucked it up.

"I'm sorry," he said. "I'm not feeling that great. Maybe we should go."

Her expression had gone sullen. "Maybe you're right."

Noah paid the bill and they left. Outside, they were slammed by ferocious winds and driving snow. Noah instinctively put a protective arm around Angela's shoulder and she didn't offer any resistance.

In spite of the bone-chilling temperature, the fresh air cleared Noah's head and made him feel a little better. "Can I walk you back to your place?" he said. "I left my vehicle at home. I didn't want to be driving in this."

"I'm okay by myself."

"I'd feel better if you let me walk you home."

"Okay."

As they walked along Grafton Street, Noah realized he still had an arm around Angela's shoulder. He removed it. "Sorry. I did that automatically."

"That's okay," she said, taking his hand. "I like it."

They silently navigated the snow and ice and pedestrian walks in opaque darkness. Occasionally, vehicle headlights would approach, blinding them momentarily before passing.

As they approached Weymouth Street, Angela said, "What was that all about back there?"

"Did you feel it too?"

"I felt something when I touched you. And it felt cold and nasty."

Noah didn't see any point in lying, but he was torn. He didn't want to frighten Angela into having nightmares, or lead her to think he was a nut-job, but he wanted to come clean on some level, if for nothing else than to warn her of possible impending danger. "I used to have a lot of bad dreams when I was a kid. Last night, they returned with a terrifying vengeance.

In the pub, flashes from my nightmare came back, and it scared me. But it was just a bad dream. That's all."

Searching his eyes, she nodded, unconvincingly.

They walked on.

As they approached the green two-story house where she rented a main-floor apartment, she stopped and looked up, her soul-searching eyes locking on his. Even in the darkness, Noah could see the concern in them.

"Are you sure it was just a bad dream?" she asked.

"Yes," he said halfheartedly.

"One day you'll tell me about them?"

"Sure. You want to know? Do you have nightmares?"

"Not that often. But I'd like to know what yours are."

They stopped at her front door and Noah half-smiled. "That means you'll see me again?"

Angela nodded. "If you're gonna unleash any supernatural stuff on me, make sure it's Casper the friendly ghost.

Noah laughed nervously. "Okay... I had a great time."

"Me too."

"It's been so long since I've had a date, I wasn't sure what to do."

"I didn't ruin it with my true confessions?"

"On the contrary," he said. "I appreciate your honesty. I didn't ruin it with my nightmare flashbacks?"

"Of course not," Angela said. "It's like you can control it."

"I'll call you," Noah said.

"I hope you do."

Noah felt like doing a lot more, but restrained himself. He kissed her on the cheek and hugged her tightly, enjoying the warm and pleasant sensations wash through his body, taking the edge off the bitter cold. He released her. She blew him a kiss, went inside her house and closed the door behind her.

They might be something I can't control, he thought, while walking home. *But I'm gonna damn well try.*

Even in the blizzard, it took less than ten minutes for him to get to the corner of Kent and Queen Street, close to home.

Trying to steer his thoughts away from the Hat Man, he instead focused on the interesting turn-of-the century architecture in Charlottetown, the birthplace of Canada. He loved the character, charm and cosmopolitan vibe of the city; even though, with a population of around 36,000, it was really just a small town compared to many other Canadian cities. But, as much as he enjoyed the vibe, he thought Charlottetown suffered from a personality complex of sorts—a downtown rich in culture, history and heritage contrasting unsympathetically with the presence of nondescript big-box stores, super-malls and fast-food franchises dotting University Drive. Culture was being replaced by commercialism.

Mulling over that contradiction, Noah paused on the curb, across the street from the Victorian-style house where his third-floor apartment was located. It had character and charm, and was within walking distance to work. He really was making himself forget all about his nightmares. And he had already chosen his next topic of contemplation—Angela.

Goosebumps sprouted and coursed up his arm, and it wasn't from the cold.

In an effort to deflect the driving snow, he adjusted his baseball cap and looked left, then right. All clear. But when he stepped off the curb, a black SUV suddenly appeared out of nowhere. Startled, he jerked back, realizing with a jolt of adrenaline-fueled panic, he'd just come within inches of becoming road-kill. He tried to take another step back, lost his footing, and landed hard on his ass on the snow and ice-covered concrete.

"Watch where you're going, asshole," he yelled, squinting to see the driver. Even through the reduced visibility produced by the darkness and blowing snow, he could see inside the vehicle. The interior light was on. *Odd*.

And, as it slowed to a crawl about twenty feet away, one thing was completely identifiable—a large, black, wide-brimmed hat.

Oh fuck, no!

CHAPTER FOUR

A few hours later, sipping a hot chocolate and lounging on his couch, Noah had all but forgotten about his near-death experience. Sure, the SUV had slowed after narrowly missing him, making him think fleetingly that the vehicle would stop and the Hat Man would get out and slaughter him. But then it sped up, spinning tires and disappearing around a corner. And he'd finally managed to convince himself that the hat was nothing more than his traumatized imagination run amuck. Angela, her endearing personality and desirous body, had replaced his thoughts now. And all he could think of was how sexy she was and how he couldn't wait to see her again.

He realized it was after one in the morning and decided to turn in for the night. He was planning on calling her tomorrow, Sunday, and invite her for lunch.

With erotic thoughts of Angela floating through his mind, it wasn't long before Noah drifted off to sleep.

******

Noah locked eyes with the black spider on the ceiling. Its eyes—eight in total—were red, glowing, pulsating. He blinked, hoping it would disappear. But, instead, the arachnid grew bigger, its menacing eyes and deadly retractable fangs filling his vision.

"No," he said. "Leave me alone!" To his ears, his voice sounded eerily surreal.

The giant spider blasted a sinewy web that landed above his head. Another one followed, then several, wrapping him in a web of death. Terrified, he knew it wouldn't be long before the spider was upon him, injecting him with its venom, and then tearing him apart limb by limb—an agonizing, torturous death.

He screamed and began tearing frantically at the web. With much effort, he freed himself. He bolted upright in bed, darted into the hallway and closed the door, trapping the spider inside his bedroom, narrowly escaping a grisly end. His heart pounded in his chest and his breath came in short gasps. He was sweating profusely. He walked into the bathroom, relieved himself, and began to leave. He bumped his head on the corner of the door and the sharp pain and warm blood dribbling down his nose, and into his eyes brought him back to reality.

He woke up in the living room, realizing it was a few minutes before 4:00 am.

He had very little recollection of the event, other than a vague unease about narrowly escaping some impending danger. But the small cut on his forehead and the blood terrified him. It meant he'd been sleepwalking, something he was sure he hadn't done since childhood.

He clearly recalled what it had been like all those years ago, hearing a thumping sound and waking up, realizing with a powerful sense of dread that he was curled up in a hallway closet, along with dust pans, brooms and cleaning supplies. His mother had woken him up, more amused than alarmed. Although he couldn't remember how he'd gotten there, he'd surmised that the Hat Man had scared him into the broom closet. He didn't dare tell Barbara. She would just make fun of him, as she usually did.

He still remembered her words. "Get out of there, Noah. Don't be scared of the bogeyman. He doesn't exist, you silly boy."

Pressing his palm to his head, he sat down on the couch and waited for his breathing to normalize and the fear to dissipate before disinfecting and bandaging the wound. Trying to drive out thoughts of the Dark Menace and the new problem of sleepwalking, he purposely shifted his thoughts to Angela, and what he was going to say when he asked her out for lunch.

Fifteen minutes later, he returned to bed. After a few minutes of anxious tossing and turning, he drifted off to sleep. But not before a dark image of a wide-brimmed black hat once again invaded his subconscious.

******

He had green ones, red ones, brown ones, black ones. He had cattleman, cutter, Dakota, and diamond-shaped ones. He had akubras, balaclavas, berretinas and beanies. He had bowlers, boaters, berets and bucket hats.

But, oh how Drake Simeon loved his fedoras, top hats and gauchos.

He removed the gaucho from a hook on the wall, alongside all the others. Placing it on his head, he posed in front of the full-length mirror in the living room of his modest bungalow fronting Highway #3, about twenty minutes east of Charlottetown. The flashlight positioned behind him cast the perfect image of the Hat Man; nearly seven feet tall, slender, draped in a black trench coat. But of course, the accoutrement that completed the menacing picture was clearly the gaucho hat. Its smooth black leather, distinctive wide rim, and the sheer joy he got from wearing it seemed to transform him into something sinister. Something that had nothing to do with Drake's Monday-to-Friday, nine-to-five job as an accountant, a boring bean counter.

Lighting a cigarette, he turned sideways and took a deep drag, watching the black-gray swirls of smoke floating up and lingering around his face and hat as he exhaled. He tipped the hat into the mirror's dark reflection and the reflection tipped back. He marveled at how the side profile of his sharp cheekbones and pointy nose added to the chilling aspect of the image.

He removed the gaucho hat, went into the kitchen and sat down, swirling it on his index finger and admiring its beauty.

"Definitely my favorite hat," Drake said to the empty house.

It had been a good night so far. Earlier, along with the trusty gaucho, he'd scared the living shit out of nine or ten people. He had played on their fears of the Hat Man—a worldwide phenomenon, a terrifying character often compared to the bogeyman—and infected their psyches. He was sure most of those people, if not all of them, would have nasty nightmares tonight.

Just what the doctor ordered, he thought, taking another long drag on his cigarette and slowly blowing smoke rings above the flickering flame of a jar candle on the table. *Or maybe, just what the Devil ordered.*

Ever since he'd been a child, he'd been haunted by the Hat Man. The spectral entity, who terrified thousands, first emerged in a terrifying nightmare. Then the Hat Man started appearing in his waking life. He'd catch glimpses of him in various locations in his childhood home; in the bedroom closet; in the hallway; in the living room; even in the bathroom. As he got older, the sightings escalated. He would see him in the fields; in trees; at night in the forest; even haunting Drake in the school bus in broad daylight.

But the Hat Man sighting in his 5th grade classroom was not only the most memorable, but the most catastrophic. The Hat Man had appeared behind math teacher Emma Filbert one day. Frightened, he'd watched as the Dark Menace began strangling her. Emma struggled frantically but the Hat Man's iron grip was too powerful and eventually she succumbed, withering to the classroom floor like a lifeless ragdoll. Then the Hat Man had turned a malevolent eye toward Drake, crossing the classroom with lightning speed, lifting him up by the throat, slamming him into a wall and choking him with a ferocious death grip.

It took many years for him to recollect what exactly had happened after that. But slowly he began assembling pieces of a macabre jigsaw puzzle. After his release from the hospital, his mother—armed with the knowledge that the math teacher had actually not been attacked by the Hat Man or anyone else—abandoned him and disappeared. Then came the foster homes... and the rebellion. Finally he'd been committed to a mental institution.

At the time, he'd thought it was the worst thing that had ever happened to him. But, he'd soon realized that he'd been wrong. It had been his cure. Drake began to recognize the Hat Man for who he really was—a powerful benevolent force whose mission was to rid the world of evil. So, like the Hat Man, he decided to lead the charge against the malignant cancers of society. He was no longer afraid of the Hat Man.

He had become the Hat Man.

But somehow along the way, his mission had become blurred. From saving the souls of the damned, he'd switched to scaring the shit out of everybody and anybody. It was exhilarating. Exciting. Fun.

A reign of terror. It gave him control.

Driving home in the blizzard earlier, he initially believed he'd wreaked enough havoc for one night. But as he parked his black SUV in the garage, he'd decided to go inside the house and wait it out. Sure the roads were bad now, some even impassable, but he wanted to see what Mother Nature had in store for him. Maybe there would be a reprieve and a path back to the city for more taunting and terrorizing. He looked out the window and that's when he saw it.

Excited, he rose and approached the window with a wicked grin. In the distance, a large bank of clouds was moving eastward, being replaced by twinkling stars and calm night skies. And when he glimpsed the full and glowing moon appear out of a mass of separating dark clouds, he knew it was a sign. He must return, if only to see her again, to terrorize the woman who had eluded him earlier.

Firing up the SUV in the garage a few minutes later, he realized with some satisfaction that the woman hadn't actually eluded him. It was simply the storm's fury that had caused him to beat a hasty retreat. But not before he'd recorded her address. He knew where she lived.

She couldn't hide behind her fake name anymore. Because she wasn't who she purported to be at all. No. She was his mother, Matilda, who'd been resurrected from the grave for the sole purpose of tormenting him.

Even though Drake had read his mother's obituary a few years ago indicating that Matilda had died in a terrible car crash, he didn't believe it. In almost every female face, he saw her dark eyes, nasty scowl and malevolent grin. But it wasn't until he saw *her* that he knew his mother had truly returned, resurrected from the dead as Angela Rosewood.

It took him a few minutes to realize he had a white-knuckled grip on the steering wheel and was grinding his teeth, bad habits spawned from Matilda's mistreatment of him. He took a deep breath, loosened his hands on the wheel and slid his tongue along his sensitive and scraped molars. A flash of pain catapulted him back to reality and kicked his agenda into high gear.

Three-thirty-six in the morning or not, it was time for vengeance.

******

She saw it as a shadow. Then it morphed into a terrifying headless black shape that descended down on her. Thick black hands reached out, gripped her windpipe and squeezed. She felt her throat tighten and in a terrifying instant, thought her voice box was going to shatter and explode. She woke up, screamed bloody murder, and the black headless attacker vanished. Her heart beat rapidly. The room was suddenly cold.

Her throat was parched. Her oversized white t-shirt was moist with sweat.

"What the hell was that?" Angela said, breathing heavily. She got out of bed, grabbed a flashlight off her nightstand and turned it on. She slowly trained the beam around the room, afraid the headless monster might at any second leap out from a dark corner. Nervously, she approached her closet, flung open the door, and jumped back, half-expecting an assault. She shone the light in the closet. There was nothing there but clothes and boxes of junk piled high on a shelf, a few more stuffed into corners on the floor. She reached inside, grabbed a fresh t-shirt, quickly stripped off her wet one and threw it on the floor. She put on the clean, dry t-shirt, went into the kitchen, and flicked on a lamp sitting in the middle of her oval kitchen table. She poured a glass of cold water, went into the living room and sat down on the couch, then drank two quick mouthfuls and tried to make sense of the bizarre nightmare.

Angela could barely remember the last time she had a nightmare. She pulled a nearby comforter up to her shoulders and thought about it. *Why now? Maybe it's him. His nightmare—the evil forces in it—rubbing off on me... when I touched him.* She shuddered, trying to dismiss the notion, but it was there, growing like a pesky weed, casting doubt on her future with Noah.

Her eyes wandered around the disarray of her living room. There were clothes scattered on an armchair facing the couch. The small simulated woodgrain coffee table was strewn with dirty dishes, newspapers, magazines, novels, and a few make-up accessories. More boxes of books were piled high by a street-facing window alongside a pre-fabricated boxed bookstand she'd meant to assemble ages ago. Five or six framed pictures of PEI beach vistas and pastoral landscapes leaned haphazardly against a wall. More dishes cluttered the adjoining open-concept kitchen island. Even the sink was full.

The disarray in the apartment was emblematic of the disarray in her life and she struggled to organize her thoughts before she returned to bed, even though it was closing in on four am. Her mother's old adage rang like the tolling of a bell in her mind. *"Cluttered house, cluttered mind."*

Vowing to clean up her act the following morning, she refocused on trying to make sense of her nightmare and its connection to Noah. Sure, she'd wallowed in a pit of grief and despair for a long time after Case had unceremoniously dumped her, but surely that had nothing to do with the headless attacker that had almost killed her in her sleep. The pressure on her throat, the pain, it was so real. Case was presumably happy with his blond bimbo, so why would he come after her now? It's not like she did anything to him, not like there was any reason for him to want to get back at her. *Because he has a dark side, that's why.* She blocked the thought out as quickly as it entered her mind.

After returning home from her date with Noah, she'd managed to clean up the remaining glass and the heart-shaped rock. She'd stuffed the rock, along with the image of Case, into the nightstand drawer. Out of sight, out of mind. And even though her date with Noah had been an emotional roller-coaster, it had served to at least apply a topical antibiotic to the injury inflicted by Case. She'd tried, but hadn't been able to remove his photo from her nightstand for a long time. And now finally, it was out of sight.

Didn't that make Noah somewhat of a savior? Still, his nightmare and the frightening effect it had on him made it a tough thing for her to get past... especially when she'd felt it too. Touching his hand in a spontaneous gesture of support, Angela had felt a powerful and fearsome evil presence penetrate the very core of her being. She shivered, tucking the comforter over her shoulders, hugging herself. *Maybe he's transferring the evil to me. Whatever is attacking him is using him a conduit to get to me. But why?*

Over the years, Angela had read her fair share of paranormal novels—enough to give her a healthy fear and respect of the supernatural. But to make sense of it, she needed to know more. As much as it frightened her, she needed to understand the details of Noah's nightmare. She had volumes of books on the paranormal. *Knowledge is power. Power is understanding. Understanding leads to answers and remedies.* As she thought about it, she realized she didn't want to distance herself from Noah because of his nightmare. If she ran away, she felt sure she would be in even more danger. She had to get to the bottom of what was bothering him.

The books, she realized. The answer might be in the books. First, she'd have to find out the details of Noah's nightmare. Then, she'd clean the house and organize the book shelf, because she couldn't possibly find anything in the current mess.

"*Cluttered house, cluttered mind.*"

"All right, Mother. I'll clean up my act."

With renewed resolve, she rose, went into the kitchen and turned the lamp off. The small room was suffused in moonlit darkness; enough light, she realized, to retrieve the flashlight from the coffee table and head to bed. As she bent down to pick it up, she saw something, a dark shadow, out of the corner of her eye. She swung around and faced the window. Through the partially opened floral-patterned drapes, her eyes widened in horror as her mind processed the image. She could see the upper torso of a shadow man. He appeared to be wearing a trench coat. He also wore a wide-brimmed black hat and his facial features were a mask of black.

"Bitch," he said in a deeply authoritarian voice. "Your time is coming."

"Aaaaaaaaaaaaahhhhh!" she screamed, slipping as she struggled to retrieve the flashlight. She landed hard on her ass, but the adrenaline boost masked the jolt of pain that shot up her spine. She rolled over quickly, not wanting to look at the Hat Man, but wanting, needing desperately to find the flashlight, as if the light would miraculously make the evil disappear. Finally, her hand touched the flashlight. She grabbed it, turned it on and pointed it at the window.

The Hat Man was gone.

When she stood up, another bolt of pain shot up her back. She winced and staggered to the front door, wanting to make sure it was locked. Sure enough, she'd forgotten to turn the deadbolt. She cranked it into the locked position, letting out a small sigh.

Thump... thump... crack!

The sound of wood splintering. As her heart raced, she realized the Hat Man was trying to kick the door down. It wouldn't be long before he succeeded.

"Please, no," she said, panicking. She ran into the kitchen, grabbed a chair and propped it up against the door, hoping it would hold; though likely, not for long. Her next instinct was to run. She returned quickly to the kitchen and rummaged through the cutlery tray, realizing as she darted into her bedroom and closed the door, that all she'd managed to grab was a butter knife.

The pounding on the door continued. Wood splintered, tiny spears flying into the living room.

Better than nothing, she thought, slamming the door. With supernatural strength fueled by adrenaline, she heaved and slid a large fully loaded dresser up against the door.

She raced into the closet and closed the door. Then she sat and waited, cold terror infusing her veins.

She heard a loud crash and knew with dead certainty that the Hat Man had just kicked in her front door.

Then she fainted.

CHAPTER FIVE

Noah had tried to reach Angela three times in the last hour, and he was beginning to worry. It wasn't that he'd had a premonition or anything after he'd returned to bed after his traumatic sleepwalking episode. Nor had he had any nightmares about what might have happened to her. As far as he could remember, he'd slept soundly on his second try. His concern had more to do with Angela's reaction to touching him during his nightmare flashback. She'd looked horrified. Had he somehow transferred the evil to her?

He thought of walking to her apartment, but realized after looking out his window, that it was a bright sunny day and the roads were clear enough to drive. Exercise could wait. He could even see signs of a meltdown. *Weird winter here. One day a snowstorm and well below freezing, the next day a meltdown and well above freezing. Strange days indeed.*

A few minutes later, he fired up his navy-blue Chevrolet Silverado half-ton pickup and was on his way. At five-to-noon, he pulled in front of Angela's apartment, his eyes widening at what he saw. Her dark red wooden front door was splintered and shattered. Large chunks of it were strewn around. Two blue coverall-clad contractors were out front, cleaning up the debris and loading it into a gray pickup parked on the snow-covered lawn.

Yellow crime scene tape bordered part of the purple picket fence fronting the house.

A cop car was parked across the street. Inside the vehicle, the cop was talking on a cell phone.

As Noah parked, the cop put the phone down, sized up Noah and his Silverado, and scribbled something on a note pad. Then he pulled away.

Noah felt his heartbeat quicken. *Oh, shit no.*

He quickly exited the truck and strode up the shoveled walkway to the house. He saw a cardboard-wrapped new door propped up against the gray pickup.

He approached one of the contractors, a burly man with a mop of brown hair and a thick beard.

"What happened?"

The man gave Noah a sideways glance. "Who are you?"

"I'm a friend. Is Angela okay?"

The man threw a piece of wood into the truck bed. "I don't know who Angela is?"

"She lives here."

"Well, I don't remember the name. I work for the landlord."

"What happened?"

"Break-in, is what the landlord said. Maybe an assault, according to that cop."

"Assault? What happened to Angela? Is she okay?"

"Landlord said the tenant is in the hospital?"

"Hospital? What hospital?"

"How the hell should I know? Why don't you try the Queen Elizabeth? It's the closest one."

The other contractor, a tall, skinny, clean-cut man, approached the work truck with a section of door and threw it into the truck bed. It landed with a large clang. He turned to Noah. "You a friend?"

Noah nodded.

"Give him your business card, Hank." To Noah, he said, "If you find the tenant, can you tell her to call us to arrange to get a new key to her house? I don't even know if the woman is alive, but it's not our job to track her down and get her new key to her. Fucking cheap son of a bitch, her landlord. Pays us jack-shit to install a door and then expects us to track down the tenant and give her the key."

Hank produced a business card from a pocket and handed it to Noah. "Can you make sure she gets this?"

"No problem." Noah took the card and put it in his pocket as a potent feeling of dread settled over him.

Hank's eyes narrowed. "And we're not telling you where we hide the key. The tenant... uh, Angela, has to call us. After all, we don't know you from fucking Adam."

Noah was too worried about Angela to bother with a smart-assed response. "Thanks. Don't worry, I'll tell her."

Although the roads were clear and had indeed started to melt, it seemed to Noah that the trip to the Queen Elizabeth Hospital took eons. Every red light seemed to last for an eternity. Every braking vehicle seemed to be going in slow motion. Passing pedestrians took forever to reach the curb. It wasn't the longest fifteen minutes of his life, but it felt damn close. He finally pulled into the visitor parking lot and was looking for a place to park when he noticed someone familiar exiting the automated sliding-glass doors of the EMERGENCY entrance.

As he quickly looped out of the parking lot and pulled in front of the EMERGENCY doors, a nearby paramedic loading an ambulance with an empty stretcher scowled at him for his Richard Petty-like maneuvers.

But he only had eyes for Angela. She stood outside, looking around bewildered.

He pulled up beside her, stopped, and quickly got out of the truck.

The paramedic shook his head. "No parking here."

Noah ignored him, rushing to Angela. Her sandy-blond hair was disheveled and matted to the side of her face and she wore a large navy-blue parka.

As she saw him, raw panic froze her facial features. She stepped back.

Now within ten feet, Noah said, "Angela, are you okay?"

The panicked expression slowly melted, and she moved forward and hugged him impulsively. After he released her, she said, "Thank God, you're here. I was just gonna arrange a cab."

Unimpressed, the paramedic turned and walked toward them. Noah turned to him. "Don't worry, we're leaving... right now."

"This isn't a patient pick-up area," he said. "It's for ambulance emergencies."

"We're going," Noah said. He helped Angela into the passenger seat of the pickup and closed the door. He got in and pulled away quickly, before the paramedic decided to turn vitriolic.

He turned right on Riverside Drive, and then realized that Angela's house was the other direction. Noah searched for delicate words to query her on the attack. He started with his original unanswered question. "Are you okay?"

"I guess it could've been worse," she said. "I sprained my spine. At least I didn't break anything. Did you hear what happened?"

Noah nodded. "Some of it. I tried calling you a few times this morning but got no answer. So, I went to your house. The contractors replacing your door told me." Noah reached into his shirt pocket and produced a business card and handed it to her. "Before I forget, you have to call them to get a new house key."

She took the card and stuffed it into her pocket. "Thanks."

He could see she'd been crying, and he didn't want to upset her. Clearly she'd been through a terrifying ordeal. But a morbid curiosity pushed him forward. "What happened, Angela?"

"Someone broke into my house last night," she said, her voice quaking. "While I was home. Where are we going anyway?"

"Sorry, I forgot to ask. Do you want me to take you home?"

"Not right now. I'm hungry. Can we get something to eat? I'll tell you all about it over breakfast. And there's something I need to know."

******

Twenty minutes later they were settled in a booth at Smitty's Family Restaurant on University Avenue. Since Angela's cell phone had been left at her apartment, she had used Noah's phone to call the contractors and obtain the secret location of her new house key—under a rock on the front porch.

She dabbed her toast into the soft yolk of a sunny-side-up egg and took a large bite.

Noah shoveled a fork full of hash browns into his mouth and, chewing slowly, set his fork down. He took a sip of coffee.

Angela took a sip of coffee too, and slowly looked up at Noah. "You wanna know what happened?"

"Please. I was pretty worried about you."

She brought him up to speed; her nightmare of the headless attacker; the chilling attack of the Hat Man; fainting in her bedroom closet. "When I came to, I was in the hospital. The cops questioned me there. They told me my upstairs neighbor, Margaret, heard all the commotion and woke up. I guess she yelled at the Hat Man and threatened to call the cops. He took off. But Margaret likes her after-dinner drinks, and didn't get much of a description. Other than the hat."

"The cops have no suspects?"

"That's what they tell me."

Remembering his sleepwalking episode last night, Noah scratched his chin stubble and wondered: *Could I have attacked Angela in an unremembered, zombie-like state?* He thought he'd heard stories of people killing while sleepwalking. As a cold chill crept up his spine, Noah shuddered. *What time did I finally wake up after sleepwalking? Right. It was 3:56 am. And I went back to bed shortly after that.*

A bead of sweat popped on his forehead and he quickly wiped it away. "Do you know what time it happened?"

"It was around four in the morning," Angela said. "I was just getting ready to go back to bed after that headless monstrosity tried to strangle me in my nightmare."

Noah let out a big sigh. *Physically impossible for me to be in two places at once.* But he wasn't totally relieved. They'd both had their nightmares at around the same time. That was creepy. And hadn't Angela told him that she seldom experienced nightmares? *Where is this leading?* He had a hundred questions and very few answers.

And what Noah found so deeply disturbing was the Hat Man. The same Dark Menace that had tormented him as a child and was now haunting him again, was also terrorizing Angela. And goddammit, the monster was real. Noah was at a loss for words.

"Are you okay?" Angela asked. "What happened to your head anyway? You didn't have that bandage on your forehead last night."

Noah thought that giving Angela too much information, too quickly, might frighten her off permanently. He already suspected she was making connections between his nightmare, his sighting of the Hat Man outside The Pilot House last night, his sudden mood change in the pub, and him, period. He didn't want to confirm a suspicion that might be growing in her mind that he was a certifiable nutcase. Hell, she already had admitted she thought he was a little weird. He decided to gloss over it and steer the conversation in another direction. "I just bumped my head. It's nothing really."

She made a small smile. "I guess you're clumsy. Like me."

"I guess so."

After a thoughtful pause, she said, "I need to know something. You said last night you'd tell me about your nightmare. Could you describe it to me?"

She'd managed to get right to the point. And, if she was in danger—which she clearly was—then he had to come clean, at least on that point. "As a kid, I used to have nightmares about the Hat Man. One time, he tried to choke me in my sleep. It felt so real. I've never forgotten it. But then he went away...

for years and years. But recently, he returned with a vengeance. My nightmare the other night involved the Hat Man. At first, he was a hillbilly-type Hat Man, trying to kill me with an axe. Then he was the one that you described, standing at the foot of my bed, leaning down threateningly. He seemed to be constricting my breathing, paralyzing me, sucking out my soul. It scared the shit out of me."

"That's what scares me," Angela said, pushing her half-eaten breakfast plate away and taking a sip of coffee. "First I meet you, and now you tell me you got attacked by the Hat Man in a nightmare the night before. Then I have a similar horrible nightmare. And I almost never have nightmares. Then I was attacked by the Hat Man—in real life! It's as if—and I dread the thought—somehow you're passing the evil to me."

"It's suspicious, I'll grant you. But I don't think so," Noah said. Not that he was sure. He just refused to believe it. "I like you, Angela. I wouldn't try to hurt you."

"I don't know you that well. And I like you, too. But you have to admit, the pieces add up.

"I think we need some answers. I don't know anything about the Hat Man. Do you?"

"A little. I read a few books on him a few years back. I have to go through my boxes of books one day and dig them out. I remember some stuff, but I need a refresher."

"What did you learn about him?"

"He's more common than you might think," Angela said. "Apparently thousands of people around the world have reported not only seeing him in their dreams, but in their waking lives."

"Really? And what do they say?"

"There are many theories. Some believe he's the Devil. Others think he's somehow linked to alien abduction. Some people even think he's from another dimension or a parallel universe. Then there are those who believe he's a ghost, and others who say the Hat Man is nothing more than a sleep disorder, or a trick of the mind."

"So what do most people believe? That he's good, or the other way around?"

"I'm not sure. But it seems to me most people think he's evil, although I've read accounts where people swear he's a positive influence in their lives. A guardian angel of sorts."

"Does he hurt people? Like really hurt them, in real life."

"You wouldn't believe some of the accounts. They're shocking and disturbing, to say the least. Many people claim he just stares at them balefully, like he did in your nightmare. But others claim he's trashed their houses, attacked them and caused physical harm. I even read one comment written by a guy who wants to interview him."

In spite of the serious nature of the conversation, Noah laughed. "I should try that. What's your agenda, Hat Man?"

Angela laughed nervously. "Well, whenever you're dealing with the supernatural—something that can't be explained scientifically—people are gonna come up with crazy ways to deal with it."

"Yeah. But what I'd really like to know is how to get rid of him."

"There are theories on that. Speaking the name of Jesus or God, blessing your house, even just ordering him to leave. Some think he feeds on our fears and attacks us when we're at our lowest point. I've even read accounts of people actually kicking the shit out of him."

I wouldn't mind smashing him over the head with a baseball bat, Noah thought. "Wow, weird stuff for sure. But that religious stuff probably only works if you're religious. Which we're not. Not really."

"It might be worth a try, though." Angela said. "Really, anything would be worth a try."

"Why don't we read some of your books?" Noah asked, while another idea was fermenting in his head. He had a sleep specialist/paranormal investigator friend who was into all kinds of trippy stuff. Neil Samuelson might be just the guy to shed some light on this subject.

Angela had mentioned sleep disorders and when Noah reflected on it, he realized he probably suffered from multiple ones. He made a mental note to consult Neil privately about his sleep-related problems and his nightmares.

Besides, with Angela's recent trauma and spine sprain, it wasn't likely she'd be in any condition to go parading around town looking for answers. He'd seen her wince at least three times during their conversation and knew she was trying hard to put on a brave face.

A disturbing thought crossed his mind. After the hillbilly attack, he too still had a nagging pain in the small of his back. He and Angela were a match made in heaven. So much in common. Both with lower back injuries, both being terrorized by the Hat Man.

"Maybe later," she said. "I need to go home and put some ice on my back... maybe take one of the painkillers the doctor gave me. Besides, my place is a mess. I'm embarrassed for you to see it."

Noah hadn't mentioned his back pain to Angela and decided now was not the time to start. She was already freaked out and he didn't want to give her any more reasons to fear him. "I'll take you home. But don't be embarrassed. If you want, you can order me around and I'll help you clean your place."

"That's very kind," she said with a smile. "I just might take you up on that."

Noah was relieved to see the evasive dimple return and dance around her cheek—the mark of a real smile. He paid the bill and they left.

It was time to find some answers.

******

As Noah parked in front of Angela's house ten minutes later, his thoughts tumbled like a Mount Everest avalanche. *Is the Hat Man a figment of my imagination? No. He just attacked Angela. Yeah, but was that the real Hat Man? Maybe the Hat Man is a guardian angel? Or is he evil? And what about the fucking sleepwalking?*

Opening the door for Angela and helping her out of the pickup, he shuddered. *Am I the Hat Man? Neil will know. Neil Samuelson always knows.*

CHAPTER SIX

Neil Samuelson had no idea what the woman was talking about. He had been working on an experiment that Sunday night in his barn/laboratory when the call came in. The ragged, aged voice on the other end of the line sounded hysterical and incomprehensible.

He listened to her mutter gibberish mixed with a horrific scream before he finally cut in and tried to calm the old woman down. "I'm sorry, ma'am. You're going to have to slow down. Please calm down and tell me what you saw."

There was a ten-second silence before she said, "It's the black man... he's... he's wrecking the house."

"Black man? You mean a real man?"

Neil heard a loud crash before she continued. "You have to come quick... before he kills me." Her voice was panicked and ragged with fear.

Neil abandoned his previous line of inquiry in favor of one important fact. "Where do you live?"

"I'm on Peter's Road."

"What's your address?"

"Four..."

There was another crash, followed by a terrifying scream. Neil switched his cell to speakerphone and held it away from his ear at arm's length. "Four... is that it, ma'am?"

He heard a rustling sound, followed by labored breathing, some static, and then the terrified woman's shrieky voice. "Four... one... four... Peter's Road. Pleeease, come qui... "

Click. The line went dead.

In an instant, Neil recognized the address and the voice. The house was occupied by 85-year-old Agnes Ingles, a native Islander like Neil. After the death of her husband, he'd even treated her for sleep paralysis, a mysterious sleep disorder occurring in that transitional stage between falling asleep and waking, during which a person becomes completely immobilized and often sees frightening images.

Now he realized why she'd called him, and probably not the police. She'd tried that a half a dozen times, claiming she'd seen ghostly apparitions, only for them to arrive and find nothing. From what Neil had learned, her last two cop calls had fallen on deaf ears. Some cops on the force had pegged her as a looney.

Agnes's house was on Neil's list of places to check out for paranormal activity, but he'd been so preoccupied with his experiments lately, he hadn't found the time to make it out there. Part of him had believed the cop version of events, but it didn't matter now.

Maybe it's nothing, he thought. *I'll check it out, then call the cops.*

He quickly pocketed his cell phone, methodically switched off flashing electronic monitors, powered down six computers, and turned off a series of overhanging fluorescent lights in what he called his Parallel Dimension Laboratory. *Damn,* he thought. *I was making such great progress with the experiment.* He disliked being interrupted during his work.

But Neil was also a man of compassion. And when someone put out a cry for help—which Agnes had not done until now—he could do nothing else but come running. At 65, he'd taken the Hippocratic Oath thirty years ago and it always flashed through his mind during times like these: *"I swear to fulfill, to the best of my ability and judgment, this covenant: I will respect the hard-won scientific gains of those physicians in whose steps I walk, and gladly share such knowledge as is mine with those who are to follow."*

But, over his years as a sleep specialist, he'd expanded on it. And it was that last part that sent him bolting out the door whenever someone needed help, often putting the safety of others above and beyond his own safety. He repeated it in his mind as he assembled his paranormal gear below a lone incandescent lightbulb at the laboratory entrance door. *"My highest calling is to always put the needs of humankind above my own."*

He strapped on his EVP wristwatch digital recorder, briefly checked its functions, and then reached for his trusty Colt .45 revolver. It might not have the stopping power of some of the fancy handguns and assault rifles used today, but it could still save his life in a pinch. And it was a damn sight better than bringing a knife to a gunfight, with all the crazies walking around in this day and age.

He made sure it was loaded and then snapped it in place in his shoulder holster. He set the alarm, locked the laboratory and climbed into his green newer-model Ford half-ton pickup. He punched the address into a dash-mounted GPS and started it up. He knew Peter's Road was only twenty minutes away from his neatly manicured ten-acre spread fronting Highway #3, but his night vision wasn't what it once was. He relied on that sexy female British accent he'd programmed into the GPS to find the address quickly and efficiently.

He ran a hand through his thick mop of gray hair. People said he looked like Albert Einstein and he took it as a compliment.

He thought about the call as he drove. There were a lot of things disturbing about it, but one thing bothered him in particular. Agnes had said 'black man.' Did she mean black *shadow* man? Did she mean the Hat Man? Since he'd retired as a sleep specialist, Neil had been doing paranormal investigations for the last six years. As a doctor, he strove to apply scientific methodology to all of his studies. Oftentimes, he found that the reports were merely the product of delusional, or indeed, mentally ill minds. Sometimes, after systematic and methodical analysis of his findings, he'd come to the conclusion the subjects were simply bat-shit crazy.

But the Hat Man was different. All but one subject (a psychiatric hospital patient high on a potent hallucinogenic cocktail of anti-psychotic drugs) who reported seeing the Hat Man, were completely sane in Neil's learned and professional opinion. Worse still, up until two months ago, all the reports of Hat Man sightings had been from people who saw him in their sleep, most often in that strange and mysterious hypnogogic state between sleeping and waking. But lately that had changed. In just two months, he'd investigated fifteen Hat Man sightings from people who'd claimed to have witnessed him while they were awake.

Neil had never seen the Hat Man. But the evidence he'd analyzed certainly suggested his existence. And people from all walks of life, some of them highly respected members of their communities, had seen the Hat Man. Some of the subjects had claimed he was a guardian angel, sent down from heaven to protect them, forgive their sins, and guide them through a life of moral fortitude. But those people were in the minority. Most of the subjects felt a powerful evil presence, often so strong it would paralyze them with fear.

And there was more. It wasn't just sightings people experienced. Some saw objects being relocated in their homes, heard doors slamming and even witnessed the Hat Man flying through a closed door or a closed window. There were eerie voices and sounds. And just recently, property damage. Last week, he responded to a call that led him to a country home in the Montague area where he saw a window smashed and three fist-holes punched through plaster walls. The young female resident, a nurse at the King's County Memorial Hospital, was hysterical, claiming she witnessed the Hat Man pummel the wall before crashing through the window and disappearing into the night.

He'd read about a similar account just this afternoon in *The Guardian*. The details were chilling. *A woman, what was her name? Angela. Right, Angela Rosewood.* By her account, the Hat Man had smashed through her front door and tried to kill her.

But was it really the Hat Man? Or some sick impersonator?

Either way, Neil concluded, events were escalating to a horrifying new level.

"Arriving at destination," the British GPS woman said seductively. "Turn left in fifty feet."

Neil recognized the old home instantly as he turned into the long and winding driveway. He parked in front of the house, turned off the truck and reached into his duffle bag, extracting a large flashlight and a small camera. He tapped his breast pocket to make sure his cell phone was intact and felt the cold comforting steel of the Colt .45.

The house was lit by a single bulb dangling from a cord above the front door. All of the interior lights appeared to be off. He shivered, not necessarily due to the cold. It was a few degrees above freezing, downright balmy compared to the sub-zero temperatures of late.

"Agnes," he called out, approaching the door. "Are you there?"

Nothing but an eerie silence met his question, punctuated by a slight breeze whistling through the trees surrounding the house.

Again. "Agnes, it's me... Doctor Samuelson."

Cautiously, he walked up the pathway to the entrance. Shining the flashlight beam on the door handle, he realized immediately something was very wrong. The door had been battered and shattered. Forced entry. Hell, if he'd been honest with himself, he knew something bad was going to happen the minute he picked up the phone a half hour ago.

Now he had a reason to call the cops. Clear evidence of forced entry. *Better late than never.* He took out his cell phone, speed-dialed his friend Detective Lamar Stevenson, and quickly gave him the address and a brief damage assessment.

"Don't fuck up the crime scene," Detective Stevenson said before hanging up.

Drawing his gun, Neil entered the house, stepping nervously over debris. His hands began to tremble. With his flashlight in one hand, and Colt .45 in the other, he proceeded slowly down the hallway and into the living room. Blocking his path was a tipped-over china cabinet. China dolls, antique plates and trinkets were smashed all over the hardwood floor, along with splintered wood and shattered glass. Someone had knocked it over with ferocious force. Shining the beam around, he quickly noticed other signs of destruction; fist-holes in the walls; a coffee table tipped over; an upside-down armchair; pictures ripped from picture hangers and smashed.

"Agnes. Agnes, are you here?"

Silence.

Some of the damage indicated signs of a struggle. Slash marks on the couch. He approached it and studied the marks. Someone had used a large butcher knife, maybe even a machete.

His jaw dropped. Against the burnt red fabric of the couch, a spray of blood droplets colored the upholstery. *Oh shit. I'm in a crime scene. Don't fuck it up. Get out of here.*

Then he noticed the trail of blood led somewhere. His modification of the Hippocratic Oath echoed in his mind. *"My highest calling is to always put the needs of humankind above my own."* He couldn't leave now. He was a doctor, a preserver of life and a healer, after all.

Stepping carefully through the trail of debris, he walked through the hallway, following the trail of blood. It led to the back door. It was ajar. With the force of the wind, it swayed to and fro on squeaky hinges.

He felt a lightning bolt of adrenaline as he stepped onto the back porch, a sense of urgency fueling him forward.

"Agnes! Agnes!"

He heard a soft moan and then a raspy, gargling voice. "Heeellp."

Through the snow-covered lawn, he quickly followed the blood-dotted footsteps to the source. He found her lying on her back on the snow-covered lawn. His eyes widened. Her throat had been slit. There were other slashes on her cheeks. Her gray eyes were still open and her blood-drenched mouth formed a wide grimace. Her floral-patterned dress was slashed and torn and her belly had been carved with a large X.

He knelt down and checked for a pulse. She had one, but it was weak.

As he started tearing at the fabric of her dress to fashion a pressure bandage for her throat, she coughed. A mouthful of blood spewed from her mouth and dribbled down her chin. "It... it... it... was him."

"Who?" Neil asked, attending to her neck wound.

"The... the... Hat... Man... "

As he watched Agnes breathe her last gurgling breath, it suddenly occurred to Neil that Agnes, just like himself, had been all alone. Her husband had died of an unexpected stroke a few years ago, the same as his wife Maggie. He choked back a lump of bile rising in his throat, then finally lost the battle and coughed it up into the snow as he fell to his knees in grief. Agnes's untimely and violent death brought back all of Neil's pain at the loss of his wife. As the tears began flowing down his cheeks, he wondered for the first time if all his experiments really had to do with a desire to help humanity. Or were his passion and dogged determination just the manifestation of his insatiable desire to be reunited with his beloved wife?

CHAPTER SEVEN

It was just past 8:30 pm when Noah finally left Angela's house. She'd sat on her couch with an ice pack pressed into her lower back and supervised while Noah opened boxes of books, assembled the bookcase and arranged everything neatly. Halfway through, his lower back started making painful protestations and he'd confessed to some lower back pain as well, though choosing to omit the cause of it. Angela had given him two of her codeine-laced painkillers, which he'd gladly accepted, then gritted through the residual pain, and carried on. It'd taken more than three hours to arrange all the books, clean up the cardboard boxes, do her dishes and deposit all of her dirty laundry into a laundry hamper. Angela had been extremely grateful, thanking him profusely.

Later, they'd shared a frozen pepperoni pizza and studied up on the Hat Man. After going through several online sites, they moved on to Angela's collection. She had three books of interest. But it wasn't long before Angela started yawning. Noah also noticed her wincing a bit. The spine sprain was evidently causing her some discomfort, in spite of the ice and painkillers.

It was just the hint Noah needed. He wanted to give Neil a call, anyway. So he'd kissed her on the cheek, gave her a warm hug, and departed, leaving the books with Angela, and agreeing to keep his phone by his side in case of an emergency. Angela had promised to do more research tomorrow, saying she'd already called in sick. She'd been through a lot and needed some time to recover, mentally and physically, before returning to work.

After recent events, Noah wasn't so sure he'd be able to sleep at all tonight. Truth be told, he was afraid to go to sleep. The last thing he wanted to experience was another sleepwalking episode, where he might harm himself. Or, even more terrifying, harm someone else.

Sitting in his idling pickup outside Angela's house, he reached for his phone and dialed Neil.

Neil answered on the third ring. His usually confident voice sounded shaky. "Neil here. Who is this?"

"Neil, it's me. Noah."

There was a long pause on the other end. It had been more than six months since Noah had seen his friend. No falling out or anything like that. Just the run of the mill drifting apart that sometimes happens with friends.

Finally, Neil said, "Noah, it's been ages. How are you?"

Noah could tell by Neil's tone that he wanted the social pleasantries dispensed with quickly. There was something troubling the good doctor. So Noah got right to the point. "Listen, I've been having some sleeping issues lately. Sorry for such short notice, but I was wondering if I could drop by and see you tonight? It's important. Really important."

******

Sipping hot chocolate on a plush brown leather couch twenty-five minutes later in Neil's cozy and capacious living room, a roaring fire burning in a stone-encased fireplace, Noah started from the beginning. He explained his first nightmare about the Hat Man in thirty-four years, and the resulting fall-out—the lower back pain, the paralysis, the feeling of complete helplessness, the raw fear.

Neil took notes while Noah spoke. Although his expression was sad, his methods were clinical, prodding him for more detail with the odd question. When Noah finished, Neil put his pen and steno pad on the coffee table, placed another log on the fire and adjusted it with a poker. Then he closed the black metal screen and sat down in his armchair. His sharp blue eyes met Noah's eyes directly. "Have you ever heard of sleep paralysis?"

"I've heard of it. But I don't know anything about it."

Neil took a sip of hot chocolate. "This could be a long discussion. Do you have time?"

Noah nodded. "You've only heard the tip of the iceberg. I need to know what's happening to me."

"Sleep paralysis is a mysterious phenomenon that occurs in that transitional stage between falling asleep and waking," Neil said. "It's a sleep disorder in which a person becomes completely immobilized. During these episodes, people may hear, feel, or see things that are absolutely terrifying and panic-inducing. Regardless of their best efforts, they're temporarily powerless to break free from an almost catatonic state. Since sleep paralysis often occurs on the absolute edges of dreaming, it's something that's difficult, if not impossible, to properly define or explain. Our knowledge of dreaming or semi-dreaming only scratches the surface of what might be going on in that complex world. But it doesn't prevent people from trying to understand it. After all, knowledge is power and might lead to a cure."

"Do you have a cure?" Noah said.

"I have my own theories on the causes of sleep paralysis and some possible remedies. But let me finish. You need to fully understand it first."

"Sorry, go ahead."

"The theories behind the causes of sleep paralysis are many and varied: sleep deprivation, psychological stress, abnormal sleep cycles, diet, lifestyle choices, a dysfunction in REM sleep, even the result of being the victim of a violent and abusive upbringing."

Noah frowned, thinking of his neglectful and abusive mother.

"Many people experience sleep paralysis as a supernatural assault," Neil said. "Millions of people. It often includes hallucinations that continue into the subjects' waking worlds."

Noah thought of his Hat Man sightings at The Pilot House and shuddered, rubbing a new crop of goosebumps that had just sprouted on his arms.

Neil went on. "Sleep paralysis often suspends the sleeper in sort of semi-dream state. They might be awake and aware of their surroundings but otherwise, they're completely frozen, leaving some to wonder if they're actually dying, experiencing an out-of-body experience, suffering a panic attack, a stroke, or even being kidnapped by aliens. Many report seeing frightening black shadow men, some with red eyes and elongated clownish grins. Others are all black, often three-dimensional. People often see the Hat Man during episodes of sleep paralysis, as you did. Tell me, when you saw him, was he by himself, or with any other shadowy beings?"

"Just the Hat Man. And I forget to tell you, it's not just when I'm asleep. I saw him at The Pilot House the other night while I was having a drink. He was peering through a window at me. Scared the crap out of me. Totally wrecked my night. Then on the way home, he almost ran me over. I swear it was him. Driving a black SUV."

Neil raised an eyebrow, scratched his chin and scribbled something on his steno pad. "Hmmm. That is disturbing." He didn't seem to know what to say to that. So, he just picked up where he'd left off. "Where was I? Right. Sleep paralysis subjects have reported witnessing all manner of frightening ghost-like images; some even claim demon visitations by the succubus and incubus. The succubus is a female demon believed to have sexual intercourse with sleeping men, and the incubus is the male version. Have you ever experienced sex during your sleep paralysis? Or sex during your sleep?"

"No. At least, not that I can remember."

"There are some common symptoms associated with sleep paralysis. Some people hear door knocking, or a thumping sound like an imbalanced washing machine. Sometimes they hear humming, hissing, static, zapping, buzzing and roaring. People also experience out-of-body sensations—numbness, electric tingles, tickling, and feelings of being dragged out of their beds or flying. Some experience pressure on the chest and difficulty breathing. Still others report flying through visually stunning colors and through some sort of a time warp and into another dimension. Have you ever experienced anything like that?"

Noah wanted to cut to the chase—the Hat Man—but he knew Neil had a methodical, systematic and scientific way of diagnosing and treating patients. So he went along, becoming curious about where this interrogation was leading. "No. Not that I can remember. But I *have* experienced numbing, tingling sensations. Tightness in my chest. Difficulty breathing."

Neil scribbled on his pad and scratched his chin. "Do you know that many psychologists and sleep therapists view nightmares as the subconscious mind's way of processing information?"

"As I said, doc, I know very little on the subject."

"Yes, they see nightmares as the subconscious mind ridding ourselves of the stresses of daily life. Solving our problems, cleansing us of negative energy, and bringing peace. You might view sleep paralysis and nightmares as the mind's way of taking out the garbage. A kind of healing mechanism."

"That's a positive spin on it."

"Yes. Still others believe strongly that sleep paralysis is the manifestation of some powerful otherworldly force. Some claim it's an evil force, others believe it's not evil at all but a powerful and enlightening force."

"Is that how you view it?"

"I have a rather complicated theory, which I'll get to in a minute. But it's a helpful view to take. Fear gives rise to more fear. So, it's healthy to try and overcome and even embrace your fears. But I'm going off on a tangent. Before we get to the Hat Man, I want to hear about your other recent nightmares. You said it was only the beginning."

"Yeah, it gets worse." Noah relayed the nightmare of being attacked by some evil presence. The presence had been vague, but as he talked, a partial recollection materialized. He'd been caught in a giant web of death, and unable to escape for what seemed like many long minutes. And then the hellish part started. "It was only after I bumped my head and cut myself on the bathroom door that I woke up and realized I'd been sleepwalking. That really messed me up."

Neil contemplated this, carefully formulating his thoughts. "I'd say you suffer from multiple sleep disorders or parasomnias. Aside from the sleep paralysis, what you've just told me is an example of night terrors mixed with somnambulism. Sleepwalking. They often occur together. Night terrors and sleepwalking are partial wakeups or arousals from deep sleep. They happen during the first third of the night, while you're transitioning from non-rapid eye movement into the REM stage of sleep."

"This is turning into a full-blown lecture."

"Bear with me. It'll get easier to understand." Neil said. "Normally when you sleep, your brain suppresses your ability to move. It's Mother Nature's way of keeping you calm and immobilized. Not so with dread-producing night terrors and sleepwalking. Signs and symptoms include intense heavy breathing, profuse sweating, screaming and flailing, punching, and intense fear and dread. Sometimes your eyes are open and you can even carry on a conversation with an awake person, although your chances of making much sense are rather slim. Sleepwalking is a form of night terrors that can become extremely dangerous. Have you heard the story of Kenneth Parks?"

Noah had a vague recollection of somebody killing someone while sleepwalking, but the details eluded him, so absorbed was he in his own plight. "Not really."

"A few years back, Parks was charged with murder after police discovered his mother-in-law bludgeoned and stabbed to death in her Toronto area home. There was no question Parks had committed the murder. But was he cognizant and therefore responsible for his actions? The defense was able to prove beyond reasonable doubt that Parks was sleepwalking at the time. He was acquitted. Not guilty, by reason of sleepwalking."

"Holy shit."

"And that's not the only case," Neil said. "In the United States in 1994, Michael Ricksgers said he'd accidentally killed his wife while being in a somnambulistic state, claiming he woke up with a gun in his hand and a bleeding wife in bed beside him. His lawyers said his sleepwalking was brought on by a medical condition called sleep apnea. But the prosecutors argued that Ricksgers was distraught and upset that his wife was planning on leaving him. The jury didn't buy Ricksgers story and, according to the Associated Press, he was sentenced to life in prison without the possibility of parole."

Noah shuddered. "Let's get through this."

"Okay. Sleepwalkers have indeed performed some strange, astonishing and complicated things during their episodes. An Australian woman would regularly get out of bed and have sex with strangers, a phenomenon called sexsomnia. A chef cooked spaghetti Bolognese and fish and chips in his sleep. Some sleepwalkers have been reported to eat entire meals in the middle of the night."

"Keep up the good stories."

"One of the most bizarre examples is that of an artist named Lee Hadwin. At night, while sleeping, he draws beautiful and oftentimes intricate art—with virtually no recollection of it. His art is even gaining worldwide attention. I wouldn't be surprised if he's quit his day job by now."

While Noah found Neil's wealth of knowledge fascinating, he needed to direct the conversation back to the Hat Man, back to a cure. "This is all very interesting stuff. But can you tell me what I can do about my sleep disorders?"

"I actually need to think about it some more, analyze my findings. Can I get back to you with some suggestions in a couple of days?"

"But what do I do now? I'm terrified to go to bed. Especially after what you just told me."

"I'll give you some powerful sleeping pills, something to knock you right out. You won't sleepwalk, won't even remember any of your dreams. In the meantime, try and keep a positive attitude. Try and view the dreams, even the Hat Man, in a positive light."

"I'll try. But as I said, you haven't heard everything."

Neil got up, threw another log in the fire, positioned it expertly, and returned to the armchair. His face became grave. "I know. I wanted to ask you, were you by yourself at The Pilot House?"

"No. I'm seeing someone."

"What's her name?"

"Angela. Angela Rosewood."

Neil wrote on his steno pad and looked at Noah somberly. "I read about her in *The Guardian*. Is she okay?"

"She's rattled obviously, but I think she'll be all right."

"Good. If she needs any medical help, have her call me. Does she know anything about the Hat Man? I mean, is she familiar with the phenomenon?"

"She knows more than me, that's for sure. I just left her house. That was one of the reasons I went over there. We did some research online, and dug up a few books on the subject. She's probably reading them now. She explained a bunch of theories about the Hat Man to me."

"Did she come to any conclusions?"

"I don't think so. Hence, the research."

"Have you come to any conclusions?"

"My knowledge is too premature. Actually, that's one of the reasons I came to see you. What do you think?"

"I've diagnosed and helped many people who've seen the Hat Man in their sleep. And I used to believe he was nothing more than a product of the subconscious mind, a mechanism the brain uses to rid people of negative forces. A healing mechanism, like I mentioned earlier. But when people started seeing the Hat Man in their waking worlds, I soon realized my definition was too narrow. That's one of the reasons I retired from my practice. I wanted to study the phenomenon of the Hat Man and the Shadow People full time."

"Shadow People?"

"People often see Shadow People, as well. Sometimes they're with the Hat Man, sometimes not."

"So you think my Hat Man sightings, I'm talking about the ones in my waking life, and Angela's Hat Man sighting, represent the manifestation of some powerful supernatural evil force?"

"I'm still trying to figure this out. I don't want to bombard you with too much information tonight. You've been through a lot, and now you're dealing with an info dump. But I do need to warn you of something."

"Did something happen that I don't know about?"

"You're intuitive," Neil said. "You know I do paranormal investigations?"

Noah nodded.

"I got a call earlier tonight from a panic-stricken elderly lady who lives on Peter's Road. Agnes Ingles. The long and short of it is I believe it was the Hat Man who trashed her house and slashed her to pieces. She's dead." He paused for an instant. "You'll read it in the papers soon enough."

Noah's right hand began trembling. *Not again.* He clutched it with his left. "Oh my God."

"Are you okay?"

"No," he said. "I'd be lying if I said yes."

"Take a few deep breaths."

Noah did. It helped. A little.

"So, as you can see, things are escalating to a disturbing level," Neil said. "But there's something I want you to know. I don't believe the Hat Man in your nightmares is the same Hat Man who killed Agnes."

"Who is he then?"

"I have a strong suspicion there's a Hat Man impersonator running around. Just as people will pervert the tenets of a religion to suit their own evil agendas, so too is this psycho perverting the agenda of the Hat Man."

"Do you know who he is? This copycat killer."

"I wouldn't use that term loosely."

"Okay, impersonator then."

"If I did, we wouldn't be sitting here having this conversation."

"Do the cops have any leads?"

"I don't think so. But if they do, they're not telling me."

******

Less than a mile away on Highway #3, while Noah and Neil discussed the Hat Man, Drake Simeon scrubbed his hands methodically in his bathroom sink. He'd been a little sloppy earlier. He had the blood of Agnes Ingles on his hands. He still had a fire burning outside of his house. All his contaminated clothing was burning—smoke, ashes and hot embers twirling up into the dark sky. That wasn't the only fire burning. Drake still had a fire in his belly for Angela Rosewood. He believed she was his mother, Matilda, tormenting him through the body and soul of Angela.

After his recent failure to end her life, he'd been furious. In a fit of rage, he'd driven aimlessly for hours the following evening. "This is turning into a monumental fuck-up. Why can't I exact my goddamned revenge?"

But then, out of the corner of his eye, he'd seen a shadow person, floating up a long and winding driveway and disappearing near the lone porchlight outside the house. He'd stopped his SUV immediately, knowing it was a sign. He knew the shadow patch was more than just nighttime trickery. It was a living humanoid figure, a supernatural presence. A spirit. An entity. An enemy.

So he'd turned into the driveway and done his duty. As the old bag screamed, he'd chased the shadow person around the house, slashing and slicing, destroying and demolishing. He might have even spared the old woman if the shadow person hadn't possessed her. That was all the reason he needed to slice and dice, chase her outside and finish her off. At least that's how Drake's twisted mind had processed the ordeal.

He finished scrubbing his hands and turned the taps off. Drying his hands, he winced and examined them. They were raw and red, swollen and throbbing with pain. *How long have I been washing them?* He didn't know. Right now, he didn't care.

He had the fire to deal with. Both fires, really, but right now the one outside took precedence. At the door, he donned a brand-new black trench coat, put on a pair of leather working gloves, and studied his ornamental wall of hats, a monument to madness to some maybe, but to Drake it was a wall of magic and miracles.

And really, it was more than that. It was a military arsenal, providing weapons of destruction to rid the world of evil, offering protection and bestowing him with supernatural powers of invisibility and stealth. He would have to remember to say his prayers later, kneel down to the framed image of the Hat Man, the centerpiece, the God really, from which all his hats and all his powers emanated.

He plucked a black fedora from a hook next to the Hat Man image, put it on and frowned. It wasn't his hat of choice. But unfortunately, the gaucho had blood on it. It would have to be destroyed and he would have to replace it. On his way out the door, he grabbed the incriminating gaucho from the hat rack, went out into the starlit, moon-glowing evening and approached the fire. It was still blazing, popping, fizzing and bubbling, expelling moisture from some wet kindling he'd used earlier to ignite it.

Looking down at his gaucho, a lone tear snaked down his bony cheek. He thought some kind of eulogy was in order. He gripped the hat tightly and, with emotion choking his voice, said, "I'm sorry to see you go. You've been a brother-in-arms, a savior and a soulmate. I love you more than words can describe. God rest your soul."

Before he changed his mind, he quickly tossed it into the blaze. He thought he heard a pain-filled cry as it instantly burst into flames. He lit a smoke, inhaled deeply and blew a misty tunnel of gray into the air.

From a nearby pile, he grabbed a pine log and placed it on the rock-encircled fire pit. He watched as a shower of orange embers exploded into the air and swirled up like dancing fireflies. He scanned the tree- line. A gentle breeze blew in.

Spidery arms and fingers from barren branches dipped down, casting dark shadows that crawled across the snow-covered lawn toward him. He blinked. *The Shadow People. Coming for revenge.*

As if in response to his summons, a dark shadow stepped out of the trees. It was human in shape, perhaps five feet tall, with an oversized bald head.

"Get the hell out of here," Drake said, unsheathing his machete. He tossed the cigarette into the blaze.

But the humanoid entity didn't listen. Striding across the clearing, it made steady and purposeful progress toward him.

Drake slashed at the air with his machete. "I said fuck off."

The pine log popped and hissed and a large flaming ember jetted from the fire, landing on the shoulder of his trench coat. It sizzled and smoked on the heavy-duty cotton fabric. He brushed it off with a gloved hand and retreated two steps. When he looked to the tree-line, he was shocked to see the shadow person had become the Shadow People. There were perhaps twenty of them gliding toward him. As they moved, they shape-shifted, bald heads growing and shrinking, growing and shrinking. Their bodies changed as well, thinning and fattening, thinning and fattening. *Shadows from the fire. Nothing more.* He closed his eyes for a second and opened them again.

But they were still there. And coming closer. Perhaps thirty feet away, moving quickly.

He sheathed the machete, pried a hatchet loose from the log pile and started swinging it in the air. "I'll chop your fucking heads off. Decapitate all of you."

Undeterred, the Shadow People glided effortlessly toward him. And Drake noticed for the first time, they all had tiny glowing red eyes.

Seized by panic, he turned quickly and ran toward the house. He wasn't afraid of the Hat Man anymore, not since Drake had become the avenging dark force. But the Shadow People were another matter. They had a different agenda, one he didn't yet fully understand, but he knew it was at odds with the Hat Man's function and purpose. Breathing heavily, he quickly opened the door, slamming it shut and locking all three dead bolts. He threw off his trench coat, gloves and hat. Still gripping the hatchet, he ran toward the bedroom. He stopped in the hallway and spun around.

Horrified, he saw one, two, three, four Shadow People fly through the window, swoop down and bee-line it toward him. "No, no, no... please."

He raced for his bedroom, pulled the door open, and slammed it shut quickly. He felt their debilitating presence. With an enormous effort, he slid a large dresser in front of the door. Then he dove on the bed, pulling the covers over his head and clutching the hatchet tightly. Raw hands. White knuckles.

Growing terrified, he felt their dark presence invade the room. He dared not lift the blankets. "What do you want? What do you want from me?"

They didn't respond. One by one they invaded his mind, blotting out reason, blotting out consciousness, blotting out cognitive function. As a fear that defied description penetrated his body, mind and soul, he felt himself growing weaker. He tried to lift the hatchet, but it was no use. Tried to scream. Nothing.

He was paralyzed. An image of Matilda popped into his head.

She'd tormented him mercilessly over the years simply because *she* was the loser. She couldn't hold down a job or a relationship, and she sure as hell couldn't hold down her booze, although she consumed copious amounts daily.

Her likeness filled his mind. Her long thin brown hair. Those hate-filled black eyes. That nasty permanent scowl. Those long and skinny but oh-so strong arms. He heard her words again, as if she'd spoken them yesterday..."*You will never amount to shit because you're too stupid... You are a consummate loser. You're afraid of the bogeyman. There is no bogeyman—only me. Now get your lazy ass off to bed.*"

And when he'd been too slow to move, he'd receive Matilda's lightning fast backhand, so powerful it almost never failed to lift him off his feet and send him flying into a wall, or a dresser. One time, he'd even hit the TV, smashing the screen to a million pieces and receiving another beating with the belt for his careless landing.

Drake shuddered at the tormenting memories. His breathing became labored and a powerful numbing sensation permeated his being. He felt himself spinning out of control, being dragged down into a black hole. Consciousness ebbed and flowed. The numbness transformed into a million tiny needles prodding and poking at his body. He felt excruciating pain as one lanced his brain. More stabbing pain as a needle lanced his heart.

A black void encompassed him. *This is what it's like to die. This is what it's like to die.* But it gave him no release. Only a profound sadness that the almighty Hat Man, his mentor and savior, had forsaken him.

******

As he rounded a corner after leaving Neil's house, Noah saw the orange dancing flames casting shadows in the night sky. He probably would've just carried on since his brain was on info overload after talking with Neil, but something else caught his eye—a black shadowy figure that swooped down and penetrated the wall of a small white bungalow. It literally passed right through the wall. He slammed on the brakes, pulled onto the shoulder, and peered down the driveway. The flames from the fire illuminated a vehicle parked near the house.

It was a black SUV, similar in style, model, and year to the one that had almost run Noah down recently—the one driven by someone who looked like the Hat Man. *Holy shit. What the hell is this?*

He rolled down the window, pulled out a pad and paper from his glove box and scribbled the address down. Morbid curiosity and a powerful otherworldly force drove him down the driveway—infusing him with a courage and determination he'd never felt before. He stopped about six feet behind the SUV, saw that all the lights were off in the house, and recorded the license plate number. He removed a flashlight from his glove box and stepped out of the truck. Shining the flashlight beam, he approached the fire. He noticed the charred black sleeve of an article of clothing, a jacket of some description, just outside the fire pit border.

He shone the light around, taking mental notes. The small white house was in need of repair, with peeling paint, worn shingles, and precariously hanging pale blue shutters. Some wooden and metal debris was strewn haphazardly about. A small outbuilding a short distance from the house stood incongruous to the disarray and disrepair. Fresh white paint. Brand-new steel roof. New double-paned black-framed windows.

What's in there? Against his better judgment, he moved toward the outbuilding.

Suddenly, reason seized him. *What are you doing, you idiot? You're trespassing.*

But, trapped and transfixed by this powerful and unearthly force, he pressed forward. The outbuilding had a freshly painted blue door. A thick steel padlock said stay the hell away. He grabbed the door handle anyway and pulled. The door barely moved. He felt an odd and powerful presence and swung around. A shadowy figure exited through the closed window of the house and began dancing around the starlit sky. It was perhaps five feet tall with a large bald head. Its form was very defined and distinct, unlike other shadows he'd seen; natural ones outlining human bodies. This shadow person landed on the ground with its feet firmly planted. In seconds, it was joined by another shadow creature, and then another. They were almost identical, and all had beady glowing red eyes. Eyes that were watching him.

Time to go. Hurrying back to his idling pickup, he gave them a wide berth, although he was somewhat unsure if what he was feeling was raw fear or nervous excitement at having discovered another life form. They seemed so damn real. But another part of his mind reasoned that if they had any connection to the Hat Man, they were dangerous. Maybe they were his minions. Disciples from hell. Noah's experiences with the Hat Man had been terrifying. He couldn't bring himself to entertain Neil's assertions that the Hat Man or the Shadow People had anything to do with positivity.

As he neared his pickup, his hand began trembling again. If he couldn't control his nerves, he would be a basket case at work tomorrow. He still had more than twenty arts grant applications to process, and that was only last week's submissions. It was the nature of the government grant business. Everybody and his dog had their hands out.

Besides, it was close to midnight and he had a few other things to do before turning in for the night. Call the cops about the evidence he'd found. He would have to edit that conversation. Call Neil about his discoveries. He wouldn't have to edit that one.

He climbed in the pickup, closed the door, and began pulling out of the driveway, gripping the wheel firmly to try and stop his hand from shaking. As he turned onto Highway #3, he glanced in his rearview mirror. The Shadow People glided down the driveway, following him.

He stepped on the gas and high-tailed it. As he drove along in the darkness, he frequently checked the rearview mirror. He couldn't be sure—maybe his eyes were playing tricks on him—but he thought he saw the occasional black flash obscure his vision. He also felt their presence—dark, surreal, ethereal. A few minutes later, he turned onto the Trans-Canada Highway and pulled into a 24-hour service station and convenience store. He parked and dug out his cell phone. He called Neil and left a detailed voice message. Then he hung up and tried dialing 911, but the phone battery died. And he'd left his car charger at home. *Damn. Bad timing.*

Stepping out into the well-lit parking lot, he scanned the area. No sign of the Shadow People. *Good.* Although he did get some strange looks from customers gassing up their vehicles.

He went inside the store, used the washroom, and then came out and poured a hot chocolate, thinking as he stood in line to pay that maybe he should relay the emergency to the bored-looking female cashier and ask her to call the cops. That might make her day. By the time the two people in front of him paid for their purchases and left, he'd changed his mind. What emergency did he have? He'd come across a vehicle that looked like the one that had almost hit him. He thought he'd seen Shadow People dancing around a campfire. Following him. The sleeve of a burning jacket, which he'd forgotten to recover. A feeling that evil presided at that residence. *Right. Overwhelming circumstantial evidence, your honor. Guilty. Call the cops. What a joke. Stupid idea.*

"Excuse me, I said that'll be a dollar seventy-five," the cashier snapped.

"Oh, sorry," Noah said, placing a two-dollar coin on the counter and leaving without taking his change.

Twenty-five cents. A quarter. Keep the change, honey. Big spender. He laughed nervously, a coping mechanism for dealing with his escalating stress level.

Entering downtown Charlottetown fifteen minutes later, he finally started to relax a little. He no longer felt the presence of the Shadow People. Sipping hot chocolate on a cold winter night helped. He'd even tried to talk himself out of the strange feeling that he'd accidentally stumbled upon the residence of the psychotic Hat Man impersonator killer. He'd gone some way to convincing himself the Shadow People were the product of an overworked imagination, but was still puzzled by some of the things Neil had said to him.

A few minutes later, he turned into the parking lot of his home, parked, and climbed the stairs to his apartment, without incident. Opening the door and flicking on the light, he half-expected the apartment to be full of Shadow People. But no, all the furniture was in its rightful place. The same scenic photographs he'd snapped—mostly outdoor shots of PEI's natural beauty and charm—hung on the burnt-orange walls.

It looked lived-in, comfortable and organized, just the way he liked it.

Fifteen minutes later, under the influence of a powerful sleeping pill, he began to drift off. Before he did, something crossed his mind that begged for clarification. He'd asked Neil about his Shadow People and Hat Man experiments. Neil's eyes had brightened at the question, as if he was on the verge of some monumental scientific discovery. But, then he'd shut down. "I'll tell you, but not right now. When you're ready."

Ready? Ready for what?

CHAPTER EIGHT

"You have a call on line three." The receptionist's tone was cheery and business-like at the same time. The perfect balance of professionalism and friendliness. Noah studied the phone speaker from which her voice had echoed, half-expecting a cop to be on the other end of the line. But instead, he heard Angela's hopeful voice.

Perfect. He was just about to call her.

They got through the social pleasantries, and she asked, "How was your night?"

"Good. Slept like a rock. You?"

"Maybe five hours, but, other than a little pain, I'm fine. I was reading up on the Hat Man after you left. And practically all morning."

"Do you want me to bring you over some lunch?"

"That would be great. I'll tell you all about what I learned."

"Fish and chips okay?"

"Perfect."

After hanging up, Noah closed a few grant application files and, on a whim, removed a grant application from a filing cabinet drawer of his desk. Before leaving the office, he told receptionist Stella Price he might be an hour or so longer than normal. He had to discuss financial aid options with a new grant applicant. Part of his job description included house calls and meeting with applicants in venues that were less intimidating than government offices.

"You have a clean slate this afternoon," Stella said. "Take as long as you want. I'll hold your calls."

A little later, he was on his way. Turning down University Avenue, Noah looked in his rearview mirror and shuddered when he saw a black SUV pull out of an intersection and begin following him. "Relax," he told himself shakily. "There are plenty of black SUVs in town."

******

"Arriving at destination," the alluring voice of the woman living in his GPS said.

"I think I should name you," Neil said. "How about Sophia?"

"Arriving at destination," Sophia repeated.

Neil drove up the driveway and parked his pickup a few feet from the fire pit. He got out and began inspecting the property. He should be safe. Drake should be working in Charlottetown at this time of day. He had harbored suspicions about Drake for almost a month now. Ever since the strange man had paid him an impromptu visit one afternoon, asking questions about his experiments. Very specific questions.

"Who are the Shadow People?"

"What do you know about the Hat Man?"

"Did you bring the Shadow People here? Because if you did, I want you to send them back."

Of course, the kicker was Noah's panicked phone message last night about seeing the Shadow People, and sensing something sinister about the property. Neil had believed he was on the verge of something amazing with his experiments but he had no idea he was this close. *Did I bring the Shadow*

People here? Did I create the Hat Man killer? Maybe everything was going wrong. Maybe everything had gone wrong.

He walked around the small house, stopping occasionally to peer through the windows. No luck. The blinds were tightly closed. He moved away from the building and inspected the fire pit. Only ashes and embers remained. Using a nearby twig, he poked around the ashes but found nothing that would give rise to more suspicion.

He spotted the white outbuilding and approached it. Closed black Venetian blinds prevented him from looking inside. He examined the door and thought of picking the padlock. He had a kit inside the glovebox of his vehicle for such invasive surgery. Scratching his chin, he paused. Maybe this was a job for the police?

After hearing Noah's phone message, he'd thought about calling Detective Stevenson, but had decided against it. Even though, during questioning after Agnes's brutal murder, he'd promised to keep the detective in the loop should he hear or see anything suspicious. This wasn't exactly keeping the detective in the loop, he knew. But this wasn't exactly a crime scene either, at least not one that could be established as such without a search warrant. *Find the evidence. Make Lamar's life easier.*

With that, he walked back to his truck, removed his lock-picking kit and returned to the outbuilding. With gloved hands, he extracted a long piece of serrated metal and glided it into the keyhole of the padlock. After about a minute of twisting and turning, he heard a satisfying *click*.

He removed the opened padlock and slowly opened the door. A powerful rotting stench assaulted his nostrils and he recoiled, drawing his gun instinctively. It took a few seconds for his eyes to adjust to the dark recesses of the building. When they did, his jaw dropped and his eyes widened.

Black shadowy shapes attacked him from all angles.

******

They'd finished their meals—halibut with delicious tartar sauce and golden brown fries, made from scrumptious PEI potatoes.

Noah licked his lips and wiped his hands with a napkin. He'd brought Angela up to speed on some of his discussions with Neil and the subsequent discovery of the suspicious property, the suspicious black SUV, and the Shadow People. She'd watched him in shocked disbelief initially but the more he talked, the more her eyes told a different story. She was starting to believe him. He waited until she finished her last fry before continuing.

"In your research, did you learn anything about the Shadow People?" Noah asked.

She opened her laptop. "I did. For starters, Wikipedia says a shadow person is 'the perception of a patch of shadow as a living, humanoid figure, particularly as interpreted by believers in the paranormal or supernatural as the presence of a spirit or other entity.'"

"What are their origins? What do they want?"

"That's a matter of debate, but they seem to date back as far as 300AD. Evidence pops up in religions, legends and belief systems. You hear about shadowy creatures all the time in folklore and ghost stories."

"And their agenda?"

She opened up a dog-eared section of a paperback. "The author claims to be some kind of an expert. Anyway, if you believe her, Shadow People are negative alien beings sent to harm or abduct us. Often they can be repelled by invoking the name of Jesus."

"So they'd be akin to the Devil in that theory?"

"Something like that. There are others." Angela opened a window in her computer and began paraphrasing. "There's a neurological theory that claims Shadow People appear during sleep paralysis. According to that theory, they're nothing more than a product of the subconscious mind. You know what sleep paralysis is, right?"

"I do now," Noah said. "It's one of the reasons I went to see Neil. He says it's a sleep disorder that occurs in that transitional stage between falling asleep and waking, where a person becomes completely immobilized and often sees scary images."

Angela opened another window in her laptop. "Have you ever seen the Shadow People during sleep paralysis?"

"Not that I can remember. Only the Hat Man."

"When you saw them last night, did they scare you?"

"A little. The property scared me more."

"Did they have eyes?"

"Beady red eyes. Black faces, elongated bald heads that shape-shifted as they moved."

"You didn't get a powerful sense of evil from them?"

"I don't know, Angela. I was a little stressed. My mind was on information overload after what Neil had told me. Why?"

She pressed a few keys on her computer. "Some people believe the Shadow People are the evil minions of the Devil; that they want to steal our souls and drag us to hell."

"Do you believe that?"

"I don't know what I believe. But it seems to me the overwhelming evidence suggests evil intentions. I don't have a good feeling about this."

"You couldn't find anything good on them?"

"Yeah, I did. Some people claim they felt a positive vibe after seeing the Shadow People. They think they're guardian angels, sent from heaven to protect our souls and shield us from evil."

"Wait a minute," Noah said. "You said that about the Hat Man yesterday at Smitty's. That some people believe he's a guardian angel."

"I might have said it, but I have a hard time believing it."

Of course she's gonna have a hard time believing it. She's still in shock. The Hat Man almost killed her. "I wonder what the connection is. If we knew the connection between the Hat Man and the Shadow People, maybe we'd find some answers."

"Well, I know one thing," Angela said, her cheeks flushing as she became more animated. "If I hear anything else about Hat Man attacks, I'm gonna ask for 24-hour police protection."

Noah suddenly felt his face flush as he realized he'd left a key piece of information out of the conversation.

And Angela sensed it. "What's wrong?"

There was no easy way to say it. "An elderly lady was killed last night. Slashed to death. In her dying breaths, she told Neil it was the Hat Man."

Angela's face turned white. "Holy shit. This is getting out of control. Why didn't you tell me?"

"I *am* telling you. I forgot earlier. Maybe I was more freaked out by the Shadow People than I thought."

"Are you saying that Neil was with this woman in her dying seconds?"

"He's a paranormal investigator, among those other credentials I mentioned earlier."

"And you trust him?"

Noah nodded. "I don't think I've ever met anyone like him. He puts everyone else's needs above his own. Agnes called him when the Hat Man was trashing her house and he came running."

They were sitting beside each other on Angela's sofa. She moved a few inches away from Noah. "Hang on a second," she said. "My mind's getting a little frazzled here. I need to back up a bit. When you happened on that property and that SUV that almost ran you over, did you call the cops?"

"No," Noah said. "I didn't find any real evidence. I did get the make of the black SUV. It was a newer model Ford Explorer. And the license number. But I'm not sure it was the same vehicle that almost hit me the other night. Besides, I was trespassing. What am I supposed to tell the cops? The Shadow People led me there, then followed me halfway home."

"Well, you could've left that part out," Angela said, scooping up the empty food containers, napkins and plastic cutlery from the coffee table. She threw the garbage into a kitchen wastebasket and sat in an armchair facing Noah. "I was attacked by the Hat Man. I think he would've killed me if my neighbor hadn't scared him off. How do you think I'm gonna sleep, knowing there's a nutcase running around killing women?"

"*A* woman," Noah corrected. "One woman."

The color was returning to her face the more animated she became. "One woman that we know about. What's he hiding in that outbuilding?"

"I don't know."

"Well, I think we should find out." Angela extracted a card from her jeans pocket and put it on the coffee table. "Detective Lamar Stevenson is the cop who questioned me in the hospital. He told me to call him if I heard anything suspicious. I think this qualifies."

"Wait a minute," Noah said. "Neil mentioned Stevenson when we talked. I gave Neil the address of the house, as well as the plate number of the suspicious SUV. Maybe he's already called the detective."

"Call Neil," Angela said. Her tone didn't leave any room for argument. "And find out if he's passed the news along to the police. I'm not gonna sit on information that may be critical to solving this case... and keeping me alive."

Noah speed-dialed Neil. After three rings, the call went to voicemail. He left a message and hung up. He felt his right hand begin to quiver and tucked it under his leg. The small of his back began to ache dully, its first protest of the day. It was unlike Neil not to answer his phone at this time of day.

Angela picked up the business card. Her eyes were penetrating; her lips tight, face white. She spoke slowly. "I think it's time."

She called the detective. Her call went to voicemail and she frowned. "Detective Stevenson. It's Angela Rosewood. I think

I have some new information on the Hat Man case. Please call me as soon as you can."

She hung up and looked at Noah gravely. "What now?"

"I'm starting to worry about Neil. He normally picks up his calls."

"Well, not everyone can answer their phones at all times."

"I don't know. I just have a bad feeling."

Angela rose quickly and grabbed her coat. "Let's go then."

"Where?"

"You know where? We'll check on Neil. You said that other property is less than a mile away on the same road, right?"

"Yeah, Highway Three."

"Let's check them both."

Noah wasn't sure he wanted to endanger her life any further, especially since she was almost killed after only one date with him. "Are you sure you're up for this?"

"Are you kidding? Now that I know about that murder, I'm afraid to be in the house by myself. I don't want you to go by yourself either."

So off they went.

On the way out of town, Noah made a hands-free call to his receptionist, informing her that he would not be returning this afternoon. He said he'd be in first thing in the morning to begin slogging through all the applications.

"Don't worry about it," Stella said. "The supervisor's gone for the day. My lips are sealed."

Hanging up, he realized there were certain benefits to remembering special occasions—a box of chocolates and a greeting card for Secretary's Week; flowers and a card for Stella's birthday; other small gifts for Easter, Christmas, and even Islander Day. He only avoided Valentine's Day, believing it might be interpreted the wrong way, given the current climate of political correctness. Besides, Stella had just gotten married and the last thing Noah needed was a jealous husband breathing down his neck.

"Sounds like you have an understanding secretary," Angela said.

"I cover for her when she needs to take time off," Noah said. He quickly changed the subject. "That reminds me. I brought a grant application for you. It's in the glove box."

"What am I going to do with that?"

"Fill it out. Maybe I can help you get some money."

"Doing what?"

"Just take it," he said. "Think about it for a bit. Maybe you'll come up with something."

Angela smiled and the evasive dancing dimple appeared for the first time today. He liked it.

"Thanks," she said. "You surprise me sometimes."

"I'm more than just a pretty face. Not much more. But a little."

They had cleared the downtown core and were now heading east on the TransCanada Highway. In about another fifteen minutes, Noah would be approaching the Highway #3 turn-off. It was already late afternoon and in a few hours the black curtain of night would start blotting out the sun's orange-yellow glow. If at all possible, Noah hoped to get the checks done before sunset. This night driving was beginning to rattle his already frayed nerves.

"Do you wanna stop up ahead for a coffee?" Noah asked.

Angela spun around and looked behind them. "Oh shit."

Noah eyed the rearview mirror and saw it—a black SUV, about a city block back, but visible enough, nonetheless. It was too much of a coincidence to ignore. He handed his phone to Angela. "Check for Neil's number and call him, please."

She took it and fiddled with it. "No bars. You have no signal."

"What about your phone?"

She rummaged through her pockets and finally found it. "Same thing. No signal."

"It's obviously a dead zone here," Noah said, not intending the pun. "Let's try again once we get to the gas station. We'll stop there, and see if he pulls in."

"Okay."

As they drove, the black SUV would alternate following distances; changing from 100 feet, back to about 75, then 50, 30, then suddenly dropping back to 100 again. He appeared to be deliberately trying to frighten them. And if that was his intention, he was succeeding.

"Maybe we should pull over on the shoulder," Angela said, her voice tight.

Noah gave her a look.

She shook her head. "You're right. What was I thinking? At least he doesn't have a hat. The guy looks clean-cut."

"That might not mean shit," Noah said. "The gas station's not far. And it's very public."

They fell silent, both digesting the import of his words.

White-knuckled, Noah gripped the steering wheel, eyeballing the rearview mirror occasionally while Angela, gripping the back of the seat tightly, would swing around every few seconds to determine the SUV's proximity to them. Noah thought about flooring it, but instead decided a constant hundred-kilometers-an-hour speed would be safer, just in case it was a garden-variety asshole driver. It seemed to take forever for the lone gas station to appear on the stretch of highway but finally, they saw the familiar green and white NEEDS neon sign flashing, maybe a thousand feet away.

But panic pummeled poise and Noah floored it. The Silverado lurched forward with such sudden force that both of their heads slammed into headrests. He jerked the wheel left and quickly passed a white four-door sedan, wrestling the wheel hard right as oncoming headlights appeared out of nowhere in the opposite lane.

Angela sighed deeply but stayed silent.

"Sorry about that," Noah said, applying the brakes evenly to slow down so he could navigate the gas station entrance without flipping the truck. The white sedan driver didn't much care for the sudden maneuver. He leaned on the horn, rolled down the window, and flipped Noah the one-finger-salute as he passed.

"Go fuck yourself," Noah shouted, pulling into the gas station parking lot and coming to a stop in a parking stall.

As if it had been choreographed, he and Angela rolled down their automatic windows at almost exactly the same time and poked their heads out. The black SUV slowed, appeared to turn into the parking lot, and then swerved away suddenly and accelerated down the highway and out of sight.

They quickly climbed out of the truck. Noah ran halfway across the parking lot, straining to see the disappearing vehicle.

"Did you get the license number?" Angela asked.

"No. He went too fast."

They went inside the gas station convenience store, Noah purchasing a hot chocolate, Angela a coffee. They returned to the pickup and as they climbed in, Noah's cell phone rang. He answered it.

"Sorry I missed your call," Neil said. "Where are you?"

"At the NEEDS gas station, maybe fifteen minutes from you."

"Are you alone?"

"No. I'm with Angela."

"Come on over, then. There's someone here you might want to speak to."

"Okay, we'll be there soon. But I have to tell you, a black SUV was following us. I think it was the Hat Man."

CHAPTER NINE

Detective Lamar Stevenson reminded Noah of a country hick sheriff right out of a B-grade murder mystery, sans cop uniform and visible badge. Probably in his mid-50s, he sported a pot belly, a head of thick brown hair, long sideburns and a bushy handlebar mustache. But his inquisitive brown eyes defied the stereotype. When he looked at you, he seemed to look right through you, digging through the recesses of your mind to try and unearth your deepest and darkest secrets. Even the firm handshake he offered when Noah was first introduced to the man sent a strong message of authority and conveyed a talent for intimidation.

When Noah and Angela first entered the house, Detective Stevenson had sized Noah up and down with evident skepticism. Then he turned to Angela, asked how she was, and told her he'd returned her call but it had gone straight to voicemail. She'd blurted out something about the Hat Man following them, but he'd silenced her by raising an open palm, telling her she'd get her turn in due time.

As they sat at Neil's kitchen table, the detective asked Neil for his story first. He'd placed a manila file folder on the table with a steno pad and pen next to it, which he looked at occasionally, but had yet to take any notes

To Neil, Detective Stevenson said, "Okay, Let's get this show on the road. Why did you call me out here?"

Neil explained his suspicions about Drake Simeon, his neighbor up the road. His unannounced visits, the questions concerning the Hat Man. Omitting the part about Noah's uninvited visit to Drake's property, Neil detailed how this afternoon, in light of Agnes's murder, his suspicions got the better of him, and he decided to visit Drake's property. Neil paused, then finally said, "I'm sorry, Lamar, but as I got closer to that outbuilding, my curiosity prevailed. I picked the lock."

The detective's face tightened and he tugged at his handlebar mustache. "Trespassing. Break and enter. You should know better. Shit, you could've contaminated a crime scene. What the fuck were you thinking?"

Neil looked at his half-full coffee for a few seconds. Then he raised his gaze to Detective Stevenson. "I guess I wasn't. But at least I was wearing gloves."

The detective's puffy cheeks reddened. "I don't care if you were wearing a fucking hazmat suit, doc. You shouldn't go sticking your nose in police business. Christ, you're a fine upstanding member of this community with an impeccable reputation. Do you want to go and ruin all that?"

"No."

Detective Stevenson took a deep breath and studied the faces of Angela and Noah, as if searching for signs of complicity. Noah felt a blush crawl across his face.

"Okay," Detective Stevenson said, returning steely eyes to Neil. "What was in the outbuilding?"

"The first thing I smelled was rotting death," Neil said. "Overpowering and rank. Then something black flew out at me. At first I thought it was the shadows, but I soon realized I'd walked into a room of hats—all black, and of various shapes and sizes. Fedoras, gauchos, top hats—the telltale iconography of the Hat Man."

To Angela, Detective Stevenson said, "Didn't you tell me that the man who smashed through your door was wearing a gaucho hat?"

"Yes," Angela said.

To Neil, Detective Stevenson said, "What about the smell of death?"

Neil flushed a little. "There was a dead raccoon on top of some of the hats. It was all curled up, as if he'd gone into the outbuilding to get out of the cold and died."

"No mutilated corpses?"

"No."

"No dead human bodies?"

"Not that I could see."

"Was there a vehicle parked there?"

"No."

"What happened next?"

"I left the outbuilding, locked the door, and called you."

"What else did you see at the property?"

"A fire pit."

"Anything suspicious in it?"

"Just ashes."

"You see anything else suspicious at all?"

"No."

"What did you say his name was? Drake Simeon?"

"Yeah."

The detective wrote the name down. He scribbled Hat Man beside it and looked at Neil. "You know what kind of vehicle he drives?"

"A 2014 black Ford Explorer. Neil produced a piece of paper from his shirt pocket. "Here's the license plate number."

Detective Stevenson wrote the information down and pushed the scrap of paper across the table. He studied the three faces and stopped at Noah. "Now, I want all of you to come clean with me. Has anyone else here been to Drake's property?"

"I have," Noah said.

"I thought so," Detective Stevenson said. His brown eyes drilled into Noah's. "What the fuck possessed you to go there?"

Noah chose his words carefully, starting with almost getting run down by a black SUV, going to visit Neil last night seeking help for his sleep disorders, and then, on the way home, suddenly feeling an evil presence outside the property of Drake Simeon and feeling compelled to stop. Omitting the Shadow People, he detailed walking around for a few minutes, examining the burning fabric at the scene, recording the make, model, and license number of the SUV and relaying the information via a phone message to Neil prior to going home. He also left out his sightings of the Hat Man outside The Pilot House and his Hat Man nightmares. He didn't want the detective to think he was bat-shit crazy.

The detective listened patiently but Noah knew a tongue-lashing would be forthcoming.

The detective stood up, paced around the kitchen briefly and then stopped, drilling daggers into Noah with his eyes. "Don't you people get it? You're not cops. You can't go trespassing on people's property and poking around in the middle of the night. What if he *is* the killer, and he pulled out a fucking machete and slashed you to pieces?"

"I'm sorry, detective," Noah said. "I'll let you do your job from now on. I promise."

"Fucking right, you will." He glared at Noah, then Neil. "Both of you, with your fucking vigilante-style snooping, might have already jeopardized my investigation."

As the detective paced, Neil got up and refreshed everyone's coffee cups. The detective finally sat down, took a few deep breaths and looked at Angela. His tone was soft and gentle, in stark contrast to his earlier just-shy-of-shouting tone.

"Please," he said. "Tell me you didn't go snooping around Drake's property."

She shook her head. "No. Noah pointed it out to me on the way here but we didn't stop there."

"Was there a vehicle parked in the driveway? This black SUV he drives."

"I don't think so."

To Noah, the detective said, "Did you see a vehicle, Sherlock?"

Noah studied his coffee cup. "No."

To Angela, the detective said, "Now tell me about this black SUV following you.

She relayed the story, her tone becoming somber and cheeks whitening as she spoke.

The detective scribbled a few notes, and when she finished, he asked, "Did either of you get a license number on that vehicle that followed you? Or, could you tell if it was a black 2014 Ford Explorer?"

Angela shook her head.

"It was definitely a newer model black SUV," Noah said.

"What about the driver?"

"Clean cut, chiseled features," Angela said.

Noah nodded.

"Hair color? Short? Long?"

"Short, I think brown or black hair," Angela said.

"Can you guess the age?"

"Maybe forty," Angela said. "Hard to say."

"I'd guess somewhere in there," Noah said. "But we didn't get a good look at him."

"Caucasian?" the detective asked.

"Definitely," Angela said.

Noah nodded.

"Was this man wearing a hat?"

"No," Noah said.

Angela shook her head.

The detective stood again, paced around the kitchen, then stopped. "Give me a minute. I'm gonna step outside."

They watched him exit the house.

Noah sighed as the door closed. "He's a bit rough around the edges."

Neil sipped coffee. "Don't worry, underneath that rough exterior is a sympathetic man and a damn fine detective. He's like an apple pie. Crusty on the outside but sweet on the inside. He's got a chip on his shoulder about people screwing with his investigations. It cost him a conviction or two in the past and it's a sore spot with him."

"Hey, Neil, thanks for trying to cover for me earlier," Noah said. "You know, on the license plate thing. I figured you were trying to save me from a tongue-lashing by omitting that I'd dropped by that Drake guy's place and alerted you to a few things."

"Don't mention it," Neil said. "It doesn't matter anyway. You have to get up pretty early in the morning to fool Lamar. He can read you like a book."

"I wouldn't make a good killer," Noah said, realizing immediately the inappropriateness of the comment.

"I sure as hell hope not," Angela said.

"Don't worry," Neil said. "I've known Lamar for years. He'll get to the bottom of this."

Five minutes later, Detective Stevenson returned. He took Noah's phone number and gave him a card. He told them he might have more questions and he stressed the importance of calling him directly should anything suspicious arise or any danger present itself.

"What are you gonna do?" Angela asked.

The detective seemed edgy all of a sudden, as if his nose for bad news was sniffing a burning newspaper. "I ran the tags on the vehicle. It's registered to Drake Simeon. The entire police force now has his photo. He has no priors, and right now, we have nothing on him. In police work, you need evidence to charge people, evidence to obtain a search warrant, and we have nothing so far. A man with a hat collection does not a murderer make. I've got some cops digging for background on him right now. At some point, when the time is right, we'll have a word with him."

"What do I do in the meantime?" Angela said. "I'm too scared to sleep at home knowing a nutcase is terrorizing people. Not to mention that murder."

The detective twirled his mustache. "In light of what's been happening... I should tell you we've had other reports of a Hat Man tormenting people at night. I wouldn't advise you to return to your apartment. Maybe you can sort something out with your friends here. I can't afford to have a man provide 24-hour security for you right now. Our resources are tapped out."

With pleading eyes, Angela looked at Noah.

He made a half-smile. "We'll figure something out."

"Listen, I have police work to do," Detective Stevenson said. He shook their respective hands and Noah noticed the second time around, his grip was a little gentler. The detective opened the door to leave and turned around. "I want to say, one last time, if you guys can think of anything you might have missed, no matter how strange or bizarre it might sound, I want to hear about it." His piercing brown eyes met each of theirs.

Noah had seen that look earlier. The detective probably suspected they were all complicit in the withholding of information, but for now, seemed willing to let it go. He had a bigger fish to fry. Drake Simeon.

CHAPTER TEN

Drake Simeon knelt down behind his house and peered down the driveway. He saw a newer model tan-colored Crown Victoria pull over to the shoulder in front of his driveway and stop. Even from a distance of fifty or so feet, he could make out a dark-haired mustached man, who appeared to be chewing on a toothpick, examining the tire tracks in the snow. Drake wasn't a fool. He recognized the unmarked cop car and even knew who it belonged to. *Fucking Stevenson, prick.* And he knew why Stevenson had slowed down. The Shadow People had alerted him. The same Shadow People who'd tormented him last night and almost catapulted him clear out of his mind. *Doesn't matter. I've done nothing wrong. Let him come.* But Drake had been careful earlier to park his SUV in the garage and out of sight. On some dimly recognized level, he did fear the worst.

The Crown Vic pulled onto the highway and drove away. Drake was about to step out but then a blue-and-white RCMP cop car slowed down to a crawl on the road in front of his house. The driver, a uniformed cop, scanned the driveway and the property for a few seconds before pulling away.

Fuck. The heat's on. Drake stepped out from behind the house and continued his examination of the new tire tracks in his driveway—one vehicle while he'd been at work and another while he was inside, being attacked by the Shadow People. He'd heard the engine noise last night, and would have gone outside to investigate. But the Shadow People had gotten in the way. Sent by his mother in the body of Angela Rosewood and, if his

112

stalker instincts were accurate, probably aided and abetted by one Noah Janzen and one Neil Samuelson. *Fuckers are going to pay*.

Following tracks in the snow, he wandered over to his outbuilding, while mentally reevaluating his plan. He examined the padlock and noticed some snow had been pushed away at the bottom of the door. It had been opened. Evidently the lock had been picked. Things were not going to plan.

He had thought earlier, while he followed Noah, that things might take a surprising turn for the better. It had been a stroke of luck that Noah had stopped at Angela's house for a few hours and then they'd both left the house together. Kill two birds with one stone. Run them right off the highway and finish them off. But he'd been careless, taunting them with his vehicle; slowing, speeding, slowing, speeding. He'd alerted them to his pursuit. And, by the time they'd pulled into the service station, it was too late. His cover had been blown by his careless cat-and-mouse game.

But he wouldn't be surprised if they'd identified his vehicle days ago. Wouldn't be surprised if it was Neil and Noah who had been the ones who'd done an unwelcome examination of his property.

And they'd called the cops. Shit. He kicked the door of the outbuilding so hard he crunched his toe and groaned in pain. His mind raced, wondering what to do next. Slowly, as the pain ebbed, his mind calmed and things started to become clear. He decided, with the exception of his brand-new gaucho hat (*nobody could blame a man for liking gaucho hats*), he would have to destroy all the evidence and wait for nightfall. Then he would systematically destroy his enemies and life would be calm again. The Shadow People would be gone. His mother would be gone forever. Life would be good again.

And, before anyone could figure out whodunit, he would be long-gone—on a plane to Bogota, Colombia, to start anew. He had enough money saved. He didn't give a shit about his job, nor his house. He didn't have any other friends or family to worry about. Everyone was inconsequential—either an enemy or on the path to becoming one.

A few minutes later, he busily gathered together all his cherished hats and put them neatly in cardboard boxes. He removed the Hat Man picture and boxed it. Reluctantly, he threw his new trench coat into the mix and took everything outside, loaded the items into his SUV and drove the vehicle into a clearing in the forest. There, he dumped everything into a ten-by-ten, three-feet-deep depression in the ground—a fire pit reserved for log-slash burning. Out of sight from his few and far away neighbors. Out of mind for same. He loaded up the fire pit with the boxes and threw a bunch of kindling on top. He returned to the outbuilding, and holding his nostrils with one hand, tossed the decomposing raccoon into a snowbank a good seventy feet away, then cleaned out all the hats. It took two trips to get the fire pit loaded with his headwear and other potentially incriminating items. He returned with a gallon of gas, a six-pack of beer, a roll of advertising flyers and a pack of smokes. Then he doused the seven-feet-high pile with gasoline, crunched some paper into balls and stuffed them in the bottom. He flicked his Bic and jumped back.

Whoosh!

Flames leapt high into the air. He sat down on a plastic lawn chair, lit a smoke and cracked a beer. A plan was starting to gel in his mind. The only question was... who to kill first?

He watched the giant flames fan out and blend in with the orange haze of the setting sun, and grinned. *Burn in hell, motherfuckers. Burn in hell.*

CHAPTER ELEVEN

It was after eight in the evening by the time they'd left Neil's house. Noah was thankful that his friend was indeed okay, and feeling somewhat relieved that most of their ordeal was out in the open and now in the hands of the police. Just for good measure, Angela had called Detective Stevenson, informing him that she would be spending the night at Noah's place. The detective had said he'd try and send a car around this evening, just to do a drive-by to insure they were both safe.

Passing Drake's country acreage, Noah hadn't even slowed down, not wanting to risk being fitted with a new derriere by the shoot-from-the-hip detective.

They'd stopped briefly at Angela's to pick up some clothes and toiletry items. It would mark the first time Noah would have a woman's toothbrush in his apartment, and he didn't know how he'd handle it. Then they'd stopped at a Chinese restaurant and ordered some take-out, before going home. Now, they sat at Noah's kitchen table, poking chop sticks into white cardboard containers.

Although Angela seemed okay with spending the night, Noah was more than a little nervous about having her over. Something Neil had said the other night clung to his mind with the weight and purchase of a cast iron boat anchor. It was the account of the Vancouver man who'd sexually assaulted a woman in his sleep. *Yeah, but he was acquitted.* But that fact did not relieve the tension Noah was feeling, especially given his recent sleepwalking episode. Noah's sleep disorders had a mind of their own and he was worried they might act out with aggressive and unprovoked violence against Angela, the last thing in the world he wanted to happen.

Watching an egg noodle snake its way up Angela's chin and into her mouth, he wondered if he should come clean about his recent sleep disorder diagnosis. Up to this point, he'd remained relatively tight-lipped.

She puckered her lips around the errant egg noodle and sucked it into her mouth with a kissing sound. Her eyes met his. "Sorry," she said with an embarrassed smile. "I told you I'm a little clumsy."

The kissing sound, the sensuous motion of her lips, quickly tossed the notion of sleep disorder confessions overboard without a life raft. "It's okay. It's kind of cute, really."

She grinned. "Here, maybe. But not in a fancy restaurant."

She pointed to one of his framed photographs hanging on the kitchen wall—a quintessential shot of a sandy beach in the foreground, back-dropped with a view out to black and pristinely calm ocean waters. An ominously large yellow-orange sun sank into the distant horizon. "That's beautiful. Is it one of yours?"

"It is."

"You're really good."

"Thank you. I'm okay, but still an amateur."

"Are you kidding? That shot rivals some professional shots I've seen."

"Thanks, but I know you're just humoring me."

"No, I'm not. You should be proud of your work. Those other ones in the living room are equally good. Where was this sunset one taken?"

"Beach Point," Noah said. "Out by Murray Harbour."

"It's beautiful out there," Angela said.

"It is. That's one thing I like about living on an island. Especially this island. Amazing beaches everywhere. Spectacular scenery. Serene forests. Tons of history. In the summer, I can just drive for hours and get lost in it."

"Yeah," Angela agreed. "And there aren't too many people. Even in tourist season, you can always find a quiet place to go. I guess you usually take your camera with you wherever you go."

Noah nodded. He picked up a spoon and shoveled a mouthful of chicken with black bean sauce chow mien into his mouth. Angela took the cue and began her battle with a spider web of egg noodles.

Noah watched the yellow tentacles crawl up her chin. He burst out laughing, spitting a few grains of rice across the table. One of them landed on Angela's cheek.

She mock-frowned and wiped the egg noodles into her mouth with a hand. Then she plucked the single grain of rice from her cheek. "Eeeeewww. You want a food fight? Is that what you want?" Before he could respond, she flung an egg noodle at him. It stuck to his shoulder.

He grinned, loaded a spoon with rice, and flicked it at Angela. A few grains splattered her face. A few more sprinkled her pink V-neck top, and a clump of rice slipped down the deep crevice of her cleavage. She wedged a hand into the fissure, rescued the rice ball and flung it back at Noah.

Pretending to panic, he leaped from his chair. "No, please." But he wasn't quite out of range. Arcing through the air, the rice ball split into three chunks, one landing on Noah's head, the other on his nose, and the third in his mouth.

"Bullseye," Angela proclaimed, laughing with a sweet melody that was music to Noah's ears. They were finally starting to have some fun and he was loving it.

He stuck his tongue out, proudly displaying the rice ball, and then in a smooth motion, slurped it up and swallowed, relishing in the knowledge that it had just been rescued from between Angela's lovely breasts. He tasted a hint of honeydew melon as it glided down his throat. "Delicious. I love it."

She grabbed a spoon and stabbed it into a container of fluffy white rice. She stood up, an evil grin on her face, a sexy twinkle in her blue eyes. "Of course you love it. Because it touched my boobs, you pervert."

Noah's eyes narrowed. "Oh no, please. Not rice. Anything but rice. God save me."

"Food fight," Angela declared, and then began chase.

In an instant, they were running around Noah's apartment, Angela in hot pursuit with a spoonful of rice and Noah circling his coffee table, flailing his hands in a comedic parody of a man running for his life. "No, please. Don't kill me with rice," he said. "I was just offering you food for thought."

"You'll get more than food for thought," she said, laughing. "I'm gonna cram this down your pants."

"No, not there... anywhere but there."

"Okay, up your ass, then," she said, and the room exploded with laughter.

As Angela neared the sectional couch, Noah saw his opportunity and seized it. He dove across the coffee table, clutching her locked-and-loaded spoon first, and then tackling her onto the couch. Tugging on the offending spoon, he landed softly on her chest. The rice spilled onto Angela, a few small clumps plunging into the crevice of her ample cleavage.

"I got you," he said.

She dropped the spoon and grinned. "You do. You do indeed."

It happened so fast. They locked eyes. Noah felt a tingling sensation pulse through his loins and then he impulsively kissed her on the lips. He had meant it to be a quick peck, but Angela pulled him close and it turned into a passionate, wet, tongue-exploring canoodle.

Noah's fingers had just started to roam across her chest when two things happened. A large round penetrating beam of light burst through his window, filling up the candle-lit quarters with an oppressive and blinding whiteness. And a cell phone on the coffee table rang.

Noah pulled himself off Angela, snatched her cell phone and handed it to her.

She answered quickly. "Hello?"

"Is everything okay up there?"

"Who is this?"

Noah scrambled to the window and peered out, trying to determine the source of the light. He saw it and sighed with relief. A cop car with a window-mounted floodlight was parked in front of his apartment. "It's okay. It's the cops."

"This is Constable Victor Sanchez of the Charlottetown Police Department. I saw some commotion up there and I just wanted to make sure everything was okay."

Noah overheard Sanchez's voice. *Wow. That Stevenson doesn't miss a beat. Maybe Neil was right.*

"Everything's fine," Angela said. "Thanks for checking in on us. You can turn the light off now."

The light went out and the cop car rolled down the dark street. But, even with the soft glow of candlelight, the mood had evaporated, replaced by a palpable fear. Together they cleaned up the remains of the food fight and put away the leftovers.

Noah closed all the window blinds and went into the kitchen while Angela sat down in a far corner of the sectional and grew quiet. She was curled in a sort of ball, hugging her knees. He knew she was probably having flashbacks of the Saturday night attack. As much as he appreciated the police checking in on them, he wished they could go back to their earlier mood of playfulness, laughter and spontaneous romance.

He opened the fridge, hoping a little alcohol might take the edge off. "Would you like a glass of wine before bed?"

He didn't immediately get a response. He turned around and looked at Angela. Her eyes were fixated on the ceiling and a slight frown played across her lips, as if she was lost inside some inner turmoil.

"Angela?"

Her vacant eyes returned to Earth. "Sorry. Did you say something?"

"How about some white wine?"

"Sure. One glass before bed might help me sleep."

Along with the half-full bottle, he brought two glasses into the living room, poured drinks, and handed one to Angela. "Cheers," he said. "To more spontaneous fun."

A bright smile returned to her face, a remarkable transformation, Noah thought.

She raised her glass. "I'll drink to that."

They clinked glasses and drank.

Noah sank into the couch, picked up the wine glass and took another sip. As if she was being controlled by puppet strings, Angela copied him.

"You know," they began in unison.

They laughed, unlike the unselfconscious and carefree guffaws of the food-fight hilarity.

"You first," Noah said. He could visualize the black cloud fragmenting and turning gray.

"No, you. I insist."

"Okay. I was just thinking, with all the running around we were doing, I didn't notice any back pain. I don't feel any now, either. How about you?"

Angela touched the small of her back. "Not really, come to think of it. But I took a few painkillers earlier."

"What time was that?"

"This morning. Maybe ten."

"That was a while ago. They would have worn off by now. You might be getting better."

"Yeah, maybe I am. But I'm not gonna tell work just yet. I think I need at least a week off to recover."

Her eyes wandered to another framed picture on the wall. It showed a dark forest, lit by a glowing three-quarters moon and a million shining stars. Spears of moonlight poked through the forest canopy transforming the trees into strange dark entities with jagged black arms reaching out in odd directions. "I like that one, even though the imagery is kind of gloomy."

"It is kind of creepy," Noah agreed. "But something about the atmosphere caught my eye, so I snapped it."

"When did you take it?"

"About a week ago. It's a forest a few miles west of town."

Angela studied it. "The trees look like people."

"Kind of menacing, don't you think?"

"Wait a minute," she said, rising and approaching the picture. She pointed to a dark image seemingly hiding behind one of the trees. "Do you see that?"

Noah joined her, inspecting the photo. "What?"

With her index finger, she traced the image. She removed her black-framed glasses, replaced them and looked again. "It's still there. Look."

Moving closer, Noah saw what she was talking about—a shadowy figure with smooth lines, more intricate and detailed than the shadowy trees. Half of a blackly draped body peered out from behind a tree. Maybe five feet tall, but difficult to gauge scale. It could be seven feet. Its head was elongated and bald and, if you looked real close, you could almost see small red slit eyes looking back at you.

"Wow, I never noticed that before," Noah said. "It *is* something."

"Is that like the Shadow People you saw at that Drake's place?"

"Yes. But the eyes are a little different."

She returned to the couch. "Either way, the picture kind of gives me the creeps."

"Do you want me to take it down?"

"No. It's your apartment."

"But I don't want the thing to freak you out."

"I think it's too late for that. You like it, don't you?"

"Yes."

"What made you take it?"

"I don't know. I was driving and I just stopped for some reason. Something caught my eye."

"The same way you felt you needed to stop at that nutcase, Drake's place?"

"I honestly don't remember, Angela."

Realizing it was getting late, Noah wanted to steer the conversation away from Drake. It seemed Angela had convinced herself he was the Hat Man killer and the last thing Noah wanted was for her to go to bed thinking those thoughts. She was traumatized enough and he didn't need to add more fuel to the fire.

For his part, he was still worried about what he might do in his sleep. But he'd decided, before the impromptu food fight, that one of Neil's powerful sleeping pills should do the trick. It had worked before.

He gently navigated the conversation away from Drake, asking Angela questions about her interest in photography, hoping it might lead to some kind of art business whereby she could escape the financial and unmotivated rut she was in. For the next twenty minutes or so, he succeeded to some degree. Angela confessed an interest in photography and told him that during her late teens, prior to meeting "him," she'd spent a lot of time finding that perfect shot, playing with light and shadows, capturing scenic moments that evoked whatever feeling she was trying to inspire. Noah wasn't sure about opening the "him" can of worms, for fear it would plummet her into another funk.

But, as she talked about some of her photos, the cogs in Noah's mental wheel drifted to Angela's mention of "him."

He remembered "him" from their conversation last Saturday at The Pilot House. Her twelve-year relationship with fiancé Seth had come to a grinding halt after he'd dumped her for an eighteen-year-old "bimbo." Apparently, he'd subjugated Angela to his will, and wanted nothing more than an unsuccessful stay-at-home trophy wife. An object. But when the gold had faded on the trophy, at least in Seth's eyes, he'd found new luster and sheen in a brand-new and much younger symbol of prestige and accomplishment. Noah suspected there was another version of Seth in Angela's recent past, but realized timing was everything.

His relationship with her was still in the early stages. She would tell him when she was good and ready. Or she wouldn't. Period. And he was also okay with that. He wasn't going to push and he didn't want Angela to view him in the same light as she now probably viewed most men. Undoubtedly her past liaisons had shaped her current perspective, probably culminating in a view of men as nothing more than shallow women exploiters.

He sighed. There was a lot of truth to that view and he hoped he wasn't like those other guys. It had been a long time since he'd been in a relationship. He no longer knew what he thought. He just hadn't thought about having a woman in his life. He'd been happy in his own company, content with his own interests and limited social contact. *But then again, no pain, no gain.*

"Are you even listening to me?" Angela asked.

Noah felt a blush creep across his face. "Sorry. My mind drifted." But, at times, his mind actually could process two or more trains of thought simultaneously. He reached into his mental machine and fidgeted with some levers. He imagined a whirring and clunking noise. Fortunately, it shifted into gear. "Did you say something about selling some of my photos?"

Angela was amazed. "Holy shit, you *are* more than just a pretty face. I said if you didn't like my photographs, or don't think they're marketable, maybe I can sell some of yours."

He needed some time to think about this. Wouldn't it be a conflict of interest to approve a grant for Angela to sell his photos? If he was selling them to her and profiting from a grant to Angela, maybe. Probably. But, what if he just gave her the photos? Better still, have her claim them as her own. But that was dishonest.

There had to be a solution, Noah knew, but right now he was too tired to figure it out. He would need to sleep on it and think it through tomorrow with a clearer head. Still, it was nice to hear Angela taking an interest in getting ahead.

"I'll tell you what," he said. "Why don't you fill out the grant application tomorrow while I'm at work? Then dig out some of your old photos and let me see them. I need to figure out how we can do this, but I'm too tired right now. Do you have a camera?"

"Yeah, but it's pretty old."

Noah knew she didn't have the money to buy a new one. "I have an idea. I'll loan you, hell, I'll give you one of mine. I've got about six of them and I don't use them all anymore. So, your project tomorrow is complete grant application, get your photos together and take my camera and start snapping photos. Find out if it's something you could become passionate about."

Angela was delighted. "You'd help me like that?"

"Of course."

"Thank you. I feel like giving you a hug."

"I'm not stopping you," he said, grinning.

They stood, amazingly, at exactly the same time, and embraced. But Angela moved too close, too fast and head-butted Noah. Still, he felt a slight tingling in his loins as her pillowy-soft bosom pressed against his chest and her fragrant honeydew melon-and-roses scent permeated his olfactory senses.

"Sorry," she said, releasing him. "I'm starting to fade."

"Me too," Noah said. "Tell you what. You can sleep in my bedroom and I'll take the couch."

"Are you sure?"

"Yes."

Noah led her into the bedroom and got her acquainted. Resisting long dormant carnal impulses, he tucked her in and gave her a quick kiss on the lips. He didn't trust himself to give her anything more than a peck, out of respect for Angela and a healthy regard for where it might lead. He removed a comforter and a pillow from a bedroom closet, wished her a good night, and left.

He got settled on the couch, a glass of water and a sleeping pill next to him on the coffee table. His eyes wandered aimlessly around the room as his thoughts drifted to Angela and his burning desire to take the relationship to the next level. *Slow down,* he kept telling himself. *You have some shit of your own to sort out first. You have a fucking nutcase stalking you. Stalking her.* But the Hat Man took a backseat to other thoughts. Fifteen minutes passed as he unsuccessfully tried to steer his mind away from Angela's ample anatomy—the feel of her soft, milky white skin; those breasts, so round, full and ripe; that dimple, so damn cute and irresistible.

Stop it already. Go to sleep. He picked up the sleeping pill. He heard the bedroom door click open.

Silhouetted by the soft glow of a streetlight beam seeping through a partially opened Venetian blind, Angela stood leaning against the door. She wore a translucent white V-neck nightgown. Her nipples poked out attentively. Noah's eyes wandered over them and then down to her dark pubic mound, barely visible as a shadowy V.

"I'm scared," Angela said. "Will you sleep with me? Please?"

Noah put down the sleeping pill, almost tipping over the glass of water in his haste.

In bed, wearing underwear and a white t-shirt, he spooned Angela, unable to keep his burgeoning member from rubbing up against her buttocks. "Don't worry," he said. "Everything's gonna be okay."

She turned around and kissed him full on the lips, long and wet. Then she looked at him and traced her finger up the side of his face. His loins were on fire with desire.

"I want you," she said. "It's been so long. So, so long."

He peeled Angela's nightgown off and tossed it onto a nearby chair. He watched her magnificent high-beams approach, stroking her rock-hard nipples as she removed his t-shirt. He raised his hands to aid her efforts. She flung it on the floor and pushed her bosom into his face, watching and smiling as he tongued her nipples voraciously.

His hands, lips and tongue freely and passionately explored her body. Soon they were locked together as one, slowly thrusting and pumping, moaning and groaning, speaking and sighing.

"That's so good."

"Yes, baby. Yes, Angela. It's so good... so good."

"Oh yes, Noah. Right there, baby. That's amazing... oohhh, ohhh, ohhh... so incredible."

Their lovemaking slowly built from a steady hum of mutually intense and satisfying carnal bliss to a raging crescendo of pleasure, finally culminating in two intense and explosive orgasms.

When it was over, they lay side-by-side, both struggling to catch their breaths. When their breathing did finally slow, Noah turned to Angela, put a hand on her breast, and sighed. "Holy fucking wow," he said. "That's all I can think of to say."

Angela smothered him with kisses and giggled. "That was amazing. I don't have words for it, either. I needed that. I needed that badly."

Locked in an embrace, they drifted off to sleep, Noah with a smile on his face, and a peaceful yet paradoxically wanting sensation in his heart. As the hand of sleep led him gently into subconscious bliss, a fragmented thought poked through dream-like pastoral images of PEI scenery. *You forgot the pill. You forgot to take the sleeping pill.*

But the thought evaporated and was replaced by a surreal and immense image of a crimson sun sinking down into a distant black horizon.

CHAPTER TWELVE

It was damn near quitting time and Noah was amazed at the speed and efficiency at which he'd processed grant applications that day. There was no other way to put it. He was simply on fire. He'd gone through the entire backlog of applications, sifting some into the clear reject pile, putting others into a possible-maybe category and still others into a vote pile, meaning some of them would find their way into this Friday's grant approval committee meeting.

And it wasn't only his energy that had changed. He had a glow about him and a smile that, despite his best efforts, he was having a hard time wiping off his face. "Why would I want to hide it," he said to a window looking out onto the darkening street. "If it feels good, do it."

Others in the office noticed his unusual enthusiasm as well. There were a few comments at the water cooler earlier in the day when he'd stopped for a short break to fill up his water bottle and grab a leftover stale pastry that had been sitting on the staff lunch room table overnight. He'd heard a colleague, Belinda, mutter not quite under her breath, "He probably got a blow-job last night."

And Stella, the receptionist, had also commented when he arrived this morning. "What do you look so happy about? You must've gotten laid last night." Too embarrassed to actually respond, he'd at least managed a wink and a chuckle before shuffling off to his office cubicle at the end of the hall.

He finished reviewing (or processing, as his supervisor Cindy Hardy liked to say) the last grant application, his 26th for the day, and carried it over to a stack of files sitting neatly on a table by the window. He put it on the possible-maybe stack and returned to his desk, going through his sticky notes and organizing them neatly onto one master TO DO list. He finished that, reached into his desk drawer and pulled the grant budget for the remainder of this year. Since it was only early February, there was a fair amount of money still available. The end of the year would be a different story, of course. He ran his finger down a column and stopped at Fine Arts, under which photography was listed as a sub-category. There were five *unapproved* applicants listed in that category. Each applicant was asking for $50,000, and there was $350,000 total to be dispersed for the year, which meant that even if all five applicants were successful, there would still be $100,000 remaining. *Good. Angela's got a shot. But she's gotta get the application in quick.*

Noah had also come up with a way to solve the conflict-of-interest issue. If, in his opinion, Angela's photos weren't commercially viable, then he would simply donate a few dozen of his own to her, free of charge. But first he had to see what she could do. Maybe she was really talented. She'd mentioned this morning when he woke from a restful and erotic-dream-filled sleep that she would sort through some of her closet clutter and find some of the better photos she'd taken. They'd agreed to meet at her apartment after work for a pizza, a photo-shooting field trip and a bed trip. At least, he'd hoped a bed trip would top the evening's activities. *That's the problem with sex,* he thought. *Once you've had it, you can't get enough of it.*

He finished cleaning his desk, grabbed his jacket from a coat hanger, flicked the light off, and left the office. Passing the receptionist desk, he was surprised he didn't see Stella. But, glancing at his watch, he realized he was running late. She'd already left.

He left the building, followed by the janitor, who locked the door behind him. The poor guy must have been waiting for him to get his act together.

Walking out into the brisk late afternoon air, enjoying the freshness as he inhaled deeply, he tried to remember the last time he'd enjoyed work so much he'd lost track of the time.

Try never.

******

"Never say never," Neil said, fidgeting with an assortment of buttons and dials deep in a corner of his laboratory. He stood in front of a steel wall-mounted panel about eight feet tall and twenty-five feet wide. Along with the buttons and dials, there were gauges, built-in computer screens, an assortment of metal handles and levers. The gauge needles quivered, the computer screens flashed with a wild and colorful assortment of different shapes and sizes. Satisfied with the settings, he stood back, his eyes tracing a long cylindrical white tube that was connected to what he called the Parallel Projector. The tube, which Neil called a Parallel Pointer, spread out like a giant tentacle, the end of which spotlighted a black circular stage in another corner of the lab. In the middle of the stage was a circular beam of light. In the middle of the circle of light was a small glass jar with a black beetle crawling around inside it.

Bennie the Beatle.

The test subject.

Neil turned around, walked over to a long computer-stacked table and sat down.

Curled up on the edge of the table, Tilly, his Oriental black cat, opened one yellow eye, studied Neil briefly, and then closed it again. He stroked her sleek and refined head gently and she began a steady sewing-machine-like purr.

"That's right, Tilly," Neil said. "You should be happy. I think it's going to work this time. Seven tries today. Seven failures. But, this is it. Never say never."

Tilly opened both eyes and raised her head slightly. "Meow... meow... meow."

"Okay, Bennie, here we go." Neil started punching a keyboard. To Tilly, he said, "That's right. Three times lucky. But in this case, it's eight times lucky. But, how would you know? You've slept through most of it."

Tilly closed her eyes, tucking her ears into outstretched paws.

He punched a few keys and a white screen flashed before him. Small metallic balls danced around and formed the image of a woman's face, calm and serene, professional and business-like.

Gemini, named after the astrological sign of his beloved wife Maggie, who'd passed away six years ago, smiled at Neil. "Good evening, Neil," she said. "Would you like to start the experiment now?"

Tilly raised an eye to Gemini and closed it again. Tilly wasn't fussed. The two were closely acquainted, if not good friends by now.

"Good evening, Gemini," Neil said. "Yes. Please start the experiment now."

Neil studied the glass jar in the middle of the stage. "Okay, Bennie, fasten your seat belt. Here we go... one small step for Bennie, one giant leap for humankind."

Gemini's face crumbled and was replaced by a large red ON button. A gloved hand appeared on the screen, extending a finger and pressing the red button. It turned green. A whirring sound began and slowly grew louder as computer screens illuminated with colorful digital charts, showing the power level and progress of the experiment.

When the Parallel Pointer targeting Bennie began rattling with the force, Neil rose quickly, hurried over and started adjusting levers and knobs.

Tilly leaped to her feet, arched, and the hair on her back and tail stiffened and fanned out.

As the humming intensified, Neil continued adjusting the controls. "Come on, baby... you can do it. Come on... don't fail me now. Please, don't fail me now."

Tilly leaped off the table, sending a file folder stacked with papers soaring into the air, fanning out, and floating gently down toward the shiny concrete floor below. She darted over to a small utility table near the lab's entrance door, ran under it, and crouched into an attack stance, her yellow eyes darting fervently around the lab.

The humming reached an ear-piercingly high-pitched intensity as the Parallel Pointer continued to rattle under its series of interlocking metal harnesses. The lab florescent lights flickered and began trembling.

"Come on," Neil said.

Suddenly a powerful beam blasted the glass jar with a beam of light. It started off small and then began growing in intensity. The laboratory shuddered and shook. There was a loud popping sound, then a zapping sound and the powerful beam vanished.

The lab lights went out and the room fell into an eerie silence.

"Shit," Neil said, rummaging around in his lab coat pocket for a flashlight. He pulled it out, walked quickly over to a large breaker panel and found the source of the problem. He clicked the breaker back into the ON position. Nothing happened. *Must have fried a wire.*

Three steps later, he arrived at a small sound-dampening building attached to an inside wall. He opened its door, fired up the generator, and closed the door, reducing the engine noise to a dull roar. It lit the bare essentials—six wall-mounted incandescent light bulbs. Not enough to run the entire lab, but enough to see where he was going and what was going on.

He looked under the table by the door. "Are you okay, Tilly?"

She was frozen in her attack stance. "Meow... meow."

"Okay, let me see what happened." He went over to the small stage and trained the flashlight beam inside the jar. Bennie stopped his restless circular pacing and looked at him. Then he continued down the road to nowhere. *Going in circles,* Neil thought. *Just like me.*

Neil balled his fists and his cheeks flushed. "Not another failure. Please, not another fucking failure."

Defeated, he began picking up pieces of paper off the floor and stuffing them into the file folder. When he finished, he sat at the computer table, covered his head in his hands, and took a few deep breaths, waiting for his head to clear and his disappointment to abate somewhat before trying to figure out what had gone wrong He hadn't even begun to troubleshoot the Parallel Projector or the computers for damage.

Six years of work down the drain, he thought. *Six years of trying to discover the true nature of reality and nothing to show for it but fried electrical wiring. Maybe fried computers. Maybe a cooked Parallel Projector. What a monumental waste of time.*

He'd tried to build a machine similar to the Large Hadron Collider, the largest and most powerful particle accelerator built by the European Organization for Nuclear Research. He knew that, aside from studying microscopic particle collisions, scientists were also using the largest single machine in the world to discover more evidence to prove alternate worlds exist. Parallel universes, alternate realties, or as string theorists would say, other dimensions.

It had been Neil's quest to save humanity. Unlocking the doors to those dimensions would create mind-boggling possibilities; being able to see into and enter the past, present and future; being able to change outcomes; being able to travel through other dimensions; becoming debt-free; meeting another version of yourself living life in much the same way you do, but in a parallel universe. Those were just a few of the amazing possibilities. And Neil had worked tirelessly to be at the forefront of those discoveries—for the chance to lead humankind into bold new frontiers; frontiers where war, famine, disease, and the destruction of the planet might not exist. Ruminating about it only deepened his sadness.

He was loath to admit that perhaps the most important reason he'd created the Parallel Projector was to find a way to be with his late wife Maggie once more. They'd been together for forty-five years. Their relationship had been intense and loving. Symbiotic. Interdependent. His identity had become fused with hers. Six years since her death. Six years of repressed heartache and grief. Six years of suffering. Six years of pain.

He removed his hands from his face and threw them open to the ceiling. "But what the hell do I have here? Years of my life down the toilet, a beetle in a jar, extra-crispy wiring and probably fried computers and a toasted Projector."

He laughed suddenly. It had an unhinged sound. "Anyone like a fried computer with a side order of extra-crispy wires and a toasted Projector? Any mayonnaise on that, ma'am? How about a slice of ham?"

As he scratched his chin stubble, he caught a glimpse of something out of the corner of his eye. He fixed his gaze on the stage, lit opaquely by the generator-powered light bulbs. Out of the Parallel Pointer, a shadowy figure emerged, ballooned into a humanoid shape and floated up to the ceiling. Soon it was joined by three more Shadow People, floating around the lab, featureless but for small glowing red eyes.

Instead of being afraid, Neil was thunderstruck. "A miracle," he said, beaming. "I've created a miracle."

This might not be what he'd intended, but it was a start. Bennie was supposed to be visiting the Shadow People in the eighth, possibly the tenth dimension, right now. Instead, they'd come to Bennie, come to Neil, come to meet and greet the world. Instead of discovering a portal to travel to other dimensions, he'd inadvertently opened a portal allowing the denizens of other dimensions to travel to Earth.

He scratched his head and scribbled a mathematical formula on a scrap of paper. This opened up incredible possibilities. He scribbled another math equation and thought: *I can reverse the formula. I can do this.* And then another thought hit him. *Wait a minute. Noah. The Shadow People. At Drake's house. Was it my experiments that brought them there?* His mind raced with a million questions. A million possibilities.

Neil looked up and saw six Shadow People floating around his lab, expertly weaving their way around—some right through—the display of hanging lights. He was filled with a sense of awe, admiration, and pride at his success.

"I brought you here," he said. "To save humanity."

They joined hands and continued silently dancing around the large lab. The only sound was the muffled hum of the generator.

Neil leaped from his chair so quickly he tipped it over. But he ignored it, dancing around the room, flailing his arms wildly and shouting for joy. He stopped, studied the Shadow People for another full minute and then finally regained control of his scientific faculties. *The camera. I need to photograph them.*

Tilly slithered silently from underneath the table and fearlessly stopped in front of Neil. "Meow," she said, her tone assertive.

Neil reached down and scratched her chin.

When he looked up, the Shadow People had vanished.

******

Driving his pickup with Angela by his side, Noah was halfway to Dalvay Beach, about thirty minutes practically straight north of downtown Charlottetown.

Earlier that day, he'd noticed a few clouds rolling in, but by the time he walked the ten minutes to Angela's house, the sky had cleared and it was only a degree or two below zero, downright tropical for a Canadian winter. It felt like all the stars were aligning.

As they walked the few blocks to Noah's apartment to retrieve his pickup truck, Angela had proudly told him of her day's accomplishments; she'd completed the grant application; arranged some of her favorite photos in a handy pocket-sized photo album, and even snapped a few images around Charlottetown. She'd showed him a few of her older shots and a few of the new ones. Noah had to admit, he was impressed. Angela had a knack for composition and lighting, as well as an eye for art and depth of field—isolating and integrating the subject from the background and foreground. If he didn't know any better, he would have sworn she'd had some formal photography training.

Without having a clear idea of where he was going, they'd climbed into the pickup and set off. But as they drove, the decision became clear—shoot for the beach and a chance at capturing an amazing sunset. The sky in PEI at dusk, at least on a clear day, never failed to produce brilliant pinks, purples, yellows and oranges—if you were in the right place at the right time.

And it looked like they would be. Looking ahead, Noah could already see a faint pink-orange haze beginning to blanket the northern horizon as the golden sun seeped away. He glanced at Angela and felt a sense of pride. She'd not only accomplished her TO DO list, but she'd obviously also taken pains with her appearance, looking alluring in a carnal sort of way. Her hair was tied back neatly in a bun, accentuating the black-rimmed glasses and evoking a sexy secretary persona. She also had just the right amount of black eyeliner, a subtle shade of red lipstick, and a few dabs of flesh-toned face powder. And whatever perfume she had on—a mysterious mixture of exotic wood, rich vanilla and white orchid—was driving Noah around the bend.

He stepped on the gas. "Almost there. I've photographed some amazing sunsets at Dalvay. Hey, what kind of perfume is that you're wearing?"

"Dead Sexy."

"It is that. It's driving me crazy. You look gorgeous, by the way."

She grinned. "Thanks."

A few minutes later, they arrived at the beach parking lot. They got out and walked along the snow-covered beach, Noah watching, Angela snapping photos. They arrived at a spot with a view straight out to the setting sun, the perfect location for a spectacular shot. And the timing was perfect. It was 5:45 pm. The sun would disappear in fifteen minutes.

"Wow," Angela said, pointing out to sea. "Isn't that amazing?" A bank of clouds had rolled out from the shoreline and was picking up a purplish-grey reflection from both the massive orange sun and the calm dark waters. In the distance, the sun stood bold, bright and orange, unobstructed by the oncoming clouds. Beyond the clouds, a pale blue sky with hints of white and yellow. It was clearly one of Mother Nature's finest works of art. Priceless, to be sure.

But does she have the talent to reproduce such beauty?

She responded as if she'd read his mind. "I can never compete with Mother Nature. It's hard for a picture to do justice to the real thing. Especially that beauty. But I can try."

She took shots from several angles and several positions, at one point even lying down on snow-covered sand.

"Aren't you worried about your jacket or your pants?" Noah asked, quickly realizing the stupidity of his query, especially considering he was just as relentless in his quest for the perfect shot.

She got up and wiped some sand and snow away from her black pants and blue parka. "Are you serious? You're the photographer."

"No, I'm not serious. I don't know what I was thinking. My mantra has always been, get the shot at all costs."

"Take a look at these," she said, moving in closer, as Noah inhaled the fragrant scent of Dead Sexy with a smile.

"Stunning," he said. "You really do know how to capture a scene."

As the last sliver of the setting sun sank beneath the horizon, and the sky was blanketed in a kaleidoscope of brilliant colors—pink, gray, purple, black and blue—they decided it was time to go. Dead Sexy was stimulating Noah's libido and he pulled Angela close, hugging her tightly and planting a wet kiss on her sensuous red lips.

"Hey, you've got lipstick on your cheek," she said, as they began to walk hand-in-hand to the truck. They stopped and she began wiping it off.

"Better there, than on my collar," Noah said. *Oops.*

Her smile evaporated. She recoiled and released his hand.

Noah knew the lipstick-on-the-collar line had become synonymous with infidelity. But that wasn't one of his character traits. *So why did you say it? It was spontaneous, that's all.* Nonetheless, he realized an apology was in order, especially since Angela's mood had swung on a dime and she now marched ahead of him, distant and cold, more figuratively than literally.

He caught up to her. "Listen, I'm sorry. I didn't mean anything by that."

Silently, she continued to the truck, putting more distance between them. Noah dropped back, surmising that she needed time to process whatever new scabs he'd scraped away from old wounds.

Hands on her hips, she waited for him to unlock the door. Using the remote, he did, moving around to the passenger door to open it for her. But she'd already opened it. "I can do that myself. I'm not helpless, you know."

On the way home, he let her brood silently, thinking, *If that's all it takes to set her off, that's her own shit. Obviously her last boyfriend cheated on her, but I'm not her last boyfriend. Am I just rebound guy who'll be dropped like a sack of hammers once I help her get her self-esteem back? Transition guy?*

As he rounded a bend in the highway, a shadow caught his eye, disappearing beyond the tree-line, but unmistakably not caused by the truck's headlights. He pulled over to the shoulder and stopped. "Did you see that?"

After a moment, Angela turned to him, a slight frown creasing her soft features. "See what?"

Noah pointed. "A shadow. Over there."

"I don't see anything."

Then a shadow emerged from the tree, red-eyed, with an elongated bald head. It floated from the dark forest and hovered above the windshield, leaving them both jaw-dropped and petrified.

"Take a picture, Angela. Take a picture."

She quickly grabbed the camera and snapped three shots in quick succession. In the opposite lane, headlights approached. And as the high-beams neared, the shadow person vanished. The car passed and the darkness returned.

"I think we better get moving," Angela said, her voice tight.

Noah pulled out onto the highway and continued on. "Holy shit, Angela. They're real. The Shadow People are real."

As she reviewed the camera images, her mouth formed a large O. "They're here. We got them." She held out the camera to Noah and he took a quick look before returning his eyes to the road. Sure enough, a dark shadow was visible beyond and above the vehicle windshield. Even the tiny red eyes could be seen staring at them, appearing to look right through them. After his last Shadow People sighting, Noah had only given it cursory consideration. Not anymore. They had photographic evidence. He decided to call Neil to get an expert opinion as soon as he arrived home.

The black curtain of night had snatched away what remained of dusk by the time Noah turned onto Kent Street. There was a cop car with flashing red lights parked in front of his apartment. A cop stood outside, and as they approached, he waved them over.

Noah parked behind the cop car. "Shit, what now?"

A uniformed cop with a flashlight approached, signaling Noah to roll down his window. Once he did, the cop shone the light inside the truck, momentarily blinding them. When the white dots cleared from his vision, Noah looked up and saw a Hispanic man with a neatly trimmed goatee.

"Are you Noah Janzen?" the cop asked.

Noah nodded.

To Angela, he asked, "And you're Angela Rosewood?"

"That's right, officer. What did we do?"

Suddenly an alarm went off, deafening.

BWEEP... bip... bip... BWEEP... bip... bip... BWEEP...

The automatic doors to the fire station directly across the street from Noah's apartment opened and a bright red fire truck pulled out and quickly turned left.

BWEEP... bip... bip... BWEEP... bip... bip... BWEEP...

The cop waited until the sound of the fire alarm faded before responding. "You didn't do anything. I'm Police Constable Victor Sanchez. Detective Stevenson sent me. He wanted me to let you know that this evening we've had some odd reports of, uh, shadowy people. And a few others from people who've been terrorized by a man with a fedora. Stevenson calls him the Hat Man. Have you guys seen anything strange tonight?"

Angela tucked the camera in her pocket and gave Sanchez a description of the shadow person. Noah added a few details, indicating the exact location as accurately as possible. They never breathed a word about the photographic evidence they had.

"Okay," Sanchez said. "Were you planning on staying at Noah's apartment again tonight? Because I don't think it's safe right now for you to be in your home alone."

"If it's okay with him," Angela said, her eyes darting back and forth between the cop and Noah.

"Not a problem," Noah said.

"Carry on then," Sanchez said. "Something very strange is happening around here. If you see anything threatening, you call me, hear?"

They nodded.

"I'm going to try to check on you guys later, but I can't promise around-the-clock security. Our resources are being stretched pretty thin."

Once the cop got back in his car and took off, Angela said, "I pocketed the camera because I didn't want it to get confiscated as evidence and maybe never returned."

"I figured that," Noah said. "That's why I kept my mouth shut."

Noah and Angela made their way up to his apartment.

Reclining on Noah's sectional sofa, they went through the photographic evidence. They were amazed at how well-defined the shadow person was and how its red eyes, instead of peering at the camera, appeared to look right into their souls.

"I almost forgot," Noah said. "I should call Neil about this. Maybe he can explain a few things." He knew Neil had been conducting some rather secretive experiments lately, experiments that might explain the rash of recent Hat Man and Shadow People sightings. It was time for the good doctor to come clean, since the tiny island was suddenly being overrun with supernatural forces.

When he reached the doctor, Neil's voice sounded edgy, his words rushed. Noah explained what he and Angela had seen earlier that evening.

"I'm tied up in a paranormal investigation right now," Neil said. "I don't think I can make it over tonight. But maybe you can come out tomorrow and show me the photos. I'll explain a few things then."

"Do you know who these Shadow People are?" Noah pressed. "Do they mean us any harm?"

"Listen, I'll explain everything tomorrow."

Noah heard a thumping sound in the background, followed by an audible shriek.

"I gotta go," Neil said. "Is Angela with you?"

"Yes."

"Protect her."

Noah heard a click and the line went dead. When he set his cell phone on the coffee table, he noticed Angela's face had gone white.

She had obviously overheard the entire conversation. "I'm getting scared," she said.

"Just relax," Noah said. "I'll look after you." He retrieved a large green comforter from a nearby closet and set it on her lap. She immediately wrapped it around herself and curled into a corner of the sofa. He went into the kitchen and opened the fridge.

"How about a glass of white wine?" he asked.

"One might not hurt, to calm my nerves."

Once he'd put two glasses of wine on the coffee table along with a wine bottle, he picked up his cell phone.

"I'm gonna order a pizza," he said. "Any preference for toppings?"

She thought about it. "How about pepperoni, salami, mushroom..."

BWEEP... bip... bip... BWEEP... bip... bip... BWEEP...

The blaring of the fire alarm caused Noah's right hand to begin trembling again and he dropped the phone on the floor.

Angela recoiled, spilling some wine on her red V-neck top. She steadied the glass, placed it on the coffee table, and started to get up.

"I got it," Noah said.

He grabbed a towel, went into the kitchen and ran some warm water over it. He returned to the living room and handed it to Angela. She began wiping her bosom and Noah felt a tingle of excitement surge through his body. *That soldier has a mind of his own.*

When the blaring fire alarm faded into the distance, Noah took a deep breath and picked up the phone to order the pizza. Angela had been so frightened from the fire truck, she'd forgotten what toppings she'd asked for.

After some thought, Noah remembered. "I think it was pepperoni, salami, mushroom... you were cut off then. Anything else?"

"Do you like those toppings?"

"Sure."

"Why don't you pick two more?"

"How about garlic and red onions?"

Angela laughed nervously. "Onion and garlic breath? I guess if we both have it, we won't notice it."

There was an underlying suggestion contained in her words that appealed to Noah, regardless of their earlier distance. "Okay, it's settled then."

******

Angela understood on some almost instinctual level that if she continued to demonstrate the behavior she'd exhibited at the beach earlier, she would be walking on thin ice with Noah. He'd made an innocent joke about lipstick on the collar and it had opened up a gaping wound of unhealed heartache and misery.

One thing she'd failed to tell Noah about when she'd brought him up to speed earlier on her list of accomplishments, was that she'd purchased a new frame. This frame was now featured prominently on her nightstand, and once again contained the image of smiling ex-boyfriend Case Blackthorn. He was an unhealed, infected and festering thorn in her side, yet she seemed unable to remove him from her life for long.

She knew also that if it hadn't been for the threat of the Hat Man or the Shadow People, on some strange level a blessing in disguise, she would have angrily ordered Noah to drive her straight home so she could wallow in self-pity, heartache and despair, while staring at the image of the thorn in her side staring back at her with that smug smile that only served to taunt and ratchet up the intensity of her pain.

Why can't I just throw the photo away and move on with my life? The answer hit her like a hammer upside the head. *Because he called me today. Case called me today.*

She struggled and finally pushed the thought away, knowing that continuing to dwell on Case would destroy this new relationship before it got off the ground. Noah, knowingly or not, had provided her with a rare combination of independence, self-esteem, and happiness that had so far eluded her.

Sure, she'd felt happiness with Case, as well as happiness with her high school sweetheart, Seth; but in both cases, the cost of that happiness had meant losing her sense of independence and self-esteem. Both of her exes had robbed her of those qualities and she'd often wondered if she'd ever be able to reclaim them. She gritted her teeth and balled her fists, suddenly feeling angry at them, and even angrier at herself for her inability to move past them.

She realized she'd been quiet for a little too long and brought her mind back to the present. Evidently sensing her need for reflection, Noah had picked up the TV remote and pressed the ON button. CNN news anchor Anderson Cooper's face appeared and started berating former President Donald Trump for "eroding American democracy."

"Could you turn that off for a minute?" Angela said.

Noah killed the TV. "Sure. I was just gonna try and find some local news. I thought there might be some coverage on all the Shadow People sightings."

"We can do that later if you want. I need to get some things off my chest."

"You've got the floor," he said with a look of apprehension.

She took a sip of liquid courage and put her glass down. "What happened back there at the beach wasn't your fault." *Maybe it was. Maybe he's infidelity-prone.* "I never told you about my other ex. He dumped me at the beach. I haven't been able to bring myself to go the beach since that happened. Being there brought all the awful memories back and I took it out on you."

"It's okay."

"No, it's not okay. It was my shit and I should own it. I'm sorry."

"Okay. Thank you. Apology accepted."

"There are a few other things I didn't tell you."

"We haven't known each other for that long. We have lots of time."

"I'm not so sure about that," Angela said. "If I keep behaving that way, you're bound to get tired of it."

"I figured it was something in your past that triggered the reaction. But I didn't think it was the time or the place to discuss it. Besides, it looked like you needed to simmer a bit."

Angela nodded. "I did. But now I'm ready to talk."

"Okay."

She took a sip of wine. "Earlier today, my more recent ex-boyfriend called me. His name is Case Blackthorn. He told me his bimbo girlfriend had dumped him and asked me to take him back."

That got Noah's undivided attention. "Really?"

"Yes, and I have to admit, I was tempted. But then I started thinking about how he treated me. Like an object. So possessive and jealous, too. So I did something for myself for a change, something for the future of our relationship. I told him I wasn't interested in taking him back, that I was seeing someone. And it felt so good, so good."

"How did he react?"

"He started swearing at me and slammed the phone down. He said something about how I'd get mine one day, something like that."

"Wow. Is he violent?"

"I don't think so. I don't know. But it felt so good to stand up to him for a change, felt so good to put my own emotions first." She studied some of the framed photographs for a moment, searching for the right words. She decided there was no diplomatic way to put what she wanted to ask. "Have you ever cheated on any of your girlfriends? I have to ask, because I like you. But I don't want to invest a lot of time in someone who might be unfaithful."

"I've never cheated."

"What about your girlfriends? Have any of them ever cheated on you?"

"Not that I'm aware of."

Angela took some comfort in the knowledge that Noah didn't suffer from the same insecurities she did. However, the comfort was short-lived. He'd hinted about his mother's neglect at The Pilot House the other day. Wouldn't that treatment give him a grim view of women? Wouldn't it create insecurities about women?

She realized that he'd expertly sidetracked the conversation away from relationships earlier. Either that, or she hadn't asked, mainly because the pain of her own relationship failures was still too raw to want to listen to someone else's. But if they had any hope of succeeding, this emotional baggage would have to be emptied sooner or later. Better sooner, when there were less emotions involved.

"Maybe you don't want to talk about this," she said, "but I'm beginning to think we should get it out in the open. When was your last relationship?"

A frown creased Noah's brow and he reached for his wine. After a short pause, he said, "Sixteen years ago."

"How long were you together?"

"Five years."

"And it wasn't a nasty break-up? Do you mind me asking this?"

"No, and no."

"And she didn't cheat on you?"

"I don't think so. But you *are* starting to hit on something—something that I guess I've kept bottled up for many years."

"What's that?"

"Natasha broke up with me because she said I had trust issues. If I stop and think about it, and I haven't for a very long time, I think those trust issues stemmed from my mother's neglect. Barbara treated me like shit. She was too busy partying and fucking around with other guys to pay much attention to me. And that was what I grew to expect. Maybe I transferred that distrust to Natasha without realizing it."

"I can see how that could happen."

"Maybe it did, Angela. But I don't want it to happen with you." He slid a little closer to her, and she did the same.

"Well, that's why we're talking about it," she said. "I think it can be therapeutic for both of us."

Noah put both hands over his cheeks and stared at the floor. "I might not have told you if you hadn't asked."

"Well, I did and you did. That's what matters. If we can both come to grips with our issues, we have a fighting chance. My issues really aren't that much different from yours. I found out after my relationship with Seth ended that he'd been cheating on me. I found out after my relationship with Case was over that he'd been cheating on me, too. You'd think that would make me hate them, but it didn't."

Noah slowly removed his hands from his face and looked up at Angela. "Well, you stood up to Case today and I'm proud of you for that. You've made progress by the sounds of it."

I didn't mention the new picture frame I bought for Case's photo just before he called. I didn't mention I'm still unable to throw it away. I didn't mention my joy at blowing him off was short-lived. "Maybe I have," she said. "I'd just like it to go faster."

"These things take time," Noah said. "I'm sure you've gotten over Seth by now."

"I have," Angela agreed. "I don't pine for Seth. Not anymore, anyway, though I did for a long time. Maybe Case replaced that yearning. I don't know." Her eyes moistened. "But, can you believe it? I still pine for Case. After everything that fuck did, I still miss him. What's wrong with me, Noah? What's wrong with me?"

******

Noah wasn't a psychologist. He didn't know what was wrong with Angela. However, whatever it was, he suffered from some of the same issues. Only he'd managed to block them out for so many years and live what he'd thought was a happy life. Now, for the first time in his life, he realized—Angela had helped him realize—that his happiness had been a lie, a refusal to accept and work through his shit. She'd peeled away scabs from old unhealed wounds and he began to realize just how emotionally bottled up he was. Did he really expect a Band-Aid to last forever? What had he been thinking? His mind tumbled into a maelstrom of emotions, and he began to painfully relive moments of Barbara's neglect and abuse.

She'd always told him there was no bogeyman and that the monster was only in his mind. She'd been unsympathetic to his terrifying nightmares. Her off-hand comments about him being afraid of his "own shadow" probably only served to perpetuate his terrifying childhood nightmares.

The general coldness and disinterest she'd exhibited cut the deepest—unwilling to hold, unwilling to hug, unwilling or unable to love him.

Bringing guy after guy after guy to the house without any regard for how multiple father figures, many of them verbally abusive, would shape his upbringing.

The loud noise and partying that went on day in and day out.

Noah sat almost catatonic on the couch until the gale force winds of the emotional cyclone of tormenting memories began to subside. And when he looked at his right hand it was shaking again. And he was finally beginning to realize why. More than his fear of the Hat Man, more than any fear of the Shadow people, *this* was the fear that was his undoing—the fear of coming to grips and moving past his terrifying upbringing. Maybe the Hat Man was just a symbol for all that darkness that he steadfastly refused to shed light on.

He sighed as a realization crept over him. If the Hat Man was merely a symbol for his unembraced dark side, then Angela, while helping herself, was transforming darkness into light. He looked into her deep blue eyes. A teardrop slowly bubbled up in her left eye. She closed her eyes and it rolled down her cheek. He was unexpectedly overcome with affection for her in a more powerful and intense way than ever before. As he felt his own eyes moisten, he slid over and embraced her in a long and tight hug, feeling his cheek moisten as her tears intermingled with his own and dripped onto the nape of his neck.

"We're gonna be alright, honey," he said. "We're gonna be okay." It was all he could think of to say.

Bzzz... bzzzzzzz... bzzzzz!

They both jumped out of their skins at the sound of the buzzer, Noah's arms rising in a protective fashion, almost tipping over his wine glass.

He scrambled to the buzzer and pressed TALK. "Hello?"

"Your pizza's here."

CHAPTER THIRTEEN

Driving into Charlottetown for his third paranormal investigation in a matter of hours, Neil was starting to feel a little rattled. Now that the Parallel Projector had unleashed the Shadow People upon the world, he wasn't sure what would happen next.

The first call came in from Deborah Crawfield, a neighbor who lived about a mile up the road. She'd called in a panic saying she'd sighted a shadow person and her husband Charlie had begun behaving violently, tossing items around the house and swearing and cursing. She was afraid his anger would eventually be directed toward her. That was nothing new to Neil. After one too many drinks, Charlie had a habit of flying off the handle and verbally abusing his wife. Neil thought it was just a matter of time before the abuse turned physical and Deborah would either wind up in the hospital or wind up dead. He'd even made it a point to report Charlie's unstable and unpredictable behavior to Detective Stevenson.

When he'd arrived at their house, Deborah, flashlight in hand, had met Neil in the driveway. She was hysterical. She'd told him she'd seen the shadow person in the living room shortly after her husband had erupted, throwing things at the wall, a few items narrowly missing her. Then she and Charlie saw the shadow person fly up the stairs and Charlie had armed himself with a shotgun and raced up the stairs in hot pursuit of the spectral entity.

She'd heard some thumping and knocking in an upper bedroom but had been too terrified to investigate. Armed with a Colt .45, a digital recorder wristwatch, cell phone and flashlight, Neil had raced up the stairs. In one of the bedrooms, a lamp had been overturned, along with a nightstand, and it appeared the double bed had been moved. But there was no evidence of the shadow person. And Charlie was passed out on the bed, snoring peacefully with an ear-to-ear grin, his shotgun on the floor below him. Neil had shone the flashlight in Charlie's face and he'd woken up with a grin, greeted Neil with a warm hug, and even offered him a beer. Stranger still, after Charlie had managed to stagger downstairs, he gave Deborah a passionate embrace and planted a wet kiss on her lips, claiming he had no recollection of anything bad happening and professing his undying love and devotion to his wife. Neil would have stayed to insure the situation was indeed calm and that Charlie wasn't merely putting on an act to escape criminal charges, but a second call had sent him rushing out the door.

His long-time friend and neighbor Norman Murphy had called, saying there was a shadow person floating around his living room. Arriving at Norman's house a few minutes later, Neil, in spite of a thorough search of the residence and property, couldn't find any evidence of Shadow People. However, during a second search of an upper bedroom, they heard some thumping coming from an adjacent bedroom. They had rushed into the bedroom only to see a faint dark remnant of a shadow person disappearing through a closed window. It was as if they were being toyed with, like puppets on a string. As Neil was about to head home to assess the damage to the Parallel Projector, the third call came in, the one he was chasing down now.

"Please don't let this be horrible," he told himself as he turned onto Weymouth Street. An eerie, dark vibe washed over him and he struggled to recollect if he'd ever conducted a paranormal investigation at the white two-story house the GPS had guided him to. Nothing came to mind. Then a thought occurred to him. *It's close to Angela's house. In fact, it's right next door to her house.*

He remembered reading the address of the Hat Man attack in *The Guardian*. He struggled to contain a cold shudder creeping up his spine, but then he remembered that Angela was safe and sound at Noah's apartment, and he felt somewhat reassured.

He parked his pickup, sorted through his gear, and packed the large pockets of his military-style green parka. In addition to the smartphone, he added an extra camera to his paranormal paraphernalia, something he'd forgotten on the first two investigations.

As he got out of his truck, the first thing that hit him was the smell—burning plastic, oil, wood, mixed with other toxins. Walking toward the front door of the house, he glanced toward the airport and in the distance saw a large orange ball of flames erupt with a whoosh and illuminate the dark sky. Then he heard the sirens, rushing to the scene of the blaze. It looked like it was in an area filled with warehouses. *My God. A fire. What's happening?* As he knocked on the door, he couldn't help the powerful feelings of guilt that cut through him like a hot knife through butter. *My experiment, gone wrong. Is this all my fault?*

A dark-haired young woman answered the door, beads of perspiration clinging to her forehead. Her dark eyes were squinty, her face tight with worry. "Are you Neil, the paranormal investigator?"

"Yes," he said, stepping inside. "You must be Bonnie."

She nodded.

Neil had been told that Bonnie's boyfriend Tyler had barricaded himself in an upper bedroom after seeing a dark shadowy figure penetrate an exterior wall of the house and glide to within a few inches of his face.

Bonnie led him into the living room and Neil sat down on an armchair, checking his wristwatch to insure it was recording. It was. He scratched his chin, trying to put pieces of the mysterious puzzle together. "Tyler's still in the bedroom?"

"Yeah."

"It's pretty quiet now. Did he make any noise?"

Bonnie, a waif of a woman perhaps in her late twenties, wiped sweat from her forehead and tucked strands of her long black hair behind her ears. "He screamed bloody murder when he ran upstairs. I checked the door. It's locked. I couldn't hear anything, so I came back downstairs and called you."

"Have you heard anything else since you called me?"

"No. It's been quiet for the last twenty minutes or so."

"Did you call the cops?"

"No. I hear they're running their asses off tonight anyway."

"That's true," Neil said. He'd checked his police radio earlier and discovered that the authorities were attending to fires, responding to domestic abuse calls and dealing with reports of Shadow People and the Hat Man all over town.

"What's happening?" Bonnie asked. "It's as if someone unleashed the Devil on us."

Neil ran a hand through his hair and crinkled his brow. "I'm still trying to figure that out. Tell me, did anything happen before Tyler saw the shadow person?"

Bonnie's eyes darted around the room, finally stopping at a fireplace, where burning logs snapped, crackled and popped. After studying the flames for a short time, she looked at Neil. "What do you mean?"

"I mean were you guys fighting or anything like that? Arguing maybe?"

"Actually, we were. He's a verbally abusive son of a bitch and sometimes I don't know why I put up with his bullshit." Her eyes welled with tears. "He lays one fucking hand on me and I swear to God I'm gonna get the cops on his ass so fast Shadow People will be the least of his concerns. I'll kick his ass curbside so fast it'll make his head spin."

Neil slid his hand inside the parka and felt the cold comforting steel of the Colt .45. "Does he have any weapons? He into guns?"

Bonnie shook her head. "No. But he's got a baseball bat inside the room he locked himself in. You wanna know why I haven't even called to him since he fled? Haven't even tried to talk to him behind that door? Well, I'll tell you. That jobless loser called me a 'dumb bitch.' He can't even hold down a job and when he does get a dime to his name, he spends it on either booze or pot. Or both."

"He doesn't sound like a very nice man."

"That's an understatement." Her voice was filling with emotion and rising exponentially with every word. "I thought if he was scared shitless for a change, I'd let him stay that way, locked in the bedroom until he learned a lesson. I probably wouldn't have even called you, but I started worrying about him killing himself or something. Even if he was killed by a shadow person, I wanted to make sure I didn't get charged with murder. I called you more out of a sense of self-preservation than out of concern for that worthless piece of shit."

A loud crunching sound caused Bonnie and Neil to tense up like lightning-infused metal rods. Before they realized what was happening, Neil saw a lean and muscular bald-headed man with a thick black beard come charging downstairs, wielding a baseball bat. He stopped at the foot of the stairs, arched the bat over his head, and stared at Bonnie with wild and vacant eyes.

He stepped toward her. "So I'm a 'worthless piece of shit,' am I?"

Eyes widening in shock, she stepped back.

He approached her with the bat raised. "When I'm done with you, you stupid bitch, you'll be the 'worthless piece of shit.' You'll be in a fucking coma or dead."

"No... no... no, please," she pleaded.

In a swift movement, Neil unbuckled the gun and aimed it at Tyler's head. "Back off," he demanded. "I don't want to put a bullet in you, but I will if I have to."

Tyler looked at Neil coldly and snarled like a wolf. "Fuck you. You don't scare me one bit."

Then, in a lightning-fast motion, he rushed over to Bonnie, aimed the business end of the baseball bat at her head and prepared to bash her brains out.

She raised her arms in defense. "Aaaaaaaaahhhh."

Neil was only a split-second away from pulling the trigger when something caught his eye. A shadow person glided down the stairs, rushed up behind Tyler and enveloped him in darkness. The bat dropped to the floor. Tyler quivered and screamed, spun around three times, tripped over the bat and landed face-first on the soft cushiony fabric of the living room sofa. Neil and Bonnie watched in stunned silence as the dark shadow seemed to melt into Tyler before his normal form and color returned.

He opened his eyes with a grin and sat up. "It's so great to see you, my dear. You didn't tell me we were having company. Please, offer the man a beer."

******

From a distance, Drake watched the warehouse burn with a satisfied grin. He was confident he would succeed this time. Earlier, after listening to the news about all the Shadow People sightings, he'd decided it was time to execute his plan. Cops were being stretched thin and, unlike last night, when his attempt had been foiled by Victor Sanchez's presence, he was now sure the cops would be everywhere else but Noah's apartment. Just to be sure, he'd ignited two fires around the city. One, a small abandoned house, had unfortunately been quickly extinguished by firefighters. But they didn't have a chance with the warehouse. After igniting it a few hours ago with a canister of gasoline and a single flick of his Bic, he'd watched rapidly advancing flames quickly engulf and ravage the large wood-framed structure. And he'd been delighted when two successive and massive explosions had magically transformed the dark sky into a brilliant fiery orange.

He steadied the binoculars, zeroing in on the action. Three fire trucks. Two ambulances. Six cop cars. A seventh pulling up to the scene. Hoses blasting. Fires raging and blazing, snapping and cracking. A small explosion blew a metal garage bay door off its hinges. The door flew about fifteen feet in the air before crash-landing with a metallic thump on the asphalt parking lot as firefighters ran for their lives. A man engulfed in flames staggered out of the flaming opening produced by the blast. He screamed in gut-wrenching agony as firefighters doused him and paramedics rushed to his aid. The man let out an agonized cry and then fell silent and still.

Too little, too late, Drake thought with a chuckle. He had other reasons to laugh. His fear of the Shadow People, he now realized, had been completely unfounded. They weren't his enemies at all. They were brothers in arms, sent to distract the cops while he terrorized residents with his Hat Man act. Maybe they were even his minions, sent from God to do his bidding. *Time will tell. Time will tell.* There was only one thing that mattered now—act three of the Hat Man Horror.

He set the binoculars down and fired up the SUV. He slowly pulled out of the dark alley, flicked his headlights on, and pulled out onto the street. *Die Mother, die. No better still... die motherfucker, die.* The quiet interior of the SUV filled up with his demonic, high-pitched laugh.

******

Since he'd decided to come clean on everything he could think of, even confessing to Angela the horrific details of his multiple sleep disorders, they'd mutually agreed that, at least for tonight, Angela would sleep in Noah's bedroom behind a locked door and Noah would take the couch. He'd told her about the powerful sleeping pills that Neil had given him, but both agreed, in light of the crazy things going on in the city lately, it would be a better idea for Noah to attempt a natural sleep. The last thing they wanted was for one or both of them to be thrust into a life-threatening situation and have Noah too groggy to defend himself or Angela.

Noah turned over on the couch and the motion woke him up. He realized, as images flooded his mind, that he'd just been dreaming. He sat up, trying to recollect the dream. Slowly the realization came to him that indeed he'd dreamt about the Hat Man. But, far from the previous terrifying nightmares, this one had left him feeling calm and peaceful.

In the dream, he walked down the middle of a street dotted with antiquated shops, saloons, a general store, even a blacksmith operation. It was a set right out of an old spaghetti-western movie. In the distance, he saw the shadowy form of the Hat Man approaching, as if it was the opening sequence of a gunfight in an old movie. As the Hat Man drew near, Noah realized the street was lined with black humanoid images on one side, white humanoid images on the other. When the Hat Man was about twenty feet away from Noah, he stopped. So did Noah. Next, Noah presumed, they would draw their guns. But they didn't have any guns to draw. Instead, the Hat Man covered the distance with lightning speed and embraced Noah in a powerful, warm and protective hug. And the words the Hat Man spoke were as clear now as they were in the dream. "I'm not *what* you think I am. I'm not *who* you think I am."

Noah retrieved a small notepad and a pen from a built-in coffee table drawer and wrote down as much as he could remember about the dream. He felt excited and exhilarated and couldn't wait to tell Angela and Neil about this newfound positive experience with the mysterious man he'd always viewed as the Dark Menace, even the Devil. What could it possibly mean and why was it happening now?

He finished scribbling, curled up, and pulled the comforter up over his ears. Within five minutes, he drifted off into a peaceful sleep.

******

She retrieved a pair of leather work gloves from a utility drawer and put them on. She turned around and went into her bedroom. She picked up the smug smiling face of Case and, with a wry grin, went into her kitchen. She allowed herself one last look at his taunting smile and then slammed the glass-encased picture frame on the kitchen counter. The glass smashed and glittering shards flew everywhere. She examined what was left of the frame, and of Case. One spear of glass had poked through his paper chest, through his heart, and another protruded precariously from his mouth. One of his eyes was obliterated by sparkling glass shards.

"Who has the broken heart now?" Angela asked, gritting her teeth. "Who? Not me, you philandering fuck. Not me." Satisfied with her reprimand, she slammed the picture frame down onto the kitchen counter forcefully several more times. When she finally stopped, all that remained of Case was a shredded, glass-embedded paper tiger. His smug smirk was gone. He was gone. She twisted the remains into a crude tube, as if she was wringing out a soppy dishtowel, and tossed it into a garbage can. Then she calmly removed the gloves and returned to bed. *Is this a dream? It feels so eerily real.*

She curled up and pulled the blankets over her ears. She listened to her heart rate slowly return to normal. She grinned. *Out with yesterday's stinky trash. Just how it should be.* Next would be the Rolex watch. And she knew just what to do with that.

A dark shadow caught her eye. She tried to move, but couldn't. She was frozen.

The shadow grew into the form of the Hat Man. He glided up to the foot of her bed and stopped.

Again, she tried to move to no avail. Then her mind began to process the strange feeling enveloping her and she stopped fighting it. The sensation was oddly pleasing. Comforting, in a guardian angel kind of way. She stared at the Hat Man and tried to speak, but no words emerged. *This must be sleep paralysis.* It was just like Noah had explained, only quite the opposite of terrifying.

Standing larger than life at the foot of the bed, the Hat Man's featureless face stared back at her. It infused her with a comforting warmth and an indescribable feeling of inner peace. He moved closer, working his way effortlessly around to the side of her bed.

Angela bathed in the peacefulness the Hat Man's dark presence exuded. It was as if the iconographic colors of good and evil were being reversed. Black was no longer evil, white not necessarily good. Or maybe it was different, she thought. Something like, out of the darkness light emerges. You can't have one without the other. She couldn't quite grasp the concept so she let it go, instead savoring this period of blissful calm, peace, and protectiveness. She was in the hands of her guardian angel, coming to grips with her relationship issues, and everything was going to be okay.

The Hat Man faded away and then vanished entirely.

Then she woke with a start.

Glass shattered and shards flew everywhere. A darkly cloaked man wearing a fedora hat burst through the bedroom window, brandishing a machete.

Angela bolted upright. "Aaaaaaaaaaaahhhh!"

Swinging the machete, the Hat Man approached quickly. "It's your time to die, Mother." He cackled insanely, approaching the foot of the bed. Aiming for her leg, he swung the machete down.

Angela scrambled to her feet as the machete sliced into blankets and bedsheets.

On the bed, she jumped and dodged as the Hat Man sliced through the air. "Come on, Mother. It's useless to resist. It's your time to die, Mother. It's your time to die, motherfucker."

Mercilessly, he swung the machete and Angela performed a death-defying mattress dance. Descending from one leap, she landed awkwardly and, terrified, watched the machete advance swiftly toward her legs. She quickly leaped up, too little too late. The blade sliced into her right calf and she felt stinging pain and warm blood gush out and soak her leg. She landed on a nightstand, picked up a lamp, and began swinging it at her attacker. "Fuck you," she said. "Fuck you to hell!"

******

"Fuck you to hell!" The words pierced Noah's erotic dream like a murderous machete. He pulled back the comforter swiftly, jumped up, rushed into the kitchen, quickly plucked a large carving knife from a wooden knife holder, and hurried for the door.

He tried the handle but, as the dream-induced image of Angela's voluminous naked breasts faded from his mind, quickly realized it was locked. Locked from the inside.

He pounded on the door. "Angela... Angela!"

From the other side, "Help me!"

With socked feet, he kicked the door. Stinging pain shot up his toe as his foot crumpled on the solid oak surface. Whatever cobwebs that remained from the dream were quickly erased by the searing pain. "Shit!"

"Help me!"

"No one's gonna help you, bitch. Least of all that weak little boyfriend of yours."

"Aaaaaaaaahh... help me, please!"

Ignoring the pain, Noah backed up a few feet, and ran for the door, hitting it hard with his shoulder. It flew open and he fell into the room. Still clutching the carving knife, he smashed into the Hat Man, knocking him ass-first into the jagged edges of the shattered bedroom window frame. For his trouble, the Hat Man received an ass full of glass. Noah landed on top of the Hat Man, narrowly escaping the glass daggers.

The Hat Man groaned and raised the machete.

With both hands, Noah pulled at the carving knife, the blade of which was embedded in the wall, inches from the Hat Man.

Angela removed the shade from the lamp and smashed it into the wall. The bulb shattered. She jumped off the bed and approached the Hat Man with jagged edges and murderous intentions.

"Step aside," she told Noah. "I'm gonna finish this sicko off once and for all."

Noah released his grip on the knife and rolled onto the floor.

Angela pointed the broken lamp like a spear and charged the Hat Man. But, as she neared, he wrenched his bleeding buttocks from his sharp-edged seat and dove on the floor, across from Noah.

Angela's forward momentum propelled her through the window. She landed halfway in the window frame and halfway on the metal balcony of the rear fire escape. A cold hard landing. During her exit, the lamp-spear had rattled loose from her grip, landing on the window ledge.

Noah picked it up and got to his feet. He slashed the Hat Man's leg. The Hat Man clutched the wound as blood gushed from it like a mini geyser. Noah slashed again and the jagged edges of the light bulb lanced his face, creating a macabre and bloody mustache.

Angela groaned. "I'm stuck."

With superhuman speed and agility, the Hat Man vaulted to his feet, wiping a hand over his new mustache and painting a garish clown grin around his mouth. He ignored the spears in his ass and his blood-spewing leg wound and raised the machete, charging Noah, head-butting him in the chest, winding him and sending him careening into the wall. The back of Noah's head slammed into the wooden door frame, and the lamp flew out of his hands. The room blackened and stars twinkled and danced around as he crumpled to the floor.

The Hat Man knelt down in front of him and raised the machete.

Even in his haze, Noah could see the blood-soaked blade hovering directly above his throat. He fought to get his breath and clear his head, but the blackness was overpowering. First there was one machete. Then there were two. First there was one Hat Man. Then there were two. Consciousness ebbed. Consciousness flowed. Consciousness ebbed. He realized it was too late. There was nothing he could do but succumb to death. And, surprisingly, on death's doorstep, there was no white light. Only the ivory white glow of Angela's sumptuous breasts, contrasting sharply with her ripe red nipples. That was the last thing he saw before succumbing to black nothingness.

******

Angela heard the metallic clanging of footsteps making rapid progress up the fire escape steps. But in the dimly lit surroundings, she was unable to discern who it was. And her leg had caught the window frame at an awkward angle, trapping her. Even in her fear, even in her panic, she knew enough to stay silent. Whoever it was, was coming for him. *Coming to rescue us.*

She smelled Old Spice deodorant as the metallic footsteps reached the third-floor balcony. A warm and comforting hand touched her shoulder and a man said, "Shhhhhhhh."

She craned her neck as he raised the gun. Still it was too dark to recognize him.

Ka-pow... ka-pow... ka-pow!

Through the deafening gunshot blasts, Angela saw the Hat Man take three bullets—two to the back of his head, and one to the back of his neck. Blood sprayed like a fountain from his neck. The machete clattered to the floor. The Hat Man groaned and slumped over onto Noah's chest.

After he'd carefully extracted her from her trapped position in the window, Angela finally got a good look at the man who had saved her life.

"Neil," she shouted, hugging him tightly as adrenaline pumped through her veins.

"It's okay," Neil said. "I got him. The Hat Man impersonator is dead. It's all over now."

"You're a lifesaver," Angela said. "You're a Godsend."

Neil released her and looked at her calf. Blood flowed freely from the large gash. He tore a large strip from a rumpled bedsheet and handed it to her. "Wrap your leg," he said. "I need to check on Noah."

"Is he okay?" Angela said, wrapping her blood-spurting calf. "He's not dead, is he? Please, tell me he's not dead." She started trembling uncontrollably, both from shock and a bitterly cold wind blustering into the apartment from the open window.

Neil quickly approached the Hat Man, pushed his dead body off Noah, knelt down and felt for a pulse.

Angela continued wrapping her calf with the improvised tourniquet. "Please, tell me he's okay."

"He's got a pulse," Neil said. "And a rather nasty goose egg on his head. He's out cold."

Angela let out a huge sigh.

And then she fainted.

CHAPTER FOURTEEN

Noah sat up in a strange bed in a strange bedroom and sipped a coffee. Neil had left about an hour ago, telling Noah he had some work to do in his lab and to make himself at home. The bedroom was painted in a soothing deep green color with tasteful chocolate-brown Venetian blinds covering two large windows. The blinds were open slightly, affording him a view of a snow-covered field that was bordered by towering pine and bearded spruce trees. Light snow drifted down. The sky was overcast and gray.

Noah rubbed the back of his head. It still ached dully and he didn't feel quite himself yet. A little dizzy. A little nauseous. According to Neil, he had suffered a moderate concussion. It would take some time for the full force of his cognitive functions to return, the good doctor had said. Noah looked at the digital bedside clock: 3:36 pm. He had been in and out of consciousness for the last thirty-six hours. He barely remembered the trip to the hospital, the doctor's diagnosis, and then later Neil driving him to his acreage in the country. The ordeal with the Hat Man had started late Tuesday night. Wednesday was a blur and now here he was rising up in bed on a Thursday afternoon. He had lost a full day and a half. He shuddered as the vague but horrific memory of the Hat Man attack formed pieces of a gruesome jigsaw puzzle in his mind.

He had almost lost his life.

Angela had almost lost hers, too. He thought Neil had told him that she'd needed thirty-six stitches in her calf. Was that right? Yeah, he was pretty sure that's what Neil had said when he'd brought him up to speed on what had happened.

A wave of dizziness swept over him and he set his coffee down and rested his head on the pillow. The bedroom and the outdoor winter wonderland rotated on its axis 180 degrees and then came to a stop. He watched for a moment to make sure everything remained stationery. When his vision cleared, he sat up again, grabbed his coffee, took two gulps, and tried to organize his thoughts.

Again, the extent of Angela's injury came back to him. Thirty-six stitches. And he'd needed thirty-six hours to recover. Thirty-six hours lost in a fog. *The time, well folks, it's coincidentally 3:36 pm, or at least it was a few minutes ago when I first started doing the math.*

From Neil's debriefing, Noah learned that the machete slash wound to Angela's calf—or the jagged glass edges of the window frame—had severed an artery and she'd come within a few inches of bleeding to death. In fact, she was still in the hospital. After numerous blood transfusions, they'd decided to keep her in for observation, as well as some trauma counselling with a hospital psychologist. As soon as he felt well enough, Noah told himself, he too would look into therapy. Besides the shock of the horrific attack, he knew he had demons that he needed to confront and overcome if he ever had a shot at a healthy relationship. He couldn't live his life forever in denial. Angela had opened that closet door and Noah had been horrified to learn it was full of skeletons and monsters that required proper burials for him to be able to lead a truly healthy and happy life.

He sighed and took another sip of coffee. At least they had started. Wasn't recognition the first step to recovery? And one very real monster, one Drake Simeon, was dead, paving the way for the other monsters to disappear. The end of the Hat Man, the end of the Shadow People.

Wait a minute. Weren't the Shadow People very much alive? The police reports. The sightings. Our photographic evidence. And then Noah remembered his latest Hat Man dream. Totally unlike the others. An overwhelming feeling of positivity. Why?

The question lingered for a short time and then evaporated. It was replaced by more urgent but jumbled thoughts and questions. *Today's Thursday. Angela's grant application is due tomorrow. It's at my apartment, along with my phone, probably. Is my apartment ready to live in? Did they fix the window, clean up all the blood? Is it still a crime scene? I need to get the application in before the deadline. I need to call Angela and see how she's doing. I need to see her. I need some answers from Neil on my Hat Man dream and the Shadow People. What the hell are his experiments all about?* A hundred other questions stung his brain like tiny steel balls of buckshot discharged from a shotgun. He couldn't afford to stay idle. He had to get moving.

He pushed through the dizziness, showered and dressed in some clothes that had been neatly arranged on a bedside vanity, along with some toiletries. His clothes, his toiletries, he remembered. *The memory isn't that bad after all.* Neil had thought of everything. He glanced in the mirror and wasn't pleased with what he saw; black sockets under his eyes, hair in disarray, three-day chin stubble. Bug-eyes.

He examined the other items on the vanity. Two white pills had been placed beside a full glass of water. He put both of them in his mouth and washed them down.

He searched the bedroom for his cell phone but was unable to find it. He went out into the kitchen and noticed a bowl of fruit, a plastic container of strawberry yogurt, and a glass of orange juice had been set out for him. Even the coffee pot was almost full with freshly brewed coffee. Fighting through nausea, he wolfed down the food, drained the glass of orange juice, found a steel thermos coffee mug in one of the cupboards and filled it up.

Then he went outside, walked across the snow-covered lawn, and opened the door to Neil's lab. In a corner of the lab, he saw Neil soldering some wires on a large steel wall consisting of dials, knobs, gauges, computer components. Neil had removed one of the panels and was operating inside the wire guts and other computer gadgetry of the mysterious machine. The place looked like a highly classified military intelligence laboratory—everything sterile and everything in its place.

Neil set the soldering gun on a small metal wheel-equipped work bench and smiled at Noah. "You better sit down, my friend. You shouldn't be out of bed yet. You're not well."

Noah sat down in front of a computer monitor, the soft-featured face of a woman on screen smiling at him.

"I've got things to do," Noah said.

Neil joined him at the table. "There's lots of time for that. What's on your mind?"

Tilly jumped up on the table and strutted proudly toward Noah, brushing him with her tail.

"Meow," she said.

He stroked the top of her head gently and she began her signature purr.

"I didn't know you had a cat."

"Tilly normally avoids people," Neil said. "Finds them catastrophic, I think... but she really likes you. That's a surprise. Animals never cease to amaze me."

Tilly curled up on the table next to Noah, watching him attentively and purring.

The "catastrophic" pun was missed on Noah. "I have a million questions."

"Why don't you start with what's most pressing on your mind."

"Have you seen my phone?"

Neil extracted it from a pocket of his white lab coat and handed it to Noah. "Yeah, sorry. I've been playing secretary while you've been recovering. I hope you don't mind."

"No. And thanks."

"Before I forget, Detective Stevenson called not long ago. He says your apartment will be ready Friday."

"Tomorrow?"

"That's right. The window has been repaired but a forensic team is still gathering evidence. When you feel up to it, Detective Stevenson would like your version of events. I told him you're in no condition to talk right now and he accepted that."

"I wanted to get something from my apartment," Noah said. "There's a grant application for Angela that I need to submit by tomorrow."

"I have that in my house. When I grabbed your stuff, I noticed it. I thought it looked important so I took it."

Even through a thin fog, Noah was impressed. "Wow. You don't leave a single stone unturned. Listen, I wanna thank you for saving my life. And for taking care of me for the last, uh, thirty-six hours."

Neil dismissed it with a wave. "It's the least I could do. And the Dark Menace Drake is dead. I've been assured by Detective Stevenson that future questioning is just a formality. He tells me it's an open and shut case of self-defense. They even found Drake's DNA at Agnes's murder scene and are now looking into a few missing person files. It seems that monster was much worse than anyone had imagined. Who knows how many bodies they might find buried on his property?"

"Agnes?" Noah asked.

"Agnes Ingles. You remember. That elderly lady who was killed a few days back. Slashed up with a machete."

Noah shuddered as he realized just how close he'd actually come to ending up like Agnes. "Right. I do have a vague recollection of that. By the way, how is Angela?"

Neil reached over and stroked Tilly's chin. The purring feline seemed to smile. "She's doing much better. That was the other call that came in not too long ago. The hospital is releasing her this evening."

"Does she have anyone to pick her up?"

"That's where I come in," Neil said. "She didn't want to involve her parents, for her own reasons. They were up to see her but she sent them home after a short visit, assuring them she was fine."

"I should call her," Noah said.

"Just give me a minute," Neil said. "I know you'll want to come along and I don't think you should. I really think you should get some more rest. I also spoke to your boss at the Arts Council. They know what happened and don't expect you back until next week some time."

Noah held up an open palm. "Angela's been traumatized. She needs me."

Neil raised an open palm. "Please, let me finish. I invited Angela to stay with me for a few days until she feels better. She agreed. We need to make sure you're both safe. Beyond my other hobbies, I'm still a doctor. And a doctor should always put his patient's needs ahead of his own."

Noah felt his eyes moisten, plucked a tissue from a dispenser on the table, and wiped them. He hoped he wouldn't turn into a blubbering idiot. He was beginning to understand the depth of Neil's caregiving nature. He could learn a thing or two from this man. And he planned on doing just that in the days to come. "Thanks, doc. You're amazing. What about the grant application?"

"I'll drop it off on my way to pick up Angela. Don't they have a mail slot for grant applications at your office?"

"Yeah, it's on the right side of the building."

"Good. I'll put it in there."

"I suppose you have the address of my office."

"Yes," Neil said. "Don't worry about the little things. Worry about the big things first. Like your health."

"Speaking of that," Noah said. "I'd like to talk to you about some issues related to my sleep disorders and the Hat Man. I had a positive dream about him the other night. Just before... just before the vicious attack. I think maybe I need to see a psychologist."

"Listen," Neil said. "In due time. I have to pick Angela up at nine tonight, after her counselling session. While I'm gone, you get some rest. If you're up to it later tonight, we can talk about a few things. Before I became a sleep disorder specialist, my major for my undergraduate degree was psychology. I know a thing or two about how the mind works. I can be your surrogate psychologist for the time being."

Confused, Noah stared at his phone. "Okay. Should I call Angela?"

Neil checked his watch. "Not now. She's having supper. Why don't you call her after your nap?"

"Okay." The information overload was starting to make Noah tired. He was beginning to realize Neil was right. He was exhausted. He also wanted to be in better shape for Angela's arrival. He studied all the high-tech equipment and realized that in many ways, Neil Samuelson was an enigma to him. He also realized he'd forgotten the obvious question. "What's all this stuff for? What kind of experiments are you conducting here?"

Neil stood, touched Noah's shoulder gently, and guided him to the door. Tilly meowed, flew off the table, and followed, thrusting her sleek black tail straight up in a gravity-defying pose.

They stopped at the door and Neil turned around and looked proudly at all the equipment. "What you see here, my friend, is the machinery that will lead to the biggest scientific discovery known to humankind. And I'll tell you all about it tomorrow. But first things first. Your health. Now be a good patient and go to bed."

CHAPTER FIFTEEN

It was exactly eleven pm when the digital alarm clock woke Noah from a deep sleep to the sound of a weather report:

"A low pressure system will approach Prince Edward Island today. Snow will develop near noon, then taper off to showers or flurries this evening. Snowfall amounts of near 10 centimeters are expected. On Friday a second system will pass south of Nova Scotia. Light rain or snow will redevelop across the island Friday afternoon then change to snow Friday evening and persist into Saturday. Snowfall amounts could possibly exceed 15 centimeters with this second system. There may also be some gusty winds and blowing snow..."

He pressed the OFF button and sat up in bed. Among other things, it appeared the sleep specialist was monitoring and controlling his sleep. He realized he'd slept soundly for six hours. The haze was a little thinner, and he felt more alert after wiping the sleep from his eyes. Even his headache had become a dull roar—a minor annoyance to be sure, but little more than that. Down the hall, he heard the muffled and friendly banter of Neil and Angela talking.

He found a black baseball cap on a nearby wall anchor, one of Neil's obviously, but he thought he'd borrow it. He doubted Neil would mind and besides, he knew bed-head wasn't a good look for him. In the bathroom, he splashed some warm water on his face, brushed his teeth and rinsed his mouth out with Scope before proceeding down the hall and into the living room.

"Alas, Sleeping Beauty has arisen," Neil said.

A savory aroma of spicy beans and beef greeted Noah's senses and he noticed a simmering crock pot on the counter next to the stove. In the living room, Angela sat on an armchair opposite Neil, who sat on the couch. Both had steaming hot beverages on tea tables beside them and Tilly sat contentedly on the arm of Angela's chair, her inquisitive yellow eyes watching her every move. Angela's hair was neatly tied back in a ponytail and her face looked fresh and alive, a healthy pink glow on both cheeks; as if she'd just stepped out of a hot shower. She wore an oversized black sweatshirt and baggy gray sweatpants, the right leg of which was rolled up to her knee, presumably to give air to a white gauze ankle-to-knee bandage.

The fireplace was alight with a blazing fire and someone had dotted the perimeter of the warm and expansive living room with candles, adding a cozy ambiance.

Seeing Noah, Angela's face lit up and she started to stand up.

Noah rushed over to her. "Don't get up. Your leg."

She sat down and the motion disturbed Tilly, who meowed and jumped off the chair. Tilly strutted over to the couch, leaped up and sat next to Neil.

Noah leaned over and hugged Angela tightly. Then he kissed her softly on the lips, not wanting to make an exhibitionist display of passion in the presence of Neil. Or Tilly, for that matter, who seemed to take exception to it.

Noah released her slowly. "Are you okay?"

"I'm better, thanks. I should be asking you that question."

"I feel much better now. I slept a long time."

"Thank God," Angela said, a ripple of relief washing over her face.

Noah joined Neil on the couch next to Tilly, who eyeballed Noah curiously but decided to stay put.

"I was sure glad to get out of that hospital," Angela said. "I hate hospitals. By the way, Noah, before I forget, I want to thank you. You saved my life. You were very brave."

Courage was not a quality Noah ever realized was a part of his repertoire. But, then again, he'd never before been put into a fight-or-flight response situation. "Don't thank me," Noah said, gesturing to Neil with a nod of his head. "He's the hero. He saved both of us."

"He *is* a hero, and I thanked him for his bravery. But if you hadn't done what you did, when you did, I might not be here to thank either of you."

"Well, you're welcome," Noah said. "You were pretty brave yourself, going after him with that broken lamp."

Angela sighed and dropped her eyes.

Neil offered Noah a drink, giving him a choice between wine, Scotch, beer, water, coffee, or hot chocolate."

"What are you guys drinking?"

"Hot chocolate," Angela said. "Neil makes a mean one."

"That's perfect," Noah said.

"Great," Neil said. "Hot chocolate it is then." From the kitchen, he added, "I've also got some decent chili here, too, if you're hungry."

"I can vouch for it," Angela said. "It's awesome."

"Thanks," Noah said. "I'll have some later."

Neil returned to the living room and handed Noah a hot chocolate. Then he sat down and scratched Tilly under her chin. The cat purred contentedly.

"Strange," Neil said. "Usually Tilly scoots off whenever people come over, but she obviously really likes you guys. I can't get over that."

After a few minutes of small talk, Neil grew silent. Angela and Noah watched him run a hand through his mop of hair, and then scratch his cheek stubble. Noah knew something serious would be forthcoming so he remained quiet.

Angela seemed to sense it as well.

"Now then," Neil said finally. "Let's get down to business, shall we?" Neil didn't wait for any nods of acceptance before continuing.

To Noah, Neil said, "Angela was just telling me about her Hat Man dream. Without going into the details—she can tell you those in her own time—it was a positive dream. I believe you mentioned earlier you had a positive dream about the Hat Man as well, after so many horrifying ones. Would you mind telling us about it? I mean, do you feel up to it now?"

"Sure," Noah said. He sipped his drink, hoping the chocolatey hot beverage would stir his memory. It seemed to help. He explained the darkly lit spaghetti western-like landscape, white angelic figures on one side, dark shadowy figures lining the opposite side, an approach and a subsequent warm embrace by the Hat Man that had left him feeling calm, protected and peaceful.

"Is that everything?" Neil asked.

"I think so. Everything that I can remember anyway."

Neil pointed to a note pad on the coffee table. "Go ahead, pick it up. I found it on your coffee table and took the liberty of bringing it here. I didn't want it falling into the wrong hands."

Noah suddenly remembered he had written details down, and anxiously scanned the pages. He quickly found what he was looking for. "In my dream, the Hat Man said something to me."

"What did he say?" Angela said. "I'm dying to know."

"The Hat Man said, 'I'm not *what* you think I am. I'm not *who* you think I am.'"

"What does that mean?" Angela asked. "Please, Neil, shed some light on it for us."

"It's complicated, my dear, but I'll do my best to simplify it. Many people have issues in their past that they fail to deal with properly. Fail to process properly. I have my own unresolved issues but that's a lesson for another day. This lesson is about you guys, *for* you guys."

Neil paused and turned to Noah. "Over the years that I've known you, you've touched on a few issues relating to your childhood. Would you say you have some unresolved issues in that area?"

"That's a fair statement," Noah said, hoping he wouldn't have to take an extended trip down nightmare alley.

"Don't worry," Neil said. "I don't want all the gory details. Not right now, anyway. Suffice it to say you've got some unresolved issues in your past."

Noah nodded and Neil turned to Angela, whose cheeks had blossomed from shocking pink to rosy red. "I'm not going to pry, Angela, but is it safe to say that you have some unresolved issues in your past as well, relating to your childhood, even adulthood for that matter?"

"Mine are more of the adulthood nature," she said.

"Okay. Now is it possible that very recently you've begun to put your issues under a microscope? Maybe you've even discussed them together, in the hope of forming a healthy relationship. Am I getting warm?"

"You're red hot," Angela said, her cheeks transforming from rosy to ruby red. "Noah and I talked a little when we first met, but we really cracked open the can of worms Tuesday night, the night of the Hat Man attack."

"Oh, but that wasn't the Hat Man," Neil argued. "That was some sick impersonator. When, exactly, did these dreams occur?"

"Tuesday night," Angela said. "The same night we started discussing our issues."

"Same with me," Noah said. "Where is this going, doctor?"

"Bear with me," Neil said. "Have either of you heard of Carl Jung?"

"He was a well-respected and admired psychologist and psychoanalyst," Noah said. "I studied him in Psych 101 in university."

"I've heard of him," Angela said. "But don't remember much."

"Okay," Neil said. "Carl Jung, brilliant mind that he was, developed a theory called Shadow Integration. The Shadow describes the part of the mind which we have denied, disowned, or outright rejected. It's our dark side. But Jung maintained that while the Shadow operates as a reservoir of human darkness, it's also a wellspring of all human creativity; not something evil or bad, just a part of ourselves that we're unwilling to face. Shadow Integration means going to the source of the fear and forming a relationship with your dark side. By doing so, the Shadow becomes a source of warmth and positivity rather than a destructive force. Do you see where I'm going with this? When both of you began to come to grips with your dark sides, embracing them if you like, all of a sudden the Hat Man, a kind of Shadow symbol, became a powerful and protective force. Even a source of joy and positivity."

"So all my bad dreams have had to do with me not embracing my dark side?" Noah asked.

"I believe so," Neil said. "Tell me, since you've started down this path of enlightenment, have you had any other problems with your sleep disorders?"

"No," Noah admitted.

"How about nightmares?"

"No."

"Even if you did have them, nightmares aren't something to be afraid of. You want to get to know them, get on a friendly basis with them. They're a part of your dark side, a part of you."

"Wow. This is kind of an epiphany for me," Angela said.

"Me too," Noah agreed.

"Do you remember what I told you last time we talked about nightmares?" Neil asked Noah.

Noah scratched his head. "Something about the mind's way of taking out the garbage."

"Exactly," Neil said. "Your memory is coming back faster than I thought. Nightmares can be viewed as the subconscious mind's way of processing information. And if you ask me, this aligns rather well with Jung's theory. Both theories, in some way, view nightmares as the subconscious mind ridding itself of the stresses of daily life. Solving our problems, cleansing us of negative energy, and bringing peace. A kind of healing mechanism."

"So you're saying I should embrace my nightmares?" Noah asked.

"If I were you, I would," Neil said. "I think they represent a gateway to limitless possibilities that we are only beginning to understand."

Noah's head was beginning to hurt from the sudden rush of realization. Perhaps Tilly, with that extra feline sense, noticed it as well. The black cat brushed her head against Noah's arm. "Meow, meow."

"I think that's about enough for now," Neil said. "It's midnight and time for Tilly's dinner. She always meows for food at midnight. You guys must be a little tired." He stood up, went into the kitchen and put out a can of tuna for Tilly. As she darted over to the bowl and began gobbling it up, Neil said, "I'm going to turn in myself. Help yourself to some chili before you go to bed if you want. Just make sure to turn the crock pot off."

Neil returned to the living room, collected his empty mug, and stopped. To Angela, he said, "There's a guest bedroom down the hall, if you'd like it. But I'd understand it if you didn't want to let Noah out of your sight. You guys can sort that out." As he walked down the hall toward his own bedroom, he stopped and turned around. "Tune in tomorrow for the Hat Man and Shadow People episode. I promise it will be an eye-opener. Good night, then. Oh, and remember to turn off all the lights before you go to bed."

After they heard his door close, down a long hallway opposite the hallway that led to the guest quarters, Angela stood. Favoring her right leg, she limped into the kitchen. "I think I'll have some more chili. Hospital food sucks."

A few minutes later, they had turned off most of the lights and sat at the kitchen island eating chili by candlelight.

"He's an interesting man," Angela said softly. "Very smart."

"I think he helped me," Noah said. "Maybe even cured my sleep disorders."

"I think he helped both of us. You know, something he said, made me think of something I've read."

Between mouthfuls, Noah asked, "Oh yeah. What's that?"

"Well, when he was talking about embracing your nightmares, it made me think of a way to do just that."

"What's that?"

"Lucid dreaming. You ever heard of it?"

"It's more than just real sharp dream images isn't it?" Noah asked. "It's on the tip of my tongue."

"Lucid dreaming is when you have a sudden awareness while you're dreaming that you are dreaming—waking up in a dream."

Noah finished his chili and set the spoon in the bowl. After six hours of solid sleep, he didn't feel tired at all, partly because he felt invigorated by Neil's revelations and partly because Angela was with him. But he didn't want to risk waking Neil, in case their softly spoken voices could be heard. "Right. I think I know where you're going with this, and I'd like to hear more. Do you wanna discuss it in bed? Do you wanna sleep with me tonight?"

"Yes and yes," Angela said.

They blew out the candles, put the dishes in the dishwasher, turned the remaining lights off, gave Tilly a goodnight pat on the head (from her reclining position on the couch, she responded with a cheerful meow), turned the crock pot off and turned in.

A few minutes later, satisfied they were out of earshot, cuddling in bed to the soft glow of a candle, they continued the lucid dreaming conversation.

"I only bring this lucid dreaming stuff up to help us," Angela said. "There's a lot of weird shit happening around town right now, stuff that we're only beginning to understand. I think it's better if we at least try to align our psyches."

"I agree," Noah said, suddenly feeling more lucid than ever. "If I follow what you're saying, lucid dreaming means waking up in a dream. And if I put it into the context of what Neil was saying about embracing our nightmares, our dark sides, I think I know where you're going. What better way to embrace our nightmares than waking up in one, realizing you're having one, and being able to control it."

"You hit the nail right on the head," she said. "Neil was right. You're recovering awful fast. Have you ever had a lucid dream before?"

"Yes," Noah said. "I've had tons of dreams, and some of them I've actually woken up in them and realized I was dreaming. I've been able to fly in some of my dreams. Talk about exhilarating."

"People all over the world have developed a love affair with this magical world," Angela said. "For over a thousand years, Tibetan Buddhists have practiced lucid dreaming. They believe it's the key to spiritual enlightenment, mindfulness, kindness, love, inner peace, all kinds of great things."

"Lucid dream your way to happiness."

"That's it. Have you ever been able to control a nightmare and turn it into something positive?"

"No. You?"

"Yeah. In one of my nightmares, I was being pursued by a rather nasty-looking killer. Or at least I thought he was a killer. Suddenly I became lucid, realized I was dreaming, and it gave me the courage to confront the attacker, face my fear. I stopped and turned around to look at him. He stopped so close to me, I could even smell his bad breath. 'What the hell do you want?' I asked. 'Why are you chasing me?' His beady red eyes rolled around in his head and you wouldn't believe what he said to me. He said, 'How the hell should I know? It's *your* nightmare.'"

"That's an amazing story," Noah said. "I guess Neil's right."

"It was a long time ago. And it helped me a lot. A monster used to chase me often in my childhood dreams. When I confronted him, he disappeared forever. And, after our near-death experience, I got myself a psychologist. I'm hoping I can make all my demons disappear for good."

"You're very brave, confronting your fears like that. I'm gonna do the same thing, Angela. You made me realize the other night that I have more skeletons in my closet than I care to admit. It's time to give them a proper burial, or set them free. Neil is going to act as my surrogate psychologist until I can find another one."

She stroked his stubble gently. "I think that's great. I'm doing it for me, but I'm also doing it for us. I don't want to screw this up."

"Neither do I, sweetie." Noah kissed her gently on the cheek and hugged her tightly. It felt good to be wanted, good to be loved.

"I almost forgot," Angela said. "I got sidetracked on the lucid dreaming thing. I saw a documentary on how to make your dreams lucid."

"Really? Tell me."

"You're not too tired?"

"Tell me and then we'll go to sleep. I want to know, so if I have a nightmare tonight, I can turn it into a positive experience. I think it's important."

"Okay. One technique to recognize a dream sign is the reality check. When you're awake, look at your hand and look away."

Noah did it.

"Now look back at your hand. It should look the same. During a dream, look at your hand and then look away. If you're dreaming, when you look back at it, it won't look the same. It might be elongated; you might be able to stretch your finger to ten times its normal size. Your hand may resemble a five-fingered water balloon. That's because the file for pattern recognition of your hand is stored in the left hemisphere of the brain and dreaming is a right-brain phenomenon. If you're dreaming, the hand-examining reality check will serve as a dream sign, alerting you and helping you become lucid."

"Wow," Noah said. "You're an encyclopedia."

"I read a lot. And watch a lot of documentaries. Obviously there are other dreams signs; flying pigs; talking to your dead father; being in your childhood home, and being nude in public. It's just a question of training your mind to recognize them."

Noah held his hand in front of the candle and repeated the exercise a few times. His hand cast large shadowy fingers on the bedroom wall. They reminded him of the Shadow People and the Hat Man and it was disconcerting.

Even Angela was beginning to get the jitters. "That's scary. They look like the Shadow People."

Noah moved his hand away from the candle. "I guess tomorrow we're gonna learn all about them."

"I'm really curious about what Neil's doing in that lab of his," Angela said. "And a little freaked out by it all. I wonder if all the Shadow People reports have anything to do with his experiments."

There was a long silence as Noah thought about it. *Hat Man nightmares. Hat Man realities. Shadow People sightings. Shadow People photographs. The firetrucks. What exactly happened with the Shadow People the night we were attacked? Why had all the Shadow People reports suddenly stopped?*

Noah suspected that everything was somehow connected, but didn't understand how. He made a mental note to check the internet tomorrow for news stories about the strange happenings on the tiny island of PEI. He was just about to ask Angela if she'd read any news reports, when he heard a gentle snore. She'd fallen asleep and he should do the same. He blew out the candle, pulled the blankets up over both of them, and six minutes later drifted off to sleep.

******

Noah walked down the street in a surreal landscape straight out of an old spaghetti western movie set. The feverish sun was setting on a desert-like crimson horizon. The buildings—a barber shop, general store, bank, and others—undulated with his every step. At first, he missed the incongruity. Suddenly a dark fang-toothed monster leaped out in front of the old saloon, growled menacingly, and charged. With an adrenaline-fueled injection, Noah dashed behind an old building. The monster's crunching footfalls grew louder. Noah began to panic. A lightbulb in his head clicked on. He looked at his hand. It was normal. He glanced away and looked back and it transformed into a five-finger water balloon. *Excellent. This is gonna be fun.* He searched the area for a weapon and magically an AK-47 materialized on the dusty ground. He picked it up. The monster approached and he fired a staccato-burst of bullets. Riddled with blood-soaked holes, the monster dropped to the ground with a heavy thud.

He continued down the street. *A larger-than-life video. The objective is to kill or be killed.* Monsters of all shapes and sizes began attacking Noah and he cut them down effortlessly with the machine gun. Soon all the monsters were dead and he was alone on the street, the smoking gun in hand. Satisfied with his efforts, he began to think of other possibilities. *Maybe I should spread my wings and fly.* But before he could focus on flying, one of the dead monsters began to stir. His spilled blood began to flow from the street and back into his veins. His bullet-ridden body magically healed itself. He rose stronger and more determined than ever. So did the others. They regrouped and attacked with vicious intentions.

He cut them down as they approached, but there were too many. Soon they were on him, biting, ripping and tearing him to shreds. With raw fear coursing through his veins, he tried to keep his composure, telling himself over and over that he was dreaming. Like the monsters, he would magically heal and launch a counter-offensive, deadlier than before.

But the uncertainty was too much and Noah woke up, albeit with vivid memories of the dream and a not-unpleasant feeling of having escaped into another wild, wonderful and powerful world—one that, in the future, he felt sure he would acquire the skills to control and manipulate positively.

CHAPTER SIXTEEN

It was almost noon that Friday and Noah sat by himself at the kitchen island eating bacon and eggs that Angela had made for him. When he'd awoken earlier, Angela hadn't been there. After he'd showered, he'd wandered into the kitchen and found a note beside the breakfast plate: *Helping Neil in the lab. Help yourself to the breakfast I made for you. Join us when you're done. XO, Angela.*

He dabbed his toast in the soft yolk of his egg and took a large bite, opening up a small laptop on the kitchen counter and checking the news.

It didn't take him long to find what he was looking for in *The Guardian.*

HAT MAN KILLER KILLED

Police are calling Neil Samuelson a hero after he gunned down serial killer Drake Simeon in a downtown apartment late Tuesday night.

According to police, Simeon, who often stalked and terrorized his victims for days, dressed in a trench coat and a gaucho or fedora hat, has been linked through DNA evidence to the brutal murder of Agnes Ingles and investigators recently unearthed the remains of two more victims underneath an outbuilding on Simeon's property east of Charlottetown on Highway #3. The identities of those victims will be released pending notification of next of kin.

Police Detective Lamar Stevenson said Samuelson happened to be in the area on unrelated business when he spotted Simeon's black SUV parked near the apartment of his friends, Noah

Janzen and Angela Rosewood. Samuelson heard shouts and screams coming from the apartment, climbed up rear fire escape steps, and entered the apartment to find the Hat Man Killer viciously attacking Janzen and Rosewood with a machete. He then shot the intruder twice in the back of the head and once in the back of the neck, saving the lives of both Janzen and Rosewood. Janzen suffered a concussion and Rosewood suffered a large slash wound to her calf.

Due to her traumatized condition shortly after the attack, doctors would not allow The Guardian to speak to Rosewood. Janzen could not be reached for comment. Both have been released from hospital and are doing well, according to doctors.

"I don't advocate vigilante justice," Detective Stevenson said. "But I can't argue with the fact that a sick serial killer is dead and two lives have been saved."

Samuelson, a retired doctor and well-respected member of the community, who lives less than a mile away from the home of the Hat Man Killer, played down his heroism. "I don't consider myself a hero at all. Anyone would have done the same thing. I'm just glad the Dark Menace is off the streets."

Prior to the death of Simeon, there were many reports of people being terrorized by a Hat Man. But now, according to Detective Stevenson, PEI has returned to "the quiet and peaceful island that it once was."

However, the investigation continues and Detective Stevenson said it may take many months, even years, before police are able to determine just how many deaths the Hat Man killer might have been responsible for.

Noah finished his breakfast, put the dishes in the dishwasher, refilled his coffee cup and returned to the computer. He had to admit, he felt much better physically. And, before reading the news report, he had been elated about his ability to manipulate his lucid dream last night and the power it offered over his demons. But that elation was now being replaced by an unsettling and visceral feeling of dread.

He surfed the net and located two stories about fires, believed to have been set by an unidentified arsonist. One, an abandoned house in Charlottetown, had been quickly extinguished by firefighters and the other, a warehouse near the city's airport, had claimed the lives of two people and injured five more.

He surfed on and soon came to another headline that caught his eye.

MYSTERIOUS SHADOW PEOPLE HAUNTING ISLANDERS

Police received no less than six reports of Shadow People haunting Islanders last Tuesday night, ironically at the same time a vicious Hat Man Killer was preying on unsuspecting victims.

Drake Simeon was shot to death Tuesday night by local hero Neil Samuelson. Simeon, now dubbed the Hat Man Killer, was attacking Noah Janzen and Angela Rosewood with a machete at the time Samuelson gunned him down. The Hat Man killer has been linked to at least three other murders.

During his recent murderous rampage, police received a number of reports of mysterious Shadow People invading the homes of local residents during their waking hours. In some cases, these Shadow People would possess the bodies of their victims and terrorize them.

Detective Stevenson would not provide many details, nor would he release the names of anyone involved. "Look, this is an ongoing investigation, so I can't say too much. Sure, some people were scared at the time, but we have no reports of any assaults or murders relating to these Shadow People. In each incident, by the time we arrived on scene, the problem seemed to have solved itself. And many people don't want their names released. Would you, if you witnessed a dark shadow float through your wall and possess the body of your spouse? People would think you've lost your mind."

The Guardian tracked down one downtown resident, Tyler Manning, who claimed his body had been possessed by a shadow person for a short time. "I first saw it in my living room. It floated right through the wall while I was having a beer. I took off running and hid in the bedroom. Finally, I thought he was gone and came out. That's when the shadow person possessed my body. It literally scared the hell out of me and I felt like the Devil was inside me. But, now he's gone and I feel great."

Detective Stevenson would not confirm nor deny the validity of Manning's claim, but The Guardian has learned that Shadow People have been seen by millions of people around the world and many believe they are a powerful and destructive force linked to the Devil and Devil worship.

Catholic pastor Thomas Sanderson said, "Next to the Hat Man, the Shadow People represent the purest form of negativity and evil that exists. They prey upon weak, vulnerable and fearful souls and feed on that weakness." Pastor Sanderson said to rid yourself of the evil influence of the Hat Man or the Shadow People, you must utter the name of Jesus Christ and you can also have your house blessed to prevent the evil spirits from entering.

However, according to Detective Stevenson, "We don't have any evidence the Shadow People are evil at all. And, since last

Tuesday, we've had no reports of Hat Man or Shadow People sightings. As I said before, Prince Edward Island has returned to the calm and gentle place it once was. So don't panic people. Enjoy your lives and leave it to us. One way or the other, we'll get to the bottom of it."

Noah reached for his cell phone and scrolled through the photos, trying to locate the Shadow People images, wanting to study them to see what kind of vibe they exuded. He didn't remember any overwhelming feelings of evil or negativity during his previous encounters with the Shadow People. He couldn't find the images, then suddenly remembered. *Right. They're in Angela's camera. She took them. Where's her camera?*

He pocketed the phone and donned a parka, baseball cap, and boots, preparing to face the bitter cold and find answers to the questions nagging at him. As he opened the door, his cell phone rang. He stepped back inside, closed the door, and answered it.

It was Cindy Hardy, his supervisor at the Arts Council.

"Noah, are you okay?" Cindy said.

"I'm feeling better. Thanks."

"I'm so sorry about what happened. My God, you could've been killed. I never thought anything like that could happen here."

"I'm very lucky," Noah said. He felt a dull throbbing pain return to his head and remembered the painkillers. He removed his boots and walked into the bedroom while he talked to Cindy.

"I want you to take as much time as you want, Noah. Don't rush back to work if you're not feeling up to it."

He arrived at the bedroom and sure enough there were two white pills on the vanity beside a glass of water. He popped them in his mouth and washed them back with a mouthful of water.

"Are you there, Noah?"

"Yeah, sorry I was just taking some painkillers. Still have a mild headache from the concussion."

"As I said, take as much time as you need. Still, I need to know, do you have any idea when you think you might be back?"

"Is Wednesday okay? I should be feeling better by then."

"Wednesday is fine. But that's not the only reason I'm calling you."

Noah braced himself for bad news. "Oh?"

"Your grant applicant. Angela Rosewood. She's been approved. I take it you two are friends, so I thought you'd want to tell her yourself."

Noah was elated. "That's awesome. She's gonna be thrilled. How much did she get?"

"The full fifty thousand. It'll be ready next week sometime. Since it's your file, you can handle the disbursements."

"Thanks so much, Cindy."

"Between me and you, I had to bend the rules a bit. Since you're part of the committee, we needed your vote to approve it. I told the committee you emailed your vote to me. They'll never know the difference. I didn't think you'd vote no, considering, you know, your interest in her."

It never ceased to amaze Noah how the gossip grapevine on the small island travelled faster than the speed of a commercial airliner. "I appreciate that, Cindy. My lips are sealed."

"Good. And here's a golden nugget of information I know you'll appreciate. I think, in fact I know, what tipped the scales in Angela's favor was the near-death experience she's just gone through. The committee felt sorry for her and believed she needed a fresh start, something to look forward to in her life."

"She *does* need something to look forward to. That grant will definitely put the passion back in her life." Noah heard a sigh on the other end of the line.

"I've always said that out of something bad, there always comes something good. You have to feel the darkness to appreciate the light, you know what I mean?"

Noah realized that Cindy might never fully understand just how right she was. "I know exactly what you mean."

******

When Noah entered the lab, Angela and Neil were crouched over at the computer table, studying images on a camera.

On the table beside them, Tilly was curled up contentedly.

Noah recognized the camera instantly as the one he'd given Angela. It seemed Neil had also thought to bring that from Noah's apartment, or Angela had. One way or the other, the camera was here and that was the important thing.

"Guess what, honey?" he said, hurrying over to Angela. "I have some good news for you."

She set the camera down. "You had a lucid dream last night?"

"Actually, I did. But that's not the only good news. You got approved for the $50,000 arts grant. You get the first installment next week."

"That's incredible. Thank you so much." Tears of joy streamed down Angela's cheeks and she hugged Noah tightly. Soon it turned into a group hug, the three of them dancing around the lab.

Neil was the first to return to the computer table, sitting down next to Tilly and scratching her chin. Even Tilly seemed to be enjoying the impromptu celebration.

"First thing I'm gonna do is quit my job at Wendy's," Angela said, as she sat down next to Neil. She plucked a tissue from a Kleenex box on the table and wiped her eyes. "I'm gonna call my boss this afternoon."

"Congratulations on the grant, Angela," Neil said, picking up the camera. "Now, can we get back to work, please?"

Noah didn't realize Neil had planned a day of work for them, but that was fine by him. Too many lingering questions were beginning to create mass confusion in his already traumatized and concussed mind. Although he had to admit, he felt better today than he had for days.

Neil showed Noah the image of the shadow person Angela had snapped while returning from their beach photo shoot. "Does that resemble the same Shadow People you saw at Drake's?"

Noah took the camera. "I'm glad we're getting to the bottom of this. I really need to try and understand what's going on." He looked at the shadowy image floating above the pickup, its black form contrasting with a pink-orange dusky sky. "Yes."

Neil scratched his head. "Hmm... that means more might've gone wrong with my experiment than I thought."

"What do you mean?" Noah asked.

Neil put the camera on the table. "I suppose I owe you an explanation before we continue. I just wanted to make sure you were ready. How are you feeling today, Noah?"

"I'm ready, Neil. I feel much better. I've been taking those painkillers I assume you've been leaving in the bedroom. They help a lot."

Neil nodded. "Codeine-laced Tylenol. Good stuff. Okay, I need to give you a little background first. My wife Maggie died six years ago of an unexpected stroke. We were together for forty-five years..."

"I'm so sorry," Angela said.

Noah added his condolences.

"It's okay. Well, it's not okay, but thanks. Maggie was a special woman. Everyone who knew her commented on her kind and loving nature. After she died, I went into a long funk, retired my practice, and did nothing for months. Then I started having dreams of Maggie. She appeared so real in those dreams. In one of them, she told me she was happy and had found peace in another dimension."

Seeing their wide-eyed stares, he changed tactics. "I'm going to try and keep this as simple as I can for now, so we can move on. Please, let me finish before you start asking questions. Are you okay with that?"

Angela and Noah nodded.

Tilly meowed her apparent acknowledgement, although Noah suspected she'd heard the story before.

"I've always had a strong interest in string theory," Neil said, "which is essentially a theory that ten dimensions exist. Humankind, in general, has very little knowledge of these other dimensions. Although they can be mathematically proven, they are hard to test otherwise. We're aware, for the most part, of only the four dimensions of our universe—length, height, depth and the concept of time. Over time, I started to believe that Maggie was not only alive in spirit, but she indeed had travelled to another dimension and was very much alive. You see, string theory contends that other realities exist, parallel universes that are not bound by our laws. Universes within which time is not linear and you can travel freely between the past, present and the future. Universes, some physicists agree—myself included—where an exact replica of yourself exists, a clone if you like, living your life, with perhaps only minor variations. In the eighth dimension, for example, you can see every possible permutation of every possible path you decide to take. Imagine living in a world where you chose one path, then see the disastrous outcome ahead, and are able to simply step off that path and choose another path with a better outcome. Literally travel back and forth through time. Mind-boggling stuff and difficult at the best of times for the human mind to understand."

Neil cleared his throat and continued. "Because of my intense love for Maggie and my interest in helping humanity, I decided I wanted to be with her in this other dimension, which my calculations tell me is the eighth dimension."

Neil waved a hand to the elaborate display of machinery and computer equipment. "That's why I created my Parallel Projector, to take me there. Now here is where the Shadow People and the Hat Man come into the picture. Many physicists, including the brilliant Stephen Hawking, believe that other dimensions, rather than being science fiction, and I quote him here, 'may be science fact.' According to Hawking,

God rest his soul, because our world may be confined to a small membrane, or bubble if you like, in a space of many bubbles, it is difficult to see or travel to these other dimensions. But because gravity spreads through these extra dimensions, it allows us to feel them and see them as dark matter. And, I believe, because of gravity, these shadow galaxies, shadow stars, Shadow People and the real Hat Man, can also be felt on a powerful and intense level."

Neil took a sip of coffee, observed their incredulous expressions and continued. "There is another theory that contends that due to climate change caused by global warming, the frequencies of these other dimensions are somehow merging with the frequency of our world and that's the reason sightings are becoming more commonplace. But that's an aside. In any event, although many theories exist, the agenda of the real Hat Man is largely unknown. Even for my part, while I believe him to be from the eighth dimension, I'm not a hundred per cent sure if he is good or evil. But I do think I've pinned down the Shadow People. You see, in my efforts to travel to the eighth dimension, something went wrong. As my test subject I used a garden-variety black beetle. But last Tuesday, during an experiment, Bennie the Beetle didn't go anywhere. Something went wrong during the experiment and six Shadow People, I believe from the eighth dimension, arrived here. And, regardless of all the crazy theories about alien abduction, or linking them to the Devil, I strongly believe they possess a benevolent agenda. Now, I suppose you're wondering how I know this."

"Are we free to ask questions now?" Noah asked.

"Ask away," Neil said.

"I just read a news story on the Shadow People," Noah said. "There were six sightings. You said six Shadow People. One guy, Tyler I think his name was, said he felt great after the shadow person left his body."

"I think I read the same news story," Angela said.

"Tyler Manning was a violent, abusive and unpredictable drunk before the Shadow People came along," Neil said. "That shadow person hasn't left his body at all. It's possessed him and turned him from evil to good. I was at their house in downtown Charlottetown the night you were attacked. After the shadow person possessed his body, he went from bad to good in the blink of an eye. Before that, he was in the process of attacking his wife with a baseball bat and I almost shot him. I just spoke to Bonnie early this morning. She said he's as sweet as pie now and catering to her every whim."

Neil took another sip of his coffee. "Now, to make a long story short, I responded to two other calls for paranormal investigations that night. One, from my loyal friend Norman Murphy. A good man. We saw a shadow person at his house. And we saw the shadow person disappear without possessing Norm. My theory is the shadow person left because there was nothing for him to do. Norman's as gentle as a teddy bear and doesn't have an evil bone in his body."

Neil cleared his throat. "I responded to another call from Deborah Crawfield, maybe a mile away from here. When Deborah had called, her husband Charlie was going berserk, throwing things around the house, fit to be tied. A shadow person appeared and Charlie armed himself with a shotgun and chased it upstairs. When I arrived, Charlie was sleeping peacefully in an upstairs bedroom, shotgun at his side. When he woke, he was as gentle as a lamb. The shadow person was nowhere to be found. Evidently a shadow person possessed him and he turned from a violent maniac to a kind and loving man. Deborah just told me this morning he served her breakfast in bed. We can go and visit them today if you want. You can see the transformation for yourself."

"It's okay," Angela said. "I believe you."

"So do I," Noah said. "But I'm still curious about a few things. So you accidentally unleashed six Shadow People into our dimension. They possessed evil people, changed their personalities for the better, and then they were done. Even the news media hasn't reported any Shadow People sightings since Tuesday. That's one thing, but here's something else to consider—something you asked me when we first started this conversation. The Shadow People at Drake's. You said you only brought six. What about the ones I saw at Drakes? Where did they come from? And if the other Shadow People were able to reverse evil in those other people, how come the Shadow People I saw couldn't reverse the evil in Drake?"

"I don't have all the answers yet," Neil admitted. "But you've hit on exactly what I've been wondering about lately. My theory on Drake is that sometimes evil can be so powerful, it trumps the good power of the Shadow People. Maybe the Shadow People tried. Maybe they succeeded to some extent, but ultimately I suppose they weren't able to stop him. And as for your other question about where the other Shadow People came from, well, you described the ones you saw at Drake's as being the same as the ones I released into our dimension. And, you're right, I only counted six. But I've had many other failed experiments. My best guess is that, unbeknownst to me, my

Parallel Projector has been hemorrhaging Shadow People into our world for some time now."

Angela sighed. "Well, at least they have a good agenda."

"I believe they do," Neil said. "And I think the sightings have stopped because their mission is complete. When you guys photographed the shadow person, you say you didn't get a bad vibe."

They shook their heads.

To Noah, Neil said, "And when you saw them at Drake's, they didn't harm you. I don't think they'll bother with already good people. They only seem to change the bad ones."

"So you're pretty sure there's a connection between the real Hat Man and the Shadow People," Noah said. "But you just don't know what it is yet."

"If you guys agree to help me fix my Parallel Projector so I can join Maggie in the eighth dimension, I'm sure we'll find the answer to that question and many more. What do you say?"

******

Using a cordless drill to assemble a large steel panel on Neil's high-tech Parallel Projector four hours later, Noah was relieved he'd decided not to go home to his apartment today, even though his landlord had called earlier and informed him that it was ready for occupancy. The fact that a killer had been killed in that apartment still haunted him on many levels and he felt sure that the work he was doing to help Neil would go a long way to crumble his fears, if not dissolve them entirely.

At the end of Neil's lecture on the ten dimensions and possible links to the Shadow People and the Hat Man, Noah and Angela had not only agreed to help him with his epic objective, they'd also been sworn to secrecy. Shortly after that, Angela had said she felt a little overwhelmed by all the information and decided to return to the house to redress her leg wound, take a little nap, and "prepare something delicious for supper." Tilly, perhaps responding to the word "supper," had followed her to the house.

Neil had removed a circuit board from the Parallel Projector and was busy removing old circuits and installing and soldering new ones. When he finished with the circuit board, he brought it over to where Noah was working. Noah finished with the last screw on the panel he was installing, turned around and watched Neil slide the circuit board into place with a click.

"Now then," Neil said. "Can you pass me that steel cover?"

Noah picked it up and they aligned it with the screw holes. While Neil held it in place, Noah removed eight screws from his shirt pocket and began fastening the panel in place. "Do you really think this is gonna work?"

"I do indeed," Neil said. "I've been doing some calculations and I think I know where I went wrong. The next test will be tomorrow."

"With Bennie the Beetle?"

"At first, yes," Neil said. "And if we succeed in bringing him back, then I go."

"You wanna go tomorrow? What if you can't get back?"

"I've already made preparations for that scenario, should something unexpected happen. But I believe I'll be fine."

"Yeah, well, what if you're not? I don't know how to work any of this fancy machinery. I won't know how to bring you back."

Neil put a hand on Noah's shoulder. His blue eyes were serious and intense. "I'm going to walk you through some basics tomorrow morning, if you feel up to it. You seem to be recovering nicely and the largely positive account of your lucid dream last night also tells me you're overcoming your sleep disorders and coming to terms with your dark side."

"I *do* feel a lot better," Noah said, realizing that Neil was trying to change the subject. "But what if I can't get you back? What if I screw something up and you get stuck?"

Noah removed another steel panel that Neil had pointed to and set it down on the concrete floor. He watched Neil slide the circuit board loose, shake his head and frown at two fried circuits, then walk over to the computer workstation with it. He set it down and began removing the damaged circuits. "Don't worry, I'm going to have the Parallel Projector largely in auto mode. You'll just have to remember a few simple instructions. And my first trip to the eighth dimension will be timed. It'll be a half hour search and reconnaissance. I'll be returned automatically."

The news went some way to assuage Noah's fears, although he still had some nagging questions and a healthy dose of skepticism. *Maybe Neil doesn't want to come back? Maybe the eighth dimension might not be a bad place to be after all? If he can't bring Maggie back, wouldn't he want to stay wherever he believes she is?*

He let the questions linger for a moment and then let them fragment and float away. Neil had helped him so much over the course of just one week, and Noah felt some reservations about raining on the man's parade at a time like this. Neil had obviously suffered countless setbacks and was still heartbroken by the loss of his wife. All he wanted to do was be with the love of his life. *What could be so wrong with that?*

Neil fell silent for the next twenty minutes, perhaps retreating into a world where Maggie was very much alive, a mysterious world where he was much happier than he was now. He smiled occasionally, reinforcing Noah's suspicions that he was thinking of his deceased wife. They worked in silence for another five minutes before the quiet was broken by the sound of Noah's phone.

It was Angela. Noah pressed TALK and then SPEAKER.

"It's supper time," Angela said. "Barbequed spare ribs, roasted potatoes with onions, garlic, olive oil and spices."

"That sounds delicious," Noah said.

"Delicious indeed," Neil said. "You are a Godsend and an angel, Angela. We'll be right in."

"See you soon," Noah said, pressing END CALL.

Neil finished with a silver bead of solder, unplugged the soldering gun and put it on the table. "One more circuit board to go. Then I can run some tests tonight to get us ready for tomorrow."

CHAPTER SEVENTEEN

Neil, Angela and Noah huddled around a computer monitor at seven the following evening. Tilly crouched under a utility table near the main door of the laboratory. Outside, the wind whistled and hissed through the buildings and trees. A bomb cyclone was pounding the Eastern Seaboard. It had already dumped two feet of snow, killed four people, created massive flooding, damaged buildings, downed power poles, and was tracking directly toward them. In spite of the risk, Neil insisted they continue with the experiment. Last night after dinner, he'd spent four more hours in the lab repairing equipment, testing and retesting. He'd cheerfully announced early this morning that "all systems are go and much of the controls have now been incorporated into voice commands."

After an early morning crash-course on shooting a Colt .45, Noah and Angela had spent the entire day in the lab being briefed on the operating systems. Neil had even brought them up to speed on the Parallel Projector's emergency procedure manual. They'd completed three "dry runs" and were now ready for the real challenge.

"Are you ready?" Neil asked.

Noah and Angela exchanged furtive glances. In spite of his uneasiness, Noah nodded.

"Yeah, I think so," Angela said tentatively.

Neil touched the barrel of the Colt .45 he'd place next to the monitor. "Remember, if anything goes wrong, don't be afraid to use this."

Noah didn't want to think about the need to fire a death-producing weapon, but he nodded tacitly, hoping to reassure Neil in lieu of the life-threatening risks ahead of them.

"I sure hope it doesn't come to that," Angela said, eyeballing the gun as if it were a venomous snake.

"I'm sure it won't," Neil said. "Let's begin." He punched a few keys and a white screen flashed before them. Small metallic balls danced around and formed the image of Gemini's face. "Good evening, Neil," she said. "Would you like to begin the experiment now?"

"Good evening, Gemini," Neil said. "Please begin the experiment now."

Gemini's face dissolved into hundreds of tiny silver balls and was replaced by a large red ON button. A gloved hand appeared on the screen. A finger extended and pressed the red button. It turned green. A whirring sound began and slowly grew louder as computer screens illuminated with flashing gauges and digital charts, showing the power level and progress of the experiment. The whirring grew louder and the Parallel Pointer began trembling with the force.

Outside, the wind hissed and began tossing debris.

Oblivious, their eyes followed the Parallel Pointer to the end, where it brightened a black circular stage in a corner of the lab. In the middle of the stage was a circular beam of light. In the middle of the beam, Bennie the Beetle sat motionless inside the small glass jar, evidently prepared to be the first life form ever to travel to the eighth dimension.

The whirring noise intensified. The Parallel Pointer shook and trembled more rigorously.

"Gemini, please reduce power by two decibels and stabilize the force field," Neil said.

"Power reduced by two decibels and force field stabilized," Gemini said.

The Parallel Pointer stopped rattling and some gauge needles ceased spiking erratically.

Suddenly, the beam of light surrounding Bennie intensified and grew.

"Cover your eyes," Neil said.

As they did, a giant white flash lit up the entire lab like a lightning bolt. It was followed by a zapping sound and then a loud pop and precipitously, but for the howling wind, the lab grew quiet.

Neil rushed over to the small stage containing Bennie's improvised orbiting capsule. Looking inside the jar, he beamed with delight. "He's gone! Bennie's gone! It's a success. Bennie's in the eighth dimension."

Before the experiment, Neil had explained that Bennie would return in exactly thirty minutes.

After the high-fiving and the congratulatory hugs had ended, Noah asked, "How do we know he's in the eighth dimension?"

"That's where my calculations put him," Neil explained. "He's too small to attach a camera to and the electronics in a camera might well interfere with a particle accelerator. I didn't want to risk fusing Bennie with shattered camera components."

"So, what do we do now? Just wait?" Angela asked.

Neil nodded. "Let's go in for a celebratory drink and come back in a half hour." He pressed a key on the computer and

Gemini materialized. "Gemini, please override manual controls and return Bennie at 7:36 pm this evening."

"Overriding manual controls to return Bennie to Earth at precisely 7:36 pm this evening," Gemini said. "Enjoy your celebratory drink."

Neil scratched his chin stubble. "Hmmm... artificial intelligence never ceases to amaze me. I didn't think she was tuned in to that part."

******

Half an hour later, Neil, grinning widely, carried the improvised orbital chamber over to the workbench where Noah and Angela sat. He set it down beneath a desk lamp and all eyes zeroed in to watch Bennie circle the jar, very much alive, very much intact.

"He's back in one piece," Neil said proudly, extending a finger into the jar. Bennie crawled up his forefinger and into the palm of his hand. Neil extended his open palm to the others.

Noah, a little buzzed from the double shot of Scotch he'd polished off earlier, watched Bennie crawl to the middle of Neil's hand and stop, raising his tiny head and studying three much larger heads.

"Congratulations," Noah said.

"Congratulations," Angela said. "But the real test will be when you go to the eighth dimension and return. Bennie can't tell us much."

Neil carefully placed Bennie inside the jar. They went to work, positioning a modified leather high-back office chair on the small stage, adjusting controls on the Parallel Projector, and testing to insure Gemini had the voice recognition patterns memorized for both Angela's and Noah's voice.

Tilly remained in her crouched position by the lab door, even refusing to follow them to the house earlier when they'd plowed through the driving snow and fierce winds in search of a celebratory drink. After they'd returned, Noah had made an attempt to coax Tilly from her defensive posture underneath the table, but he'd been met with a defiant meow that made him feel even more uneasy than he'd been at the start of the Bennie experiment.

They were ready to go now, both Noah and Angela huddled next to Gemini while Neil sat comfortably on the high-back leather chair surrounded by a soft yellow circle of light. In the house earlier, both he and Angela had expressed some reservations about Neil putting himself in front of the Parallel Pointer, but the doctor had silenced them immediately, reaffirming that his ultimate dream was to be with Maggie once again.

As Noah studied Neil's relaxed demeanor, it occurred to him that he might never understand the depth and intensity of a 45-year bond of love and devotion. Neil had dedicated the last six years of his life to being reunited with his late wife Maggie. He was willing to risk everything for the chance to spend his remaining years with her. She must be one hell of a woman.

In a spontaneous outpouring of emotion, Noah touched Angela's shoulder and, seeming to read his mood, she spun around and hugged him tightly.

"Come on," Neil said from center stage. "We can get the hugging done when I return. Let's get going."

Noah released Angela as she wiped a tear from her left eye. Choking back a lump of emotion swelling in his throat, Noah looked at Neil. "Are you ready?"

"Ready as I'll ever be. And no soliloquys, please. Just get the show on the road."

Noah pressed a key on the keyboard.

"Good evening, Noah," Gemini said, after her face materialized. "Are you ready to begin the experiment?"

Noah checked the time. 8:00 pm. "Good evening, Gemini. Please begin the experiment."

They both stood back from the table as the Parallel Projector performed its mysterious magic. This time the whirring noise was smooth and the gauges and computer monitors danced around in a strange sort of synchronicity. As before, it ended with a zapping sound, a brilliant flash of light, a loud pop and Neil vanished.

Noah moved over to the computer monitor, voice overrode the manual controls and instructed Gemini to return Neil to Earth "safe and sound at exactly eight-thirty."

Ten minutes later, Noah and Angela were biting their nails. Uneasily, they watched the large clock hanging above the door to the lab. Every second seemed like minutes, every minute like hours.

Finally Angela broke the silence. She picked up the glass jar containing Bennie and studied the insect. "He's not moving." She picked up a pen and gently poked at him. "He's dead. Bennie's dead!"

"Don't panic," Noah said, trying to reassure Angela as much as himself. "Some beetles only live for ten to fourteen days. Maybe he was at the end of his life span."

Angela frowned and set the jar down. "I can't handle the stress," she said. "Do you wanna go back inside for another drink?"

On the way out, they tried again to coax Tilly out of hiding but it was no use. Shielding themselves from driving wind and snow, they made their way back to the house and went into the living room where Noah poured strong glasses of Scotch from a bottle of Glenlivet. Saying little, they counted down the minutes.

At 8:28, they returned to the lab.

Four minutes later, Noah quickly checked the clock again, adrenaline animating his features. "Shit. He's not back. He's two minutes late... he's not back!"

Now it was Angela doing the reassuring. "Take it easy. Maybe the time delay is because he didn't go to the eighth dimension precisely at eight. Give it a few more minutes."

Like hours, the minutes passed and still nothing happened. It was now 8:40 pm. As his body shuddered with the onset of panic, Noah stepped closer to Gemini and was about to override the automatic controls and attempt to manually bring Neil back, when suddenly everything went haywire.

The Parallel Projector whirred to life. The computer monitors flashed on, displaying fiery red circular patterns. Needles on gauges danced frenetically. The noise intensified to a loud hum. Noah grabbed the gun off the counter.

"Gemini," he said. "Override automatic controls and manually return Neil safe and sound immediately."

Gemini didn't respond. The humming escalated to an ear-piercing steady hum. The overhead lights flickered and then the entire lab fell into darkness. Noah instinctively grabbed

Angela and crouched underneath a workbench, hugging her tightly and wondering what to do next. The humming sound abruptly ended and the lab fell deathly silent.

"I... I have a flashlight," Angela said.

"Turn... turn it on," Noah said.

"Meow... meow," Tilly said.

As their heartbeats began to pound, Angela turned the flashlight on, training the beam to the Parallel Pointer, searching for Neil. They watched in stunned silence. Outside, the wind intensified into a high-pitched whistle and they heard a loud thud as something smashed against the exterior wall of the lab.

It pushed Angela past the point of composure. "Aaaaaahh!"

"It's okay," Noah said. "It's just the storm... tossing debris around."

"That's not okay."

Angela trained the flashlight beam on the door of the lab, near where the thud had originated. The light caught Tilly's yellow eyes for a split-second and Angela and Noah practically jumped out of their skins.

They heard a soft whisper coming from the Parallel Pointer. As Angela slowly moved the beam over to it, their mouths dropped open simultaneously.

A shadowy oozy substance began flowing out of the oversized nozzle. Slowly, the black wispy waves joined, forming the image of a larger-than-life, terrifying Hat Man. Even through the darkness and the distance, Noah recognized the beady red eyes, the long pointed nose, jutting chin and sallow cheeks. It was none other than Drake Simeon, either resurrected from the dead or a body-double inadvertently returned from a parallel universe.

And either way, it wasn't good news.

"We gotta go," Noah said in a voice that did not sound like his own.

Angela released Noah and began sliding out from underneath the table.

The Hat Man magically produced a machete and raised it high in the air, stepping off the stage. "The only place you're going, Mother Matilda, motherfuckers, is straight to hell."

"Fuck you," Angela said, heading for the door. "I'm not your mother and I sure as hell am not going straight to hell."

Noah was right behind her. They were operating on that giddy, euphoric sensation produced by an adrenaline rush. "I'm not sure that came off the way you intended," he said.

As they neared the door, the Hat Man tipped over a small wheel-equipped work bench and charged at them. Tools scattered everywhere and the bench clanged metallically as it slid along the floor.

Noah weaved around Angela, reached the door, and fumbled frantically with the door knob. *Why isn't it opening? You're panicking, that's why.*

As he got it open, he turned around and realized the gun was tucked in his jeans. *Shoot the bastard.*

The Hat Man covered the distance in a flash and as Noah pulled out the gun, the Dark Menace dove forward, the machete raised in a fatal arc aimed at Angela's throat.

"Sssssssssss... mereeooow!" With that, Tilly sprang from her hunched position underneath the table, landing on the Hat Man's face. She sank her teeth and all four claws in, and sent him catapulting backward. The machete dropped loose from his grasp.

They hit the floor together, rolling in a black mass that was punctuated by meows and hisses from Tilly, grunts and groans from the Hat Man. In the confusion, Noah couldn't get a clear shot. He and Angela just stood and watched Tilly's life-saving bravado in action.

As he waved the gun back and forth, Noah saw Tilly's yellow eyes spring from the black ball and disappear out the door and into the black and white haze of a full-blown blizzard.

As the Hat Man struggled to his feet, Angela and Noah bolted outside and ran for their lives.

Noah followed Angela's flashlight beam, saw it disappear under a blanket of snow, tripped over Angela and landed on top of her. He quickly turned her over and brushed snow from her face.

She opened her eyes. "We gotta stop meeting like this."

In spite of the impending danger, Noah laughed nervously. "I wish we could."

"Where to?" she asked, retrieving the flashlight.

"The truck," Noah said. "Neil's truck. I have the keys."

Following Angela's lead, they scrambled to the vehicle in the near-zero visibility, brushed away snow, opened the doors, and climbed in. Noah began to wonder if this plan had been flawed from the get-go. *What about Tilly? Lost in a sub-zero blizzard.*

On top of that, the Ford was covered in several six inches of snow and he could barely see six inches in front of him. It was too late now. Guided by Angela's flashlight beam, he put the key in the ignition and started it up. It instantly roared to life. The wipers cleared some snow away but there were still a smattering of white patches right in his sight line. The good part of the plan, if there was one, was that Neil had parked on the driveway's turnaround, pointing the vehicle to Highway #3. In the distance, Noah could barely discern a highway light that marked the exit from Neil's driveway.

It was as if Angela read his mind. "Aim for that light, then turn right."

He glanced out the driver-side window and even through the black and white haze, saw the Hat Man glide out of the lab and into the blizzard. Noah didn't waste any time, slamming the Ford into four-wheel-drive-low. As he accelerated, the tires spun for a second before they found traction. He tilted his head at an angle, away from the snow-covered splotches on the windshield, and rumbled toward the highway.

As he neared the guiding light, he heard a loud thump and then the truck started spinning. Her flashlight beam leading the way, Angela looked out the back window. "Floor it. That bastard is on the tailgate."

Noah jammed the gas pedal to the floor. The truck fish-tailed and the tires spun, but nonetheless continued to make slow forward progress toward the light.

Thump... thump... thump!

"You knocked him loose," she said excitedly. "He's buried in snow. Keep going."

The truck reached the highway and Noah prayed that the snowplow had done at least one shift. If the highway was semi-clear, he would be able to switch it into four-wheel-drive-high and make much faster progress. Making the turn, he sighed. The snowplow had come and gone. He quickly shifted into four-wheel-drive-high, fish-tailed out of the driveway, and began making decent progress.

"Hurry," Angela said. "He's coming."

"Can you see him?"

"No," she said, her face turning as white as snow. "I can feel him."

As Noah accelerated, an angry gust of wind blew a mountain of snow in front of the Ford, blinding him. "Oh fuck," he said, as the truck started careening off the road. "Hang on!"

The Ford spun 360 degrees and then nose-dived into the ditch. It blasted up the other side of the trench, caught two feet of air, landed in a large snow drift, smashed through a barbed-wire fence and came to a stop as the tires whirred and spun.

"Are you okay?" he asked.

"Yeah," Angela said. "I took your advice. I hung on. You?"

Noah had gripped the wheel tightly during the wipe-out. He loosened his white-knuckled grip and took a deep breath. "Yeah... I'm good."

Noah quickly tried four-wheel-drive-low, but the tires still spun. "We're stuck."

"Try backing up."

He did, to no avail, so he put the truck in Park. He opened the glovebox, grabbed a flashlight, turned it on, opened the door and stepped outside into waist-deep snow. He shone the light around the perimeter and quickly realized there was no getting out without a winch or a tow.

Angela opened the passenger door and, with her flashlight, plunged into waist-deep snow. "Shit. This is not good. Not good at all. Any ideas?"

Through the blinding blizzard, Noah could barely see Angela. His mind raced. Overdosing on adrenaline, he was having trouble finding traction with his mental wheels, never mind the wheels of the pickup.

He felt it before he saw it—a dark, powerful evil force, rattling him to the core. He shuddered, shining the flashlight in front of the truck's headlights, and simultaneously reaching for the gun. It wasn't there. It must have dislodged during the crash. *Shit, fuck, shit.*

"He's there," Angela shouted. "Look!"

Descending from a dark, blizzardy sky, the Hat Man emerged fully, illuminated by four beams—two headlights and two flashlights.

An ominous voice spoke as the machete swung at Angela's throat. "You're dead this time."

Angela stepped back. "Aaaaaaaaaaaaahh!"

Noah shone the flashlight into the cab of the truck, spotted the gun on the passenger-side floor mat, and bent down to reach for it. But he stopped instantly.

Out of the corner of his eye, he saw one, two, three, then four, five, and six Shadow People appear out of nowhere and attack the Hat Man from behind. Shadowy arms reached out and grabbed him.

It was only for a split-second and Noah thought his panicked mind must be playing tricks on him. But, he was sure he saw his own reflection in one of the Shadow People, nodding, grinning, and even giving him the thumbs-up.

As the Dark Menace shouted and screamed horrifically, more hands and arms clutched his extremities and lifted him higher in the air, tearing him apart limb by agonizing limb, piece by agonizing piece.

They watched in stunned silence as the last remnants of the Hat Man dissolved in a dark haze and the Shadow People regrouped, joined hands, and floated away in the distance.

"Did you see that?" Noah asked.

No response. Only the whistling wind and the idling Ford.

Noah trudged through the snow to the passenger side of the truck and found Angela lying on her back in the snow. He shuddered. *Oh God, no. Did the Hat Man get her? Am I too late?* He quickly worked the flashlight beam over her prostrate body and saw no red flags. He sighed, kneeling down and gently cradling her head on his knee. He wiped snow from her face. "Angela, Angela!"

She didn't respond. He felt her neck for a pulse. There was one.

She slowly opened her eyes and looked at Noah, her mouth quivering as she spoke. "Is... is he gone?"

"He's gone. He's gone for good." Noah retrieved her flashlight from the snow and helped her to her feet.

A distant, wind-whipped husky voice floated in from the dark and stormy night. "Who's gone?"

Noah gently stuffed Angela into the passenger seat and grabbed the gun.

CHAPTER EIGHTEEN

Noah studied the man sitting in an armchair across from him. He had a head of cropped gray hair and a short, scruffy beard. He wasn't much taller than five-feet-two, but he was muscular and stocky, with dark, penetrating brown eyes that seemed to belie his hillbilly appearance. When the man had come along about an hour ago, Noah had almost put a bullet through his head, and then recalled, at the last second, who the man was and stuffed the weapon back into his pants, narrowly avoiding an accidental murder.

The man rose from his chair and busily began lighting a fire, obviously quite comfortable in Neil's house. He turned to Noah. "Gotta get this going in case of a power outage."

Noah nodded.

The man was Norman Murphy, Neil's dear friend who lived two houses down from Neil. After Norm, as he preferred to be called, had pulled the truck out of the ditch, and they were on their way back to Neil's house, Noah remembered more about what Neil had told him about the man. And Angela, who was taking a nap now after the terrifying ordeal, was the one who'd reminded him. Norm had encountered a shadow person before and, because of his innate goodness, according to Neil's theory, the shadowy entity had left him alone and moved on to darker and more sinister pastures to sow seeds of benevolence.

During their brief conversation when Norm had rescued them, Noah hadn't said anything about Neil's experiments. He'd told Norm that Neil was taking a nap, they had borrowed the truck for a romantic outing in a blizzard and, yes, actually they would like to get it out of the ditch and return to Neil's for a warm fire and a shot of Scotch. After they'd returned, it was Angela who showed Norm into the house and offered him a drink while Noah locked up the lab (without finding a single sign of Neil), found Tilly taking refuge in an outbuilding, and returned to the house with a grateful and purring black cat cradled in his arms.

After feeding Tilly and tucking Angela into bed, Noah had only five minutes ago sat down on the couch beside a comfortably dozing Tilly, who, aside from being a little moist and matted, looked none the worse for wear.

Noah lifted the glass of Scotch and poured a generous swallow down his throat, enjoying the stinging sensation that reminded him poignantly that he was very much alive. *Thank you, thank Norm, thank God, thank the Shadow People, thank somebody very much.*

Wiping his hands, Norm turned around and grinned as a fire erupted and cast a warm glow over the room. His top middle incisor tooth was missing. "There, that's better," Norm said.

"Thanks," Noah said, holding up the bottle. He wondered how much Norm really knew about Neil and his experiments. "Want another drink?"

"Sure. Don't get up." Norm approached, scooped the bottle from Noah's hand and sat down. He filled his glass, and set the bottle on a tea table in front of the armchair.

For a minute or two, they discussed how nasty the storm was and how lucky Noah and Angela were to be alive. While disclosing little else, Noah thanked him repeatedly for the rescue. Then the conversation shifted to the minor damage to Norm's fence, which, in spite of Noah's offers of financial compensation, Norm insisted on repairing free of charge.

The conversation eventually shifted to the damage to Neil's truck.

Norm took a large swallow from his glass. "Just a few scratches and a small dent. But Neil keeps that thing in mint condition. It might be nice if you got it fixed for him. Or at least offer to take care of the damages."

"I'll definitely do that," Noah said.

"Good." Norm's casual and relaxed demeanor turned serious. He gave Noah a penetrating look. "Did you say Neil was sleeping? Funny that, he's usually a night owl."

Noah was about to open his mouth, but then realized it was a trap. He felt like a lobster about to crawl into the man-made, net-ringed hole of no return. He closed his mouth, took another swallow of Scotch, and waited for Norm to make the first move.

It took less than two seconds. "I know where Neil is," Norm said. "You don't have to bullshit me. I know more about Neil, more about his experiments, than you'll probably ever know.

"Really?" Noah said. He hoped it didn't sound sarcastic, because that was not the way he meant it. "Where is he?"

"He's in the eighth dimension. He's with his wife Maggie. And he's not coming back."

CHAPTER NINETEEN

In spite of everything, it's a beautiful morning, Noah thought, admiring the snow-covered landscape at 11:00 am Sunday morning. The almost cloudless sky was bright blue and the contrasting stark whiteness blanketed the trees. It looked pristine and pure, almost sacred and innocent. He walked over to the kitchen sink, poured a glass of water, and popped two codeine-laced Tylenols into his mouth. He washed them back with four mouthfuls of water. It wasn't the concussion this morning that he needed the pills for. It was an alcohol-induced headache. A hangover. He and Norm had gotten a little carried away with the Scotch, drinking more than a bottle and a half between them before Norm finally left, which to Noah's cobweb-filled recollection was somewhere around two in the morning.

He refilled a coffee mug, added cream and sugar, then sat down at the kitchen nook to gather his thoughts. He and Norm had become fast friends, discussing everything from Neil's idiosyncrasies to Maggie's magnanimous heart. They'd even discussed the Hat Man and the Shadow People, including Noah's experiences, before the drunken conversation finally degenerated to boobs and babes. But through it all, Noah realized a few things. Although Norm was reluctant to disclose certain details about Neil and the experiments, Noah could clearly see that he had a strong ally and a good friend in the likes of Norman Murphy. Steady indeed was he, and loyal to a fault.

It was Norm's conviction last night that Neil was happy and safe in the eighth dimension that gave Noah a sense of peace now as he rubbed his temples, trying to massage the headache away. It didn't entirely work, but it didn't matter. He knew that soon the codeine would smooth over the rough edges. Maybe he should have taken it easy last night, but the stress had reached a boiling point and he really needed the booze binge to blow off some steam. Besides, he thought, if it weren't for the alcohol, there was no way he would have been able to sleep last night. As it was, as soon as he'd staggered to bed and laid his head on the pillow, he'd passed out, dead to the world.

And, for a change, Angela had been the one who slept in. *I better go wake her up. See if she's okay.* He felt a soft touch on his shoulder. He looked up.

Angela, her wet hair wrapped in a white towel, smiled at Noah. "How's your hangover?"

He noticed the 36-stich angry red scar on her calf and the terror of their situation began to settle in like an anchor. "Better. I took some pills. They'll kick in soon."

She poured herself a coffee and joined him, giving him a quick peck on the cheek. "I heard you guys a bit last night."

"Sorry," he said. "I guess we got a little carried away."

"Nonsense. You needed to blow off some steam. If I hadn't felt so jittery, I probably would've joined you. But I know how my body works. Once it's overloaded with stress, it starts to shut down. I have to go with the flow or else I'll be a mess." She rose and began busying herself in the kitchen while Noah navigated the cobwebs. "Do you need any help?"

"No. You relax."

"Did you have any dreams last night?"

She paused. Her brow crinkled. "No. But nothing could be worse than the nightmare last night. And that was real. I imagine you were too drunk to dream at all."

Noah nodded. He saw her frown and wasn't sure if it was due to the recent trauma or a recent nightmare that perhaps she didn't want to talk about. He thought it might be a sign, but let it go. "I don't remember much after I passed out. Did you sleep okay?"

Angela cracked an egg into a frying pan. It sizzled. "Not bad, considering."

Over the sizzling of the egg, Noah heard the rumble of an engine outside. He grabbed the gun and rushed over to the bay window overlooking the property.

Outside, Norm stopped the snowplow truck momentarily, tipped his black baseball cap, gave a thumbs-up sign, and carried on plowing. Noah tucked the gun in his pants and concealed it with his green sweatshirt. "It's Norm," he said. "He's plowing the driveway."

"That's good," Angela said, emptying some frozen hash browns into another frying pan. "I'd like to go into town today, if possible. I need a few things at my place and we're running low on supplies."

Noah returned to the kitchen island and sat down. "That's a good idea. I'd like to replace Neil's booze in case he *does* come back."

An uncomfortable silence hung in the air.

Angela cracked another egg into the frying pan.

Noah broke the silence. "I never asked you... do you have a car?"

"No."

"A driver's license?"

"Yes. Why?"

"I was thinking..."

"You think?"

"Sometimes, but it's rare." Neither of them laughed. Noah continued. "I was thinking maybe we can drive to my place with Neil's truck. I'd like to get my Silverado, just in case we need another set of wheels. I can drop you at my apartment. You can take my truck and go get your things, and I'll pick up some groceries and replace Neil's booze. Then we can meet back here if you want."

"That sounds like a plan. I imagine you'll want to take a look at that Parallel Projector later."

"You read my mind, baby."

Tilly jumped off the couch, slithered over to her food bowl, and meowed. Noah grinned and picked her up. She put a paw—claws retracted—gently to his lips and he put her back down. "I get it, Tilly. Food first, cuddles later. Well, you deserve it. If it wasn't for you, we might not be having this conversation."

She meowed knowingly as Noah cracked a can of cat food and emptied it into her bowl. Tilly purred and began eating as Noah put down fresh drinking water.

Over breakfast, he and Angela discussed grocery items, departure and arrival times. When they finished eating, the doorbell rang.

"Well, the timing could be worse... I'll say that much," Angela said, collecting a few dishes off the kitchen island, dropping them into the sink, and walking into the hallway.

She stopped as Noah approached the door, his right hand tucked under his sweatshirt, hovering near the waistline of his jeans. "It's Detective Stevenson."

She frowned. "I'm going to get changed. Yell if you need anything." She disappeared down the hall as Noah opened the door.

Once the social niceties were dispensed with, and they were seated comfortably in the living room, each with a coffee in hand, Detective Stevenson asked, "Where's Neil?" He scanned the room.

"He's taking a nap," Noah said, shifting in the armchair slightly.

"Really? He's not feeling well?"

"That's right. A headache."

"Well, I notice his Ford truck looks a little worse for wear today. And the neighbor's fence is damaged. And there are some ruts in the snow. That might lead a thinking man to conclude that someone drove Neil's truck into Norm's fence last night. Do you know anything about that?" Detective Stevenson's eyes pierced right through Noah.

"That's the reason Neil has a headache," Noah said. "He lost control of his truck in the storm and smashed through Norm's fence."

Detective Stevenson's eyes found the empty Scotch bottle. "Really? He'd been drinking?"

"No... that was... err, Angela and me." Noah knew he was digging himself a shallow grave and he considered the possibility of coming clean with the detective. He also realized Norm could quickly blow his cover if he didn't call him and fill him in on all the lies before the detective got to him. But what was he gonna say? *Neil is perfectly happy with his wife Maggie in the eighth dimension. He sends his fondest regards. Now please, be a good detective, fuck off and leave us alone.*

The detective scratched his long sideburns, looked at Noah for a moment and then studied his coffee. It seemed as if he wanted to let the matter go, but his detective instincts wouldn't let him.

"How is Neil?" Detective Stevenson finally asked.

Angela entered the room with vitality and vigor in her step. "Hello, detective."

The detective nodded.

"I just checked on Neil now," she said. "Just a little bump on his head. He's fast asleep. I think it's a minor concussion, just like Noah suffered.

"I hope he's gonna be okay," Detective Stevenson said.

"He'll be fine," Angela said. "It's a good thing we're here to look after him though." She swept up the detective's coffee cup before he had a chance to protest and went into the kitchen to refill it.

"How are you guys doing?" Detective Stevenson asked. "I mean, you've both been through a lot."

"My stitches are healing nicely," Angela said, returning and handing the detective a fresh, piping hot coffee. She turned to Noah. "And his head is doing fine, but he can speak for himself."

"I'm better," Noah said. *Keep him off balance.* "Back to work Wednesday. By the way, detective, have you heard anything more about the Shadow People or the Hat Man?"

Frowning, the detective sipped his coffee. "No. Not since Neil gunned down that sick fuck. But we found two more dead bodies buried at his house. Haven't identified them yet. I've been busy at the killer's house since Neil put a bullet, no two bullets in his head—one in the back of his fucking neck. That's actually why I stopped by. As you know, Drake only lived a mile or so away from here and I realized that I don't have your statement yet. It's just a formality, really, but I would like your account of what happened that night."

As Noah started to tell his story, the detective's phone rang. As if he knew what the call would be about, the color drained from his face. He answered it. "Stevenson here. What do you want? Oh, for fuck sakes!"

Eyes narrowing, Detective Stevenson stood. "I have to go. They just found another fucking body under that goddamned cursed outbuilding of his. I need to go babysit some rookies before they fuck this investigation all to hell."

"I hope it goes well," Noah said, realizing immediately how stupid it sounded.

"You have my card," Detective Stevenson said. "For now, why don't you email me your account of what happened? If I need any clarification, I'll call you. If I decide to have it typed into a statement, I'll contact you for your signature. That sound okay?"

"I'll do it later today, detective."

"Good."

They walked the detective to the door and Noah opened it.

Detective Stevenson said good bye and stepped out onto the porch. Halfway down the walkway, Noah and Angela watching him from the partially opened door, the detective stopped and turned around. "By the way," he said. "When Neil wakes up, have him call me. I'd like to know that he's okay. If

I don't hear from my friends, I start to wonder what happened to them."

"We'll do that," Noah said.

They continued to watch the detective as he climbed into his Crown Victoria, drove once around the freshly plowed turnaround and down the driveway.

Noah's jaw dropped when he saw it. He pointed. "Did you see that?"

"What?"

"A black fedora hat. I swear to God I saw a black fedora hat on his rear dashboard."

CHAPTER TWENTY

Inside her house later that afternoon, Angela walked cautiously into her bedroom, half-expecting at any second a monster to leap from the closet and attack her. She sat down on the bed and collected her thoughts. The room felt odd somehow, as if it wasn't her home anymore. So much had happened in just over a week that she felt her life would never be the same again; that maybe she could never feel at home in her apartment ever again

She thought about her dream last night. It was the first time she'd ever lied to Noah, and she hoped it would be the last. The dream was a different version of the one she'd had last Tuesday when she was staying at Noah's apartment. In that dream, she'd viciously shattered the picture of her ex-boyfriend and tossed the shredded remains of it into the garbage can. In the more recent one, she was fawning over the picture, tears streaming down her face, pining for him. She'd been unable to trash the photo, afraid that to do so would be to lose Case forever, lose the faint hope that she'd clung to for so long that somehow they'd be reunited again.

And there was something else in the dream, vague and shadowy, that painted a very grim picture of a man with a malicious streak. Had she repressed his dark side for all these years? Was she in denial of it? She pushed the thought away, hoping to eradicate all memories of Case once and for all.

"And that's exactly what I'm gonna do," she said, finally allowing herself to look at the image of the man who'd broken her heart just over seven months ago. His dark brown eyes appraised her, his broad inviting smile seemed to mock her emotional frailty. She touched the photo and withdrew her hand quickly, stung by heartache and fear.

But why should she be afraid to move on? Noah had done more for her in a week than Case had done in three years. Noah wanted her happiness and although he'd never verbalized it, she believed he loved her; whereas to Case, she'd just been a trophy to display and exploit on a wall of self-aggrandizement.

She remembered Neil's words about coming to grips with her dark side, with her Shadow. *What did Carl Jung call it? Right, Shadow Integration. Meaning essentially that to find the light, you have to pass through the darkness. Even embrace it.*

She struggled with and finally pushed aside a rising tide of emotion. In a smooth motion, she stood up, snatching the picture off the nightstand and charging into the kitchen. "That's what I'm gonna do, you piece of shit. Come to grips with my dark side. Get rid of my skeletons. And I'm gonna start with your ugly mug."

Fuelled by anger, hatred, and a sense of disgust at her own weakness, she smashed the picture on top of the kitchen counter, carefully keeping her hands on the cardboard backing to avoid injury. Case had caused her enough pain already to last a lifetime. Glass splintered and shattered. She released the picture frame and, just as in her earlier dream, she retrieved a pair of gloves from a utility drawer. Putting them on, she carefully lifted the picture, turned it around and inspected it. Similar to the dream, a spear of glass had poked through his paper chest, through his heart, and another protruded precariously from his mouth. One of his eyes was obliterated by tiny glass splinters.

"Who has the broken heart now?" Angela asked, feeling a powerful sense of déjà vu. "Who? Not me, you philandering fuck. Not me."

She carefully extracted the photo from the frame, placed it on the counter, swept the counter clean and tossed the glass, along with the twisted wreckage of the picture frame, into the recycle bin. She plucked a fork from the cutlery tray drawer, picked up the photo and began savagely stabbing it repeatedly, until it was completely shredded. With each plunging jab, she felt a weight being lifted from her shoulders. When she finally stopped and wiped her tear-stained cheeks, she realized with a powerful sense of relief that for the very first time, they were not tears of heartache, sadness and despair.

They were tears of joy.

Feeling a sense of euphoria at having gotten through the process of letting go, she removed a dinner plate from her cupboard, placed it on the counter, and deposited the shredded remains of Case Blackthorn, the proverbial thorn in her side, into it.

Using a nearby Bic lighter, she lit the pieces of paper and grinned as she watched Case Blackthorn burn in hell.

A few minutes later, considerably calmer and more relaxed, Angela reclined on her couch with a celebratory glass of red wine. A certain fitting irony, perhaps a paradox, occurred to her. *Angela Rosewood. Case Blackthorn. I'm the rose. He was the thorn in my side. Roses have thorns. But not this one—not anymore. That thorn has gone up in smoke.*

She grinned, amused at her clever analysis. She finished the wine and began moving around the apartment with a renewed energy and enthusiasm in her step. She found a suitable knapsack and began packing necessary toiletries and articles of clothing to take back to Neil's place.

In the bedroom, she picked up a few items of clothing, moved over to a dresser and began clearing the clutter. She found an address book underneath a t-shirt and it reminded her of her parents, Jonah and Linda. She hadn't spoken to them in some time. Although they hadn't called, she thought they might be worried. As well, she was dying to tell them the good news—that she was about to start her own business. Something else was compelling her to call them, but for some strange reason, she was unable to put a finger on it.

As she punched in her mother's number, she glanced at the nightstand and felt great satisfaction that there was a pleasing empty space next to her bed.

Her mother picked up on the second ring. "Honey, are you okay?"

"Better than ever, Mom."

After inquiring about the rest of the family, she decided to get to the point. "Guess what, Mom? I quit my job at Wendy's. I got approved for a government grant to be a photographer. I'll display my best shots on my upcoming website, and I might even get some of them in a gallery if I'm lucky."

Her mother's tone was nothing short of elation. "That's great, honey. I'm so proud of you. Your dad is going to be thrilled. I knew you could do it."

It was just the kind of validation Angela was looking for. "Thanks, Mom." She felt suddenly overcome with a sense of foreboding, though she couldn't understand why. "Listen, Mom, if something happens to me, I want you to know I love you. And I want you to know I'm gonna be okay. I'm always gonna be okay. Please pass that on to Dad for me, and to Jerry and Selena."

There was a transitory silence on the other end, before her mother finally spoke. Her words were tinged with emotion. "I love you too, honey. We all do. But what on God's green Earth are you talking about? What could possibly go wrong?"

******

Noah pressed SEND on the email statement he'd crafted for Detective Stevenson's benefit, killed the power, closed his laptop and packed it away in a computer bag. He moved into the kitchen and soaked a dishtowel in hot soapy water. He went into his bedroom and began scrubbing Angela's blood off the wall and floor next to the fire escape. The landlord and the police version of "ready for occupancy" obviously hadn't included a thorough cleaning.

He'd just returned from running errands that included grocery shopping, alcohol purchases, and a surprise gift for Angela—a necklace with a silver leaping dolphin pendant. He'd picked it up on a whim, and the cashier had assured him it would "bring heaps of good luck."

He'd also called Norm and brought him up to speed on the detective's curiosities. Norm offered to cover for him if necessary, and Noah had expressed his gratitude, although he realized it didn't really matter. Detective Stevenson would be calling to speak to Neil sometime this evening and if Neil wasn't available, there would be a lot of explaining to do. Regardless, Norm assured Noah that, using a house key Neil had furnished him with "eons ago," he would check the house and feed Tilly in their absence.

Fifteen minutes of scrubbing later, Noah was reasonably pleased with his efforts. He couldn't get all the blood stains out, but for now it was good enough. At some point, part of the blood-spattered wall would have to be properly sealed and repainted. In the kitchen, he rinsed the dishtowel, hung it up to dry on a kitchen chair and went into the small laundry room where the dryer had just shut off with a loud buzzing sound. He folded all the clothes neatly, added a few items to a knapsack, and sat down to take a break.

He started to feel deeply troubled and anxious concerning Neil's absence and hoped that this evening's efforts would return him safely home. Neil had done so much for Noah, and he was really starting to miss the man. His mind began meandering down the dark stream of events concerning the Shadow People, the mysterious eighth dimension, the Hat Man and, he shuddered, the fedora hat he was sure he'd seen in the rear dashboard of Detective Stevenson's Crown Victoria earlier today.

He had just begun to mull over what that might possibly mean when his phone rang.

It was Angela. She sounded absolutely jubilant. "Hey, why don't we have dinner at my place before we head to Neil's?"

******

Noah was impressed. Angela had gone to a lot of trouble. Her apartment was neat as a pin and tastefully lit with candles, strategically dotting all four corners of the room; with two adorning the kitchen table. They'd just finished a delicious meal of lasagna with meat sauce and Caesar salad.

Dinner conversation had been light and playful, as if there was an unspoken but mutual understanding that serious matters were reserved for after dinner.

Noah raised his glass of wine, admiring Angela's radiance. She absolutely glowed. "Cheers, honey. Thanks for the delicious meal. You look stunning tonight."

She clinked glasses, said "Cheers," and they drank.

She stood. "Thanks for the compliment. I'm starting to get over some hurdles and I feel good. I have a surprise."

She went into her bedroom and returned with a small black leather box with a bright red plastic bow affixed to it. She set it on the table and, beaming, looked at Noah. "Go ahead, open it."

Noah grinned, reached into his jacket pocket, and produced a small black leather box with a bright red plastic rose fastened to it.

To Angela's incredulous eyes, he set it on the table.

"You first," he said.

She reached over and hugged him warmly, planting a long wet kiss on his lips. The words were out of her mouth before she'd even realized what she said. "You're awesome, baby. I love you."

Noah had wondered when those words would come, words of endearment that typically marked another deeper and more meaningful level in any relationship. He'd imagined they'd be difficult to utter, since they were so often loaded with the promise of long-term commitment and responsibility. But they slipped from his tongue like a hot and sweet butterscotch sundae. "I love you too, Angel. I love you so much."

They embraced in a passionate hug and an even more intense kiss. When they came up for air, both of them were wiping moist eyes.

Angela laughed suddenly. "Did you just call me Angel?"

"You *are* an Angel," he said. "You're my Angel."

"Thank you, baby." She pointed to the gift. "Go ahead. You first. I insist."

Noah removed the bow and popped open the case. A gold-plated Rolex watch glittered and winked at him. "I love it. Thank you so much. This must have cost you an arm and a leg."

"It cost me a little more than that," she said ironically. "But I want you to have it. I noticed you don't wear a watch."

When Angela opened her gift, she was equally impressed. Noah helped her put it on and complimented her on how much the good luck charm suited her.

With admiring eyes, she examined the smiling dolphin. "I love dolphins. They've always been one of my favorite ocean creatures."

"The sales clerk, she says it will bring good fortune."

"I hope she's right," Angela said, and began cleaning the dishes. "Sit down. I've got this."

As Noah relaxed and sipped wine, Angela's front door abruptly burst open and, silhouetted by the glowing yellow setting sun, a man wearing a balaclava and a gaucho hat aimed a pistol and fired two quick shots at Angela.

At the sound of deafening gunshot blasts, she screamed and dove on the floor.

It was pure preservation instinct that propelled Noah to his feet. He quickly removed the gun from the crotch of his jeans and, as the hat-wearing man aimed the gun at him, he shot twice, striking the assailant once in the chest and once right between the eyes.

The man groaned, fell into the wall, staggered forward two steps and face-planted the coffee table.

Operating on adrenaline, Angela got up off the floor as Noah, in shock, examined the smoking gun in his hand. "I've just killed a man."

She rushed over to the coffee table, pulled the intruder onto his back, pushed the hat from his head, and removed the black balaclava.

Dizzy from the ordeal, Noah slumped onto the couch. "Who is it? Detective Stevenson?"

Her eyes bulging, Angela said, "No. It's my ex-boyfriend. Case Blackthorn."

EPILOGUE

Noah stood in a dimly lit room unlike any he'd ever seen. To his left, there were ten doors, each of them labeled PAST. In the middle, five doors, all labeled PRESENT. To the right, ten more doors, each labeled FUTURE. He walked around the room for a minute or so and then made his decision. He went to one of the PAST doors, opened it, and stepped inside.

Suddenly, he slipped back in time. The surroundings were familiar. A picture of Batman on the wall. His favorite brown and black-eyed teddy bear on the nightstand. His single bed, with the familiar green-and-white-polka-dot comforter. The dreaded closet with all the skeletons. He was in his childhood bedroom. Only, he wasn't a boy anymore. He was an adult. He walked cautiously over to the closet door, took three deep breaths, and shuddered. *You can do this. You have to do this.* With an unsteady hand, he slowly turned the doorknob, opened it and stepped back, willing himself to embrace his fears. With astonishment, he watched as a hundred ferocious-looking demons and monsters hissed and snarled, then took flight and disappeared.

With a satisfied smile, he closed the closet door.

He heard the drone of conversation. He approached his bedroom door and opened it. He stepped out into the hallway. Closed the door behind him. Walked quietly and slowly down the hallway. He entered the living room, saw the TV glowing with the form of a dark and menacing, white-fanged monster, and recognized the bulbous form of Barbara Janzen, his mother, slumped on the couch in front of the TV intently watching what looked like a B-grade horror movie.

With one hand, she reached into the glass bowl cradled on her lap and shoveled a mouthful of potato chips into her mouth, unaware of a few chips that slid down her gray sweatshirt, one lodging in the crotch of her sweatpants, a few others spilling onto the sofa. She grabbed the remote, adjusted her bulk, and turned up the volume. The crotch-pinned chip crunched into powder. Oblivious, she flicked the channel quickly six times and finally stopped at *Bride of the Monster*, a 1955 B-grade cult horror film. She leaned back and grinned, exposing crooked, decaying and nicotine-stained teeth.

Now standing beside his mother, a horrific picture of her past swept through his mind, striking Noah like a speeding locomotive. Like a real-life horror movie, hundreds of images of Barbara's past flashed through his mind with one consistent theme—she'd endured a life of physical and verbal abuse, much of it unleashed from the powerful hands and caustic tongue of her alcoholic father.

Overcome with sadness, Noah shuddered as a wave of realization washed over him. He suddenly understood everything clearly. Wiping a tear from his eye, he bent down and kissed his mother gently on the cheek. She recoiled as if she'd been electrocuted. The glass bowl toppled from her lap, chips spilling everywhere.

"Who's there?" she said, waving her hands furtively around the room.

"It's okay," Noah said. "It's me, Mom. Noah. Your son. I understand why, Mom. I finally understand. I'm sorry you had to grow up like that. I forgive you."

As Noah experienced his weightless form soar high into the air, he felt a huge sense of relief even though he saw a lone tear snake down his mother's cheek.

******

It was a bright sunny day and Noah, Angela, Neil and Maggie were reclining on beach towels, enjoying the spectacular view out to sea.

In real life, Noah thought Maggie was much better than all the stories he'd heard. She exuded positivity, kindness and warmth and did it all with a relaxed and easy disposition. And she looked ten years younger than the photos he'd seen. She had wavy shoulder-length grey-black hair, lively green eyes, small, soft facial features and a smile that was a clear room-illuminator. She was the kind of person you always wanted to be around, knowing that in whatever circumstance, she would cheer you up.

And Neil's trip to the eighth dimension had been kind to him as well. He too looked ten years younger and had even trimmed his Albert Einstein-like mop of hair and shaved off his scruffy facial growth. But why wouldn't he be happy? He'd been reunited with his soulmate and he was once again on fire with desire.

And since Noah had entered, come to grips with, and closed the door to his past, releasing his skeletons once and for all into the cosmic sphere of infinity, he too felt alight with passion and desire.

Angela reached over and touched his arm gently. "What are you thinking about, baby?"

"I'm just so happy, honey. Happy I went through that door last night and released all my demons. I think I'll be much better now. I think *we'll* be much better."

"I think so," Angela said. "We both released our skeletons. The only difference is I did it on Earth and you did it in the eighth dimension."

Maggie sprang to her feet and looked at Noah with concern in her soft eyes. "What do you think about all those doors? All those choices. I mean, it's just amazing here. You can take a path and if the outcome isn't what you want, you can simply change your mind."

"There are a lot of things I'm still getting used to here," Noah said. "Like the new reality where Angela and I are already married and we own twenty acres in PEI with this beautiful beach. And she owns a successful art gallery and I'm a regular contributor."

Neil jumped to his feet. "You'll get used to it. Here—more literally than figuratively—you're living in a world with infinite possibilities. You're only limited by your imagination. But just ease into it until you get used to it. Go with the flow."

"That's all I *can* do," Noah agreed. "As for the doors and Maggie's question, I'm gonna try and avoid the doors of the past and the future and just stick with the ones in the present.

"Good idea," Neil said. "You've come a long way. Both of you have. Overcoming your demons has opened up a world of endless possibilities. But even though you can live your life in the past or the future here, I still agree it makes more sense to live it in the present. At least until you adjust."

Neil and Maggie joined hands, turned and ran into the water, splashing each other playfully and laughing.

******

The dark sky was lit by an ominously glowing full moon. Twinkling stars and Mother Nature's Northern Lights danced across the heavens, adding a sense of drama and intrigue. Thousands of chairs were positioned around a large dark stage lit by a single spotlight beam. In the chairs sat shadowy entities. Shadow People, but in this dimension they were the residents of Prince Edward Island.

Scanning thousands of beady red eyes, Noah was amazed. He began to wonder if, to others, he too looked like a shadow person. He looked at Angela. She looked the same as she did on Earth. Neil and Maggie, seated next to them, also resembled Earthlings.

He squeezed Angela's hand gently. She squeezed back tenderly. Noah abandoned the thought. As Neil had said, ease into the eighth dimension. Besides, he was minutes away from hearing a big speech from the benevolent leader of PEI. Noah was anxious to see the man in person and hear his words. He'd been told that many questions would be answered.

A soft murmur echoed through the crowd as a man walked out on stage. He stood larger than life, perhaps a full eight feet tall, and wore a black trench coat and a black fedora hat. He stopped in front of the microphone, tapped it twice, and cleared his throat.

The audience erupted with raucous applause. Shadow People chanted, "The Hat Man, the Hat Man—the all-powerful Hat Man."

Noah anxiously adjusted his binoculars to get a better view of the real Hat Man. He wondered if he was right about his identity. His eyes widened in amazement as the binocular lenses focused and black transformed into white. He recognized the unmistakable bushy sideburns and handlebar mustache of Detective Lamar Stevenson. At least on Earth, he was a detective. Here, he lived a parallel life as the Hat Man, a man of peace, love, good will, kindness and generosity. Indeed, according to Neil, a leader akin to God.

A hushed silence fell over the crowd.

"I was right," Noah said, handing Angela the binoculars.

She focused on Hat Man Lamar Stevenson for a few seconds and handed the binoculars back to Noah. "I can't wait to meet him. I wonder if he's got the same caustic tongue as his body-double on Earth."

"All along, the real Hat Man has been getting a bad rap," Noah said. "But he's not an evil presence at all. He's the opposite of evil. He's good."

Neil turned to them and held an index finger to his lips. "Shhh. The Hat Man is starting now," he whispered.

Maggie squeezed Neil's hand and smiled, lighting up the night.

The Hat Man cleared his throat. "Good citizens of Prince Edward Island. Good Shadow People of this beautiful island. I am here today to inform you of some breaches to our dimension, as well as some breaches to Earth's dimension. Due to these breaches, we have lost some of our citizens. But rest assured, the ones we've lost are serving a much higher cause on Earth. They've possessed evil souls and have transformed them into morally upright, kind, caring, and law-abiding citizens. Three of those we lost have been replaced by their body-doubles on Earth—Neil Samuelson, Angela Rosewood, and Noah Janzen. I'm sure they will become fine and respectable members of our peaceful community."

The Hat Man paused, pointed to the three, and said, "Welcome. Please stand up and take a bow, folks."

To uproarious applause, Neil, Angela, and Noah stood up and bowed.

When they sat down and the crowd had quieted, the Hat Man leader continued. "Unfortunately, these breaches have caused our people and even myself to be portrayed in a bad light. But nothing is further from the truth. Shadow People are good, benevolent souls. And, as you know, I am not the purest form of negativity or evil at all. I represent the purest form of positivity and goodness. I am not the Dark Menace. The Dark Menace is dead. I am the dark light...."

******

In the bright light of the afternoon sun, Norman Murphy stepped out onto the porch of what was once Neil's house but was now his. According to all the meticulous preparations Neil had made before his departure, Norm was the new beneficiary of the property. Maybe it wasn't quite legal yet, but it would be soon enough, once a few minor details had been dealt with.

He sniffed the fresh air, marveled at the sound of swallows chirping in budding trees, and smiled. It felt like it would be an early spring. He went over to an outbuilding and retrieved a five-gallon can of gasoline. He went inside the lab, doused it liberally, and then doused the perimeter. Just as he started to manufacture a Molotov cocktail, a tan Crown Victoria turned into the driveway, pulled up to the house, and parked.

Right on time, Norm thought

Detective Lamar Stevenson, sporting a black fedora hat, stepped out and waved to Norm. The detective approached Norm. "I'd shake your hand, but it's probably covered in gas."

"It is," Norm said. "What's with the hat, Lamar?"

"I don't know. Lately, I've started to think I live another kinder and gentler life in another dimension. Maybe I started believing some of the things you told me about Neil and his experiments." He removed the hat, brushed a piece of lint from it and placed it back on his head. "And this hat here plays a big part of that life."

Norm adjusted his black baseball cap. "Hmmm... it suits you."

"Thanks."

"Hear anything about any copycat Hat Man killers lately?" Norm asked. "Or terrifying Shadow People?"

"No. Not since that Case Blackthorn was killed. But it's only been a few days."

Norm raised the Molotov cocktail and produced a Bic lighter. "Do you really think this is a good idea?"

The detective scratched one of his sideburns. "I can't think of any other way. Do you really think anybody's gonna believe me if I tell them Angela, Noah and Neil are living happily-ever-after in the eighth dimension?"

Norm sighed. "I guess not."

"This way, we can say there was a terrible accident and they lost their lives in the fire. You can legally inherit the property and we can do away once and for all with that thing Neil calls the Parallel Projector."

Norm lit the Molotov cocktail. "And you're sure you don't want to salvage that piece of machinery? For scientific reasons?"

The detective's brow crinkled in thought. "I don't think so," he said. "I don't think we're ready for it."

Norm tossed the fire bomb onto the roof of the lab and it exploded. A river of flames snaked down the roof and ignited the gasoline below. Within seconds the lab erupted into a ball of flames.

As Norm and Detective Stevenson walked toward the house, Tilly sprang from an outbuilding, leaped into Norm's arms, and meowed. Norm stroked Tilly as he carried her onto the porch.

He turned to Detective Stevenson. "How about a beer?"

"Don't mind if I do," the detective said, following Norm into the house. "It's been a hell of a week."

Detective Stevenson stroked the black cat's chin and Tilly began purring affectionately.

"Pretty friendly... for a black cat, isn't she?" Norm asked.

The detective sighed. "Well, black is not always black and white is not always white. Sometimes white is black and black is white."

Also by William Blackwell

Phantom Rage, Poison Rage, Infected Rage
Nightmare's Edge
Resurrection Point
A Head for an Eye
Rule 14
Assaulted Souls
Assaulted Souls II
Assaulted Souls III
Blood Curse
Black Dawn
The Strap
The End is Nigh
Orgon Conclusion
Freaky Franky
The Witch's Tombstone
In Your Dreams
Tales of Damnation
Macabre Alley
Brainstorm

In Your Dreams Preview

"On the surface, it's a gripping horror thriller with brutal, shocking twists. But beneath that, it's a thought-provoking exploration of obsession, loneliness, and the terrifying power our subconscious holds over us. The writing is bold, cinematic, and immersive—it reminded me of a cross between Clive

Barker and early Stephen King, yet with a unique, modern edge." -Amazon

"I have finished reading *In Your Dreams*. WOW, just WOW! What an amazing tale. You are one hell of a gifted writer." -Amazon.

"This is an amazing book. Great ending." -Goodreads

Alienated from humanity, Oliver Gimble is a self-indulgent sloth who finds vicarious comfort in binge-watching horror movies and gorging on junk food. During sleep, he escapes into a meticulously constructed dream world where he discovers carnal delight with an enigmatic woman called Stella.

His bizarre lifestyle begins to unravel when he meets Carmen Weathersby, a lonely woman, who in Oliver's mind's eye mysteriously transforms into Stella, the woman of his dreams.

But soon Oliver realizes Stella is actually interfering with his new relationship and will go to any lengths, even murder, to possess him.

When Carmen's elderly mother suffers a heart attack, fingers point to Stella. Suddenly, people close to Carmen start dying—brutally and inexplicably.

Careening helplessly down into a cryptic and otherworldly realm somewhere between reality and perception, Carmen and Oliver struggle to try and solve the macabre mystery before it's too late.

A multi-layered, horrifying journey of self-discovery, *In Your Dreams* examines the powerful and shocking connections between our conscious and subconscious worlds—boldly questioning the very nature of reality.

About the Author

Canadian dark fiction author William Blackwell studied journalism at Calgary's Mount Royal University and English literature at Vancouver's University of British Columbia. He worked as a journalist for many years before pursuing his passion for storytelling. His novels have been characterized as graphic, edgy, and at times terrifying. Currently living on a secluded acreage on Prince Edward Island, Blackwell finds much of his inspiration from Mother Nature, odd people, bizarre nightmares, and traveling around the world.

Author Comments

Thank you for reading this book. I would be eternally grateful if you would post a book review on your favorite book retailer website. A positive review is the highest compliment a writer can receive. Reviews are crucial to the success of any author and they help readers discover new books. You don't have to say much. A few sentences will suffice.

In other news, I have a gift for you. Complete the signup form below with your name and email address and download a FREE copy of *Resurrection Point*, a dark tale about the horrifying consequences of experimenting with death and resurrection. You're only agreeing to be kept up to date on blog posts, new releases, and freebies. I promise I won't spam you and you can unsubscribe at any time.

Thanks again for your support.

http://www.wblackwell.com/free-ebook/